UNBREAKABLE

BY KALLIE ROSS

Have you read *Evelyn*, the prequel to *Unbreakable*?

Learn more at
www.TheCupidChronicles.com

KALLIE ROSS

UNBREAKABLE

THE CUPID CHRONICLES

Unbreakable: The Cupid Chronicles
By Kallie Ross
Copyright © 2016 by Kallie Ross
All Rights Reserved

ISBN 978-0-9983532-0-3

Edited by Maria Pease, The Paisley Editor.

Cover Art by Drew Rodgers at Living Stone Design.

Interior by Kristie Cook at Ang'dora Productions, LLC.

First Edition: 2016

This story is dedicated to the most unbreakable person I know, Melissa.

THE CUPIDS

When the heavens witness the most selfless of love,
Immortality usurps death.
A Cupid rises with a promise and the sharp sting of loss,
Never able to find rest.
Tied to the earth and heavens by bow and string,
A Cupid must choose the match wisely.
Not one heart, but two hearts call,
The Cupid's golden arrow tuning itself to their melody.
A match made for a lifetime,
Its blow marks only the beginning.
Cupids fight for new love and old,
Throughout the years, triumphs and quarreling.
Hearts shatter if unsuitably paired,
Leaving the heavenly warrior in agony.
With each battle won the pain subsides,
Love is not a conqueror, but a boundless key.

Chapter 1

Heaven should be the end-all-be-all, most epic finale of your life. At least that's what Evelyn Bowden had assumed.

Evelyn, with her favorite jeans and green T-shirt, rushed across the heavens. She looked like a mall-walker trying to keep up the pace during peak Christmas Eve shopping hours. Inspecting the fluffy clouds she traversed was tempting, but she wouldn't allow her curiosity to distract her. She had appeared in the heavens once before but was still bewildered by the transparency of the somehow solid air beneath her feet. Clouds weren't easy to trust, but she was coming to terms with being more than a mere mortal, with being a Cupid.

Flexing her supernatural powers, Evelyn's gold tattoo glinted along the inside of her forearm. The arrow had appeared on her skin after she had marked her first couple, but it looked different than her mentor's tattoo. She didn't know why her tattoo was so much more embellished. Her brilliant arrow donned delicate vines like a maypole wrapped in ribbons.

Around her, Cupids paraded through the gleaming city set on air. Some armed themselves with their bow and arrows as if on a mission. Others strolled along the sidewalks, enjoying the perfect weather. One man passed by her in a pinstriped three-piece suit, leaving Evelyn wondering if she should turn around and change. Her nineteen-year-old college student attire didn't seem to measure up to the heavenly dress code.

Evelyn had a meeting with the Elders. She didn't know if the invitation required a more formal Cupid look, so she summoned her bow and quiver full of arrows with a simple thought. Her weapons appeared strapped across her torso. Evelyn grinned, pleased with herself.

"You can put those away. And you can also slow down. The Elders are not going anywhere," Andel suggested. He'd been following her. As her mentor, he should have been leading the way, but Evelyn's nervous energy had her bouncing ahead. Her feet stuttered, but Evelyn found herself distracted by the different buildings and Cupids they passed. Each one resembled a different era that Evelyn recognized.

Andel stopped in his tracks, but she kept walking just a few paces more before fully processing what he was saying. "Remember, they called *us* in for the meeting."

"Should I be wearing something else?" Evelyn asked with the hint of a Southern accent. She took in Andel's six-foot-and-change frame. He wore jeans, but they were tailored to fit him perfectly. His boots and belt matched, and his white T-shirt was somehow classic and trendy the way he had the hem tucked in at his hip.

"Of course not. I'm practically wearing the same thing. Our appearance is usually determined by our assignment, but while we are in the heavens, you should feel comfortable being yourself. We are heavenly warriors, not supermodels." Andel's constant voice of reason grated on her nerves. Technically they both sported jeans and a T-shirt, but Andel looked like he could grace the cover of GQ magazine.

"Thanks." Evelyn rolled her eyes.

"What I meant—"

"It's okay," Evelyn waved off Andel's backpedaling. She knew she wasn't a Kardashi-whoever, and she also knew Andel didn't really mean anything by it. As her mentor, he had always been focused on the job at hand. He'd welcomed Evelyn when she first woke up in this afterlife and he had never left her side.

She had died. It was still hard to believe.

And while taking a deathly blow for her boyfriend had seemed like a good idea at the time, Evelyn had lingered in the second stage of loss: anger. She spent the first few months of her immortality fighting Andel, even though his job was to teach her how to fight. Andel had trained and encouraged her during the process of becoming a Cupid, despite her lack of enthusiasm. Every person chosen to be a Cupid died for someone they loved, and those chosen always had a choice: move on or commit to being a Cupid. The promise of immortality could only be sealed with a perfect shot through two hearts. The only problem was Evelyn had marked an immortal unknowingly, and in the process, found out she had a power distinctly different than any other Cupid.

"You need to keep up," Evelyn said over her shoulder to Andel. She continued to walk as fast as her legs would take her in the direction of the Elder's headquarters. Evelyn's face was new to the meandering Cupids around them, so some staggered and stared like she had two heads. She caught a white-haired Cupid with a combover double take in her direction and didn't know if she should be more surprised that he wouldn't need a neck brace or that she'd gotten used to the feeling of shocking others. Unaffected, she hurried right on by the Armory building; its medieval turrets and brick outer walls looked a lot like

Dover Castle. And as she passed the Placement Office, she noted it resembled the Parthenon.

The Cupids moved with purpose. As their arms swung at their sides, Evelyn caught a glimpse of a few golden tattoos, but none of them looked like hers. Not even Andel's incandescent arrow-ink looked similar to hers. In fact, they all looked as if they differed in one way or another. The only thing they all had in common was the point of the arrowhead touched their wrist and the end reached to the inside of everyone's elbow. The feathers making up Andel's fletching had hundreds of lines. The other tattoos she caught a glimpse of had fewer lines, but every tattoo was structured and streamlined. Evelyn's feathers were more chaotic and looser, swirling as if they'd been caught in a breeze.

"The sooner we get there, the sooner I get answers," Evelyn said, hoping the Elders could tell her why she was different. But she also wanted to get her next assignment, so she could get back to the mortal realm. The staring and glaring she'd gotten from every Cupid up here, excluding Andel, was worse than being the girl who dropped her tray of food in the cafeteria. She had experience being the new kid, even the new foster kid, but the wide berths the other Cupids gave her as they walked around her were starting to make her wonder if they were threatened by her.

"Evelyn, stop." Andel used his entire six feet and four inches to catch up to his protégé. Grabbing hold of her elbow, Andel forced Evelyn to face him, super-soft cotton T-shirt first. She considered the awkwardness for a moment before being sidetracked by the muscles underneath. There was nothing soft about those.

"Excuse me, but"—Evelyn regained her composure, straightening her smooth, shoulder-length brown hair—"why?" She was fed up with not knowing the truth, and she wanted answers. She was different now.

She'd accepted the terms of her immortality, but the agreement felt more like a compromise. Evelyn needed to know why she, of all Cupids, could pierce *immortals* with love.

"For one thing, I believe we will be better received if we arrive calmly. You are not calm," Andel said through gritted teeth. He never lost his cool, but it didn't stop Evelyn from trying to push his buttons.

"And by calm, you mean we should take our orders and be on our way? No fritter way!" Evelyn's twang emphasized each word with an extra syllable.

Language was yet another change Evelyn was coping with. Evelyn's fists clenched, sending her nails digging into her palms. You'd think after helping the Cupids out and saving the world, or whatever it was she'd done in her last stint, she'd be allowed to express herself more explicitly. The transformation she had undergone, from human to Cupid, however, required sacrifice. A whole lot of sacrifice. In this case, language. She couldn't cuss! Ever. "Donut!"

"Thank you for considering my advice." Andel placed his hands on his hips. "You have definitely captured calm."

Evelyn tugged at one of her earlobes, trying to relax and keep herself from returning Andel's sarcasm. She could have sworn it was a reflexology technique, but it didn't seem to help. "Fine. I'll channel my inner comatose state."

"There is no way you could ever stay quiet long enough to be considered comatose. You even talk in your sleep." Andel's smile was a scarce addition to their banter, and it hinted that Andel was attempting to joke with her. Everything Andel did, he did perfectly. Evelyn thought everything about the Grecian archer was annoying when they had first met, but his attempt at humor had since been slowly making up for his weird way of speaking and impeccable posture.

A shrill soprano voice sang from behind Evelyn's personal life-sized action figure. "Andel!"

Evelyn peeked around Andel and spotted a statuesque woman with long silky black curls approaching. The closer she came, the higher pitched her voice got. Her skin was the color of cinnamon, and she wore a red blouse with a sultry, black pencil skirt and stilettos.

"Wowzers," Evelyn let slip. She wondered what kind of assignment this Cupid had in order to dress that way. After all, weren't Cupids supposed to wear clothes to blend into their surroundings? But this woman would have stood out in any place she went.

Andel put a hand out to keep Evelyn tucked behind him. "Let me handle this," he whispered.

"How have you been, Darling?" The Cupid asked Andel. "I'm glad to see you're still standing after your last assignment. I heard it was…challenging."

The woman patted Andel's arm, either choosing to ignore Evelyn's presence or being completely drawn in by Andel.

"The word 'challenging' does not begin to cover it," Andel said with a grin. Evelyn poked a finger at Andel's side, and he jumped, revealing his charge.

Evelyn smiled widely, while the woman's face contorted. First, her eyebrows furrowed in thought, and she pressed her lips together, taking Evelyn in. Then, the corner of her mouth quirked up at one corner.

"Well, hello." The Cupid stuck her hand out to shake Evelyn's. "I'm Zora. I'm sure Andel's mentioned me. We go way back."

Evelyn slipped her hands into her pockets. "Hi."

When Evelyn didn't offer her own hand, Zora waved it off. "Evelyn, right?"

"Right."

"So, is it true you pierced a witch during your induction?" Zora asked, getting right to the point. "I heard your arrows turn—"

"Zora, hold off," Andel interrupted.

"Red, yes," Evelyn finished, ignoring Andel's interruption. "Yes, it's true. If your friends really want something juicy, you can tell them I talk in my sleep. At least, that's what Andel tells me."

"So our gold arrows turn red when you point them at supernaturals?" Zora's smirk tightened. "Interesting."

Andel looked back and forth between the two women. Gossip tantalized Cupids the same way riddles tasted sweet on the lips of Faeries.

"What's so interesting about me?" Evelyn asked.

Zora squinted as if searching Evelyn for the answer. "You're young, new. A sparkly thing that will dull with time."

"That's enough, Zora." Andel reached for Evelyn's hand and pulled her in the direction of the Elders' headquarters. "We'll be late."

Evelyn turned to look back at Zora, and her smirk had shifted into a grimace. Zora's eyes honed in on Evelyn's hand in Andel's, and Evelyn debated how far she wanted to take the stunt. It only took a few more steps before she felt guilty. She pulled her hand out of Andel's grip to create some space between them, but she still felt a pang of shame at being so petty.

"What was that all about?" Evelyn asked once she was sure Zora couldn't overhear her.

"Nothing."

Evelyn rolled her eyes. "That wasn't nothing. Zora doesn't like me, and I've never met her before. How's that even possible?"

"It has nothing to do with disliking you. It is a fear of the unknown." Andel's straight forward approach to communicating with Evelyn left her hungry for more emotional explanations. It baffled her that a Cupid like Andel who felt every mortal emotion around him couldn't express one sentiment verbally.

"That Cupid is jealous. Did you mentor her, too?"

"No, and there is no reason for her to be jealous."

"Well, it's not like I was going to shoot her with one of my arrows. And, even if I did, it wouldn't do anything unless I caught another person in the crossfire."

"But you are different, and the unknown evokes apprehension," Andel's voice grew serious.

"Did you read that off a fortune in a cookie?"

Andel tilted his head to the side, raising his eyebrows. "No, but it would make a good one. You know the fortune I would give you? Welcome the change coming into your life."

"Whatever. Patience is a virtue unless it's against a brick wall."

Andel let out a laugh that caught the attention of a few Cupids passing them. "Speaking of brick walls—" Andel eyed Evelyn and pointed toward an ancient red-brick hall. It reminded Evelyn of places she wished she'd gotten a chance to visit while she was still alive. Growing up in Louisiana, there were some historical sites, but nothing like touring Westminster Abbey or Windsor Castle.

Evelyn sighed. "The Elders could choose to send me out on my own."

"They might." Andel slowed his pace. "If they do, you are ready. But I think they will take your request for me to join you seriously."

Evelyn let hope fill her lungs. "Oh, really?"

She knew Andel wouldn't give anything away, even if he knew something. He respected the chain of command too much. "Yes, but we must show a united front...and arrive on time." He had promised to help Evelyn find out if there were more Cupids with her ability to pierce immortals. She didn't know how long it would take or if the Elders would allow either of them the time they needed.

"You know, I wouldn't blame you if you'd prefer another partner." Evelyn used her thumb to point back in Zora's direction. "She looks like a less complicated candidate. I could even use one of my trusty red arrows to seal the deal." Evelyn waggled her eyebrows.

"If you shoot her with your arrow, I will—"

"You'll what?" Evelyn countered, narrowing her eyes.

Andel folded his arms across his chest, creating a barrier to block Evelyn's implication. "You know Cupids do not technically work in pairs." As Evelyn's grin faltered, Andel moved forward. "I am strictly an advisor," he clarified.

"Why is that? That chick over there is gorgeous. I could send an arrow flying, and you two could have supermodel Cupid-babies."

Andel's mouth drooped into a deep frown. "How about a deal?"

Evelyn nodded, curious.

"I will explain why Cupids avoid shooting and consorting with each other, but only after you keep your cool in this meeting."

"Consorting?" Evelyn slowed down and wrinkled her nose as if the word smelled like souring milk. "Fine, but I want the lowdown on Zora, too."

Andel moved past Evelyn and she fell into step behind him. Consumed with her thoughts and questions, she tripped over the front steps of the building. Andel caught hold of her shoulder before she bit the dust—or clouds. From afar, the set of structures had resembled those standing on a prestigious, ancient college campus: tall columns, intricate leaded windows, and oversized doors. But the scale was off. These columns made earthly structures look like Lego sets. The brick walls were held together with gold, and the doors were decorated with metallic arrows in a criss-cross pattern.

"I might have believed you sooner about being a Cupid if you'd brought me to see this place. It's awesome," Evelyn said. Her mouth fell open and her eyes grew wider as she took two steps at a time to catch up to Andel.

"That is exactly why I avoided bringing you here. You would have gotten the wrong idea. This is not Heaven. It is the heavens. There is a big difference."

"Close enough for me, for now." Evelyn didn't wait for another lecture. Andel had explained when they first arrived that the heavens served as a realm for the Cupids before they eventually moved on to Heaven if they chose to.

She reached for the golden door handles, but the entrance opened before she could take hold. A cozy room, a library, revealed itself. Three walls were lined with dark wooden shelves, and each ledge was covered in leather-bound books. Four overstuffed chairs sat at the center of the room, surrounded by a few tables and chairs. But Evelyn couldn't quite place the farthest wall. The shelves appeared to stretch infinitely.

It was her dream library.

"Whoa! This is definitely my kind of Heaven."

"It is a magnificent feature, isn't it?" A woman with a loose gray bun on top of her head stepped out from behind one of the never-ending bookshelves. Her smile pushed past heavy wrinkles and lit the room. "I do appreciate your idea of the perfect place. I'd like to spend time curled up here, reading each book. Is this room somewhere you've been or is it a conjured dream?"

"Wha—? Um…I think a mixture of both." Evelyn twisted her lips, trying to remember. Time had started to erase some of the pain of letting go of her mortal existence, but it also endangered her most precious memories.

The elderly woman walked across the room with ease, grazing her fingers over the books and rich, stained shelves. Her simple gray dress fell to the floor and created the illusion that she floated over the area rug positioned under the chairs at the center of the room. She wore a blue cardigan that Evelyn envied as it appeared to be as cozy and inviting as the room. But then, the feeling may have been emanating from the woman herself.

Evelyn had never known her grandparents, and if this room created her perfect place, she wondered if it included the perfect grandmother.

"It's nice to finally meet you, Evelyn." The older woman stopped a few feet shy of the doorway. "My name is Neomi. I'm one of the Elders you've been eager to interrogate."

Evelyn's eyebrows lifted, anticipating a lecture. Andel was so good at them, she figured it was one of the Cupids' supernatural powers. Neomi waved her in, and Evelyn caught Neomi nodding to Andel. Evelyn sank into one of the chairs and picked up a stack of books. Perusing the titles, she expected the other two Cupids to get comfortable as well.

"I'll give you two some privacy." Andel's voice had softened in the presence of Neomi.

"Wait!" Evelyn popped up out of her seat as the books on her lap tumbled onto the floor. "Why are you leaving? We need to find out if they're going to let you help me."

Andel's mouth flattened into a line and he dodged eye contact with Evelyn. "I will wait for you outside."

Before Evelyn could reach him, Neomi placed a hand on her shoulder. Not exactly a Vulcan nerve pinch, but the Elder's hand suspended Evelyn in place both emotionally and physically. Andel pulled the doors closed behind him. After the snick of the latch catching, Neomi let her hand fall to her side. She moved to the chair closest to Evelyn and sat down.

Evelyn remained standing in a stubborn display of her immortal youth.

"Dear girl, you can relay to Andel what you want after our discussion. Now, please, sit." Neomi patted the chair Evelyn had vacated.

Evelyn complied and sat, crossing her legs. "Why won't you tell us if you plan to let Andel keep mentoring me?"

"I have informed Andel, and I'll be happy to let you know our decision if you will relax."

"But how? When?"

Evelyn and Andel hadn't spent much time apart since they'd arrived in the heavens, and at no point had Neomi addressed Andel or the topic at hand while he was still in the room. Evelyn hadn't heard a whisper, even with her super-Cupid-hearing.

"I will explain if you'll let me." Neomi pushed herself back into the cushion of her chair while Evelyn leaned forward to pick up the books strewn on the floor in front of her.

"I'm listening," Evelyn said.

"As Cupids, we're able to communicate telepathically." Neomi grinned as Evelyn attempted to comprehend her. "It is not mind reading, and the communication is allowed with permission."

"Are you sure you're not mind melding with me? Because I'm pretty sure you read my thoughts just then," Evelyn pointed out, and Neomi's smile grew. "So, why didn't Andel teach me this earlier?"

"It's not an ability that shows itself before the full acceptance and commitment of becoming a Cupid."

"Oh." It was all Evelyn could bring herself to utter.

Neomi nodded to Evelyn. "May I?"

Evelyn half-nodded, unsure of what to expect. She stilled the moment she felt Neomi's soft voice tiptoe through her mind. *Hello, Evelyn.*

Evelyn smiled. The invading thoughts tickled. She thought, *Hi,* in response. Evelyn stared at Neomi as if her eyes could push the greeting.

Very good, but the more forcefully you press your thoughts, the louder they are in my head. Neomi turned away from Evelyn and walked over to a shelf lining the wall. She appeared to be reading the spines of a row of books. *Try it more gently.*

Which book is your favorite? Evelyn thumbed through one of the novels in her lap. Shakespeare's sonnets filled the pages.

Better. Neomi thought. *Hmm... It's been a while since I've enjoyed a good story, but I always go back to* War and Peace.

"*Really?*" Evelyn thought and said aloud with a frown. "But it's so tragic. And the droning on and on about the war. I'm not too sure where the peace comes in."

Neomi broke out into a bubbling laughter. The airy sound filled the room with joy that could practically be inhaled. "Good point. I hope that you've been able to get Andel to laugh like this."

"Speaking of Andel—" Evelyn shifted in her chair. "Is he going to be able to help me on my next assignment?"

Yes. Neomi's lips quirked to one side.

Evelyn had a feeling the Elder thought more but held her tongue. She ignored the curiosity bubbling up in her gut because she was flooded with relief at knowing Andel could continue working with her. She had hoped the Elders could also fill in a few blanks about her Cupid status. Was she a Cupid or something else? Evelyn wanted to find out if there was really another Cupid like her.

Someone cleared their throat behind one of the bookshelves, and a child revealed himself at the back of the room. He couldn't be older than seven or eight years old. The boy wore a white kimono with a blue belt, and his black hair was cut close to his scalp.

"Sheng, I'm so glad you made it." Neomi nodded to the boy, and they both made their way to two chairs across from Evelyn.

"Neomi." Sheng dipped his head low in greeting and repeated the action in Evelyn's direction. "Evelyn, at last, we meet. I would like to express my gratitude. Your selflessness in New Orleans, choosing to let go of your earthly life and serve in love, is an example Cupids will aspire to for centuries."

"To be honest, there wasn't much to choose from. Anyone would have done it."

"Honestly. I don't believe they would," Neomi interjected. "You come from a culture that rivals the Golden Age in both material wealth and moral poverty."

"Oh. Well, thank you." Evelyn wasn't quite sure how to respond, to Sheng or Neomi or the Elizabethan Era, but she hadn't left her Southern manners back on Earth. A list of questions reeled through her brain, so she started with something simple. "Why did you ask me to meet you here if you could have just mind melded with me?"

"Our telepathic abilities have a tendency to unhinge new Cupids." Neomi leaned forward and placed a hand over Evelyn's. "We also realize your unique circumstances warrant some special attention."

"I simply want some answers." Evelyn slid her hand away from Neomi.

"What kind of answers?" Sheng asked.

Evelyn had to remind herself that this Elder was likely older than Andel. Her mentor looked 24, but he was actually a couple hundred years old.

"Hmmm… Let me think." Evelyn rubbed her chin. "How about we start with why I'm different than every other Cupid in the heavens?"

"We are not sure," Sheng replied.

"What?! Why don't you know?" Evelyn fired back.

Sheng's eyes darted to Neomi, and she fidgeted, crossing her legs toward the boy-Elder. Evelyn had taken a communications class in college and knew exactly what the two Elders' nonverbal cues meant. She wouldn't be getting anything out of them.

"This is baklava!" Evelyn attempted to cuss, but her sweet tooth got in the way. After piercing her first couple with an arrow full of love, Evelyn had transformed fully into a Cupid. Andel had explained their immortality and described their abilities. Cupids can *poof* anywhere on Earth, cloak themselves or glamour the way they look, and they had super speed, hearing, and sight. But not once had he mentioned that their human vices would bounce back and bite them in the ambrosia. "Good Lord! Just tell me why I'm here!"

Both Cupid Elders froze in their seats. Evelyn couldn't tell if they were stunned by her use of *Lord* or by her outburst. One thing she was sure of was that they were having a telepathic conversation about her. The eerie silence threatened to push Evelyn over the edge.

"Since your transformation"—Neomi carefully began. She'd obviously lost a mental match of Rock, Paper, Scissors—"the Cupids have received several threats from other immortal races."

"What does that have to do with me?" Evelyn threw her arms out in question.

"At first, many supernatural races requested your assistance." Neomi winced at the words. "Then, as rumors spread about your ability, some Nox started bullying other Cupids for answers. They wanted to find out if the rumors were true—if you really gave a witch eternal love."

Evelyn sat dumbfounded. She didn't know which Nox were involved, but it couldn't be good since Neomi looked like she swallowed a bag of Sour Patch Kids. "What kind of Nox?"

"Small factions of dark supernaturals are planning attacks. We understand the groups include Fairies, Witches, Shifters, and Vampires." Sheng explained. "Even Lux, our allies, are threatening to withdraw from peace treaties."

"And, what am I supposed to do about it? I don't know why I am the way I am, and I don't know what my crazed red arrows will do if I shoot again. What if I can only use them on certain immortals? Or what if I pierce a werewolf-couple and it kills them?"

"One step at a time, my dear." Neomi's soft voice had a calming effect on Evelyn's racing heart. "We have an important assignment for you. Your mark will include a Gargoyle named Roscoe."

Evelyn stood to her feet and placed her hands on her hips. "Wait a Ding Dong minute!"

Chapter 2

"Ah, ah, ah"—Neomi waved her finger in the air like a mother silencing her child—"please, let me finish." She waited for Evelyn to nod before going on. "The Cupids have always been allied with the Gargoyles. They're ancient protectors who've agreed to help with those pesky Nox. That is, in exchange for your assistance."

"So, you're using me as a bargaining chip?" Evelyn exhaled through her nose. She was so heated she wouldn't have been surprised had smoke puffed into view. The only reason she had become a Cupid was to save the world. Well, if you didn't count the friend she'd made in Andel and the couple she pierced with true love. Having the weight of the world set on the frame of an average-sized college girl's shoulders would eventually end in knee buckling. But she'd stood strong.

"It was the only way to ensure safety for *all* of us," Sheng admitted. He looked down at his bare feet.

Evelyn lifted her chin. "And, if I don't do this, we all get our lunch money stolen? Come on you two, isn't there a way to put these bullies in their place? It's in their best interest if I take the time to find out if there are other Cupids like me."

"Cupid lives are at risk…" Sheng stood up.

"We're. Immortal," Evelyn stubbornly pointed out.

"Look at me," Sheng demanded. At his full height, Evelyn only had to look up a few additional inches from her position in the chair. "I am not playing games. Two Cupids have already been *rescued*. One of them gave up his existence to keep you safe."

"What?" Evelyn placed her forehead in her hands. She didn't understand why or how the stakes had changed. "Someone died?"

"Both Cupids suffered great agony. Zora held on until the Gargoyles found her, but Jonathan moved on," Sheng reported with the same amount of emotion a news anchor would read with on the six o'clock news.

"Moved on?" Evelyn looked from one Elder to the other for an explanation. The Elders traded glances, and she was sure the two mentally discussed how to answer.

"That's a question for your mentor," Neomi answered.

After a few moments of silence, Sheng spoke. "I don't understand your eagerness to find a Cupid like yourself, but to be clear, we aren't aware of any who currently exist. If we were, we would not be dealing with Nox abducting our kind. They want *you*."

The truth stung. Evelyn's desire to find someone like herself felt like an untrained dog on a leash. It pulled and, at times, yanked her aimlessly. She had a gut feeling about it, and no one would be able to convince her otherwise. If she had to spend her afterlife differently, she wanted the label to be worth it. As a teen, she'd been identified as the *foster kid* and it had left her bone tired. By the time she entered college, she decided to leave that label behind.

"I think I deserve some answers. Why can't you at least tell me more? Or let me take a sabbatical and look for answers myself?"

Neomi and Sheng made another mental exchange, and Evelyn began picking at her fingernails. Her nails had never been this strong or pretty. Evelyn had chalked it up to another super power. She'd always cut her nails short as a human because they would split and peel. But, now, she could probably cut through glass with them!

"There was one. Before," Sheng began. He sighed as he settled into one of the chairs across from her. "Her abilities were more heightened than the rest of ours."

"It was before my time," Neomi interjected. "I only became a Cupid in the late 1400s."

"There are only a few of us who existed that long ago. Some chose to move on over the years. I had just made my covenant, but I remember rumors about a Cupid whose targets were all immortals. There was hearsay about her ability to mentally communicate with every supernatural. But, back then, things were more chaotic. The line between Lux and Nox had not been established."

"I can't imagine any Cupid, other than myself, surviving in chaos. There are so many rules and guidelines." Evelyn tried to imagine Andel going a day without taking inventory of his arrows.

"Cupids chose their own assignments. We all came and went as we pleased." Sheng grinned at the memory.

"Sheng, let's—" Neomi patted him on the arm the same way a grandmother would lovingly get the attention of her grandchild. She must have been in her sixties or seventies when she gave her life for a loved one.

Sheng blinked and focused in on Evelyn's arm. "I also remember hearing the arrow tattoo on her forearm had space for twice as many scores as any other Cupid. She was considered ancient to have filled most of her fletching."

Neomi's eyebrows raised in Sheng's direction. "Now, we should move on to…"

Evelyn's eyebrows furrowed in response. With every step she plowed forward, she felt someone pushing her three steps back. "Why? Why do we have to move on?" Evelyn turned her arm over to inspect her tattoo. The arrowhead pointed to her palm and a vine wound around its shaft. The opposite end reached the inside of her elbow and had a wisp of a line protruding from it where feathers should be. Over time, she had been told, a new line would appear with each couple she pierced.

"We are only trying to protect you." Neomi's lips tightened in a smile not reaching her eyes.

"Respectfully, I'm not asking for protection. Something in me wants, no, needs to connect with someone like me."

"That's what we're afraid of." Sheng squeezed the leather on the arm of his chair and closed his eyes. "Have you considered why the Cupid like you is no longer with us? When that line was drawn so long ago, she chose to side with the Nox. That decision destroyed her, and if you stray from our way of operating, I'm afraid the same will happen to you."

"We have revealed enough, Sheng." Neomi stood and walked over to a bookcase near Evelyn. She ran her fingers over a row of books and tapped the top of a leather bound edition of *Catch-22*. Evelyn had a gut feeling her picture-perfect grandma was playing tug-of-war with some of the facts.

"But, I want to know…" she pleaded with Neomi.

"Tsk, tsk. Let me finish, Evelyn." Neomi patted Evelyn's arm on her way back to her seat. "We need you to assist Roscoe, *a Gargoyle*, in New York city. If you don't go, they will stop protecting Cupids while they fulfill their covenant on Earth. We will *all* be in danger."

"I'll think about it." She grinned with her lips pulled tight, struggling to hold her ground. Not wasting any time, she stood to leave. The Elders had controlled every moment of the meeting, and Evelyn reacted like a toddler.

"Evelyn, there are lives at stake," Neomi reasoned.

Evelyn hung her head. "I know, I'm sorry." She couldn't do it. She was soft like the creamy center of a cannoli. "I'll do it. Of course, I'll do it."

Her heavenly library began to crumble as she stepped toward the towering doors. Instead of toppling books, thudding on the floor, they simply evaporated out of existence. Evelyn wondered what would appear if she ever came back into this room and if her imagination had been tainted by these circumstances. She'd always feel the weight of being guilt-tripped when she thought of this place from now on.

The Elders didn't stop Evelyn from leaving, and before she could grasp the door's handle, it flew open. Without pausing to look over her shoulder or close the doors behind her, Evelyn stepped outside. In her peripheral vision, Andel leaned against one of the pillars. His hands shoved into his pockets, he was looking up at the clear blue sky that stretched over the heavens.

"At least one thing good came out of this," Evelyn began. "You don't have to get all awko-taco and tell me about Zora. I might have lost my cool."

"It went badly?"

The courtyard in front of the headquarters buzzed with more Cupids than earlier, and the walkways stretched into an endless, cloud-landscape lined with buildings resembling significant historical landmarks.

Andel. Evelyn gave him a mental knock.

She didn't want the Cupids walking around them to have another reason to stare at her. He nodded, opening his mind to her.

I lashed out at two of the Cupid Elders. I'm pretty sure I'll be cast out any moment.

Andel's lips spread into a smile. "I am sure it was not as awful as all that, but seriously? You yelled at them?"

"Not exactly…"

"Evelyn, I can honestly say I have never met a soul who raised their voice to an Elder."

"Does it count if I did it telepathically?" Evelyn started down the stairs toward the courtyard. "They'll probably give me a good reason to *move on* after my reaction." Evelyn flexed her fingers into quotation marks in the air, and Andel's smile turned into a grimace. It was as if she'd flipped him off. "What?"

"If you truly understood what it means for a Cupid to *move on*, you would not reference it so lightly." Andel had lowered his voice, looking out over the courtyard.

Evelyn felt like she recognized the fountain at its center. The golden statue of a woman was posed with her bow and arrow. Her soft round feature combined with her fierce expression tied the two images of Cupids that Evelyn had become familiar with together. Cupids were definitely not chubby little babies with wings. The covenant required a passion for love and life. From what Evelyn understood, every Cupid existed through a sacrifice for their love.

Follow me.

Evelyn jumped at the mental direction from Andel. His nonverbal communication was as no-nonsense as his speech. She followed him closely, unsure if their mental connection would grow weak with distance. Passersby kept clear of the two, and Evelyn even noticed a few of the Cupids changing direction to avoid walking near them.

Do I smell? Evelyn asked.

Andel's shoulders rose and fell with a light chuckle. Evelyn couldn't get a good look at his face, but she was glad he didn't seem to be in such a serious mood anymore. The more she learned about being a Cupid, the more she felt like she had no idea why'd she'd been chosen. How was she supposed to know everything about being a Cupid after a few weeks of training and a rushed initiation assignment? Granted, it had actually been over an earthly year, but something happens to time when traveling to and from the heavens.

You do not stink. They are scared of you or, rather, scared of what you can do.

"I don't even know what I can do!" Evelyn exclaimed, her arms flailing. She watched as a few Cupids turned to see what all the commotion was about, while others avoided eye contact and walked away faster. "Ugh." Her whole body slumped in defeat.

One thing at a time. Andel continued walking and sharing his thoughts. *Recently, one of our own gave up while being tortured by a group of Winter Fairies.*

Evelyn's footsteps stuttered. *Okay, fairies. I'm guessing they don't spread pixie dust.*

No. They were looking for you. Jonathan would not tell them where you and I were, so they tortured him for our location. It was too much for him to bear, and Jonathan gave up his Cupid status. He gave up on love and hope.

Evelyn let the idea sink in. She was close to giving up when they were in New Orleans on her first assignment. *What happens to a Cupid after they give up?*

Andel stopped in front of the gleaming fountain, and a cool spray of water brushed against his skin. "Cupids always have a choice, Evelyn. If one loses all their hope and passion, they may decide to give up and move on. None of us can be sure what lies ahead."

"That sounds to me like dying, but he was already dead."

"Jonathan died on Earth for love just like the rest of us. As a Cupid, he served almost a hundred years. We all like to think he has moved on to Heaven now, and eventually, we all hope to follow him there." Andel explained, taking a seat on the marble edge of the fountain.

Evelyn ran her fingers through her hair while deciding which question to ask. Stating the obvious felt like a better way to get to her point. "But we're immortal."

"Yes."

Evelyn folded her arms over her chest. "Do you plan on giving up someday?"

"It is not that simple."

"Nothing ever is here. I thought death would be easier than the *snickerdoodle* life I had growing up." Evelyn rolled her eyes at how ridiculous she sounded. She never imagined her addiction to sugar would cause anything more than a few cavities. It was unclear what was worse, having to be reminded of her vice or feeling guilty about wanting to cuss so much.

Andel pushed up his sleeves and turned his arm over, revealing his tattoo. The metallic arrow had a fletching, or feather at the end, that was practically filled with scores. Evelyn turned her own wrist over. Her feathered end looked so different from Andel's. She ran a finger over the only line in her fletching. It represented the one couple she'd pierced with love a few days ago.

"Why is my fletching wilder looking than yours?" Evelyn asked as she reached over to touch Andel's arm.

Andel, determined to not flinch at her touch, watched her finger trace the edge of the arrowhead. "I would point out the obvious, but honestly I'm not sure. If I were to guess, I would say it probably has something to do with your abilities. It looks like your service as a Cupid will require more marks."

"But, your fletching is full."

"Almost." Andel pulled away from Evelyn slowly. "I will fulfill my Cupid covenant after piercing four more couples successfully."

Self-conscious of another Cupid passing by and seeing her tattoo, Evelyn turned her palm over and rested her arm against her leg. "How many couples have you— Wait." She wasn't sure she wanted to know the answer to the question that crossed her mind, but if she didn't ask now, it would nag at her thoughts until she did. "What happens? What'll happen to you after the fletching is full?"

Andel stood. He looked everywhere but at Evelyn. Shoving his hands into his pockets, he paced a few steps away and returned. Evelyn didn't want to rush him. She just wanted the truth.

"This is a lesson you were rushed past, and you should have been briefed before your first arrow was shot. I am sorry for that."

"It's not your fault." Evelyn stood and tapped Andel's bicep with her fist. "My arrow being the only thing that could stop an apocalypse kinda took precedence."

"This is serious, Evelyn." Andel looked down at her through thick, dark lashes. "After a Cupid reaches the end of their service, they are given two options. One, he or she can move on. They are ushered into Heaven to live out eternity with their loved ones. At least, that's what we hope for. Two, he or she can move into an Elder role. They take on the responsibility of making assignments and training new Cupids."

"What are you going to do?"

"I honestly have not made up my mind. The Elders hope I will join them. That is why I was assigned to train you. It was my training, as well."

"But, your family…" Evelyn thought back on how Andel ended up a Cupid over two hundred years ago. He had sacrificed himself to save his wife and children when their house caught fire. When Andel told his story, it convinced Evelyn that she could work through her own grief at losing her boyfriend. Cupids practiced some backward-psychology to help dead people grieve for their living loved ones.

"I like to think my family is in Heaven, and I hope they are at peace...as I am." Andel began walking toward their Cupid living quarters, and Evelyn walked alongside him. "I have experienced great joy uniting couples and fighting for love when those same couples struggled. There is honor in this work, but I am unsure I will find as much passion on the administrative side."

"Even after mentoring me?" Evelyn elbowed Andel.

"Actually, mentoring does not involve transcending to Earth. It does not allow for any *poofing,* as you would call it, anywhere. Your case was not like any the Elders had ever anticipated. Most of them have been out of practice for half a century, so they believed it to be destiny when I was assigned to you." Andel grinned, and Evelyn was glad she could make him smile. Her reference to a Cupid's ability to *poof* anywhere was used to annoy Andel when they first met.

"Selfishly, I'd like you to avoid shooting love birds with your arrows. The longer I have you around, the longer I get to look for other Cupids like me. The Elders are pretty sure none exist, but I'm not so sure." Evelyn took a deep breath, trying to accept what the Elders had told her and Andel's limited time with her, but it felt like inhaling sawdust.

Chapter 3

Ahem. "Evelyn," Andel warned in a low voice. "You already know Zora, and this is Douglas."

As Evelyn looked up, she came face to face with the gorgeous Cupid from earlier and, behind her, a sweater-vest-clad Cupid half-waved with a cheesy grin. Evelyn couldn't help but wonder why this woman was so determined to interrupt her and Andel.

"Hi," Evelyn welcomed with an eye roll. She'd hoped to ask Andel about the Elders and their determination to control the Cupids and their assignments, but it was a discussion best left for when she and Andel were alone.

"How did your meeting go with the Elders?" One side of Zora's mouth lifted in a smirk.

"Really? How does every Cupid know my business?" Evelyn let her arms flail, and the gesture brought more attention to her, completely obliterating her desire for privacy. Zora's mouth turned down, and she started to take a step back. She looked wounded by the outburst. Then she remembered the Elders had been talking about Zora. She was the one! The one who'd been tortured because of her. If the shoe had been on the other foot, Evelyn would have been pissed, not introducing her friends to the freak show.

Andel cleared his throat. "Zora, I am sure what Evelyn means to ask is, how are you?"

"I'm sorry, Zora." Evelyn grabbed Zora's hand, and instead of shaking it she squeezed it gently. "Is there anything I can do? I mean you look like you're doing pretty good…" She tapered off, not wanting to make false promises or compliments.

"Thank you." Zora pulled her cool hand out of Evelyn's. "I think the only thing that would make me feel better is if the Elders swapped Douglas' assignment with Andel's." She stepped closer to Andel and set her pointer finger on his chest. "Could you handle that?"

Evelyn quirked her eyebrow at the spectacle Zora made of herself, and Douglas moved to stand next to her. His perfect posture, parted hair, and clean-shaven face resembled a character from The Great Gatsby. Evelyn remembered being forced to watch an old version of the movie in her tenth-grade English class. Douglas' tailored khaki pants, oxford shoes, short-sleeved button-up shirt, and baby-blue sweater vest were a picture of one of the less illustrious characters.

"Evelyn, nice to meet you." Douglas nodded. His sincerity and chipper tone brought a smile to Evelyn's face. "Andel, it is a pleasure to see you again. Zora here has been a peach since getting back to the heavens. She's really bounced back and looks better than ever. Don't you think?" He patted Andel on the shoulder like they were old buddies.

Evelyn slid away from the train wreck about to take place. Andel had no way to escape a compliment unless Evelyn decided to take pity. Andel's eyes skittered from the passing Cupids to Evelyn to the ground, never meeting Zora. Evelyn debated whether being entertained was worth Andel's frustration. She knew he'd give a teeth-gritting lecture to make sure she knew he wasn't sticking around for her entertainment.

Andel took a step back in discomfort at Zora's proximity, and her finger fell to her side. Douglas smiled, proud of his attempt to keep Zora happy. The whole scene was kind of sad. Sad enough that Evelyn couldn't let Andel or Douglas suffer the animosity of an unhappy, immortal woman.

"I would never have known any different, Douglas," Evelyn answered. "Zora, I absolutely love those heels. You'll have to show me how you train in those things."

With a tight-lipped smile, Zora chuckled. "It comes with practice, dear. I can do anything in these." She winked at Andel, but that was the wrong move. Andel took another step away from her, and Zora's smile faltered.

"How are you feeling?" Andel inquired with a long face.

"As good as you can expect, I guess," Zora began. "Hearing Jonathan as they tortured him was tormenting. And, if those Gargoyles hadn't shown up, I'd have been next."

"Who kidnapped you?" Evelyn blurted.

Andel's hand flung to grip her arm, and his brows furrowed. "Evelyn."

Zora stepped forward, passing Andel. "It's fine," She assured, coming face to face with Evelyn. "I was beaten unconscious, and when I came to, I was alone in a dark concrete room. Jonathan's screams were all I heard for two days."

"I'm sorry," Evelyn offered, but her words felt weightless like they floated away as she said them.

"Just don't let it be in vain. If what I've heard is true, you know what sacrifice is firsthand."

Evelyn went from envy to dislike to respect for Zora in the course of one conversation. Evelyn understood Andel's hesitation toward her and Douglas' attraction to her. Evelyn wouldn't be sorry if their paths crossed again.

Chapter 4

Andel watched Evelyn look over at the fountain at the center of the courtyard. She'd fallen abnormally quiet while the Cupids around them continued to scurry from building to building. He worried she'd take what happened to Zora and Jonathan personally.

"So, I've recently been assigned to protect Zora. Where are you guys off to?" Douglas broke their silence as he straightened his sweater vest, rocking his weight from one foot to the other. Andel was thankful for Douglas' struggle with awkward silence.

"Evelyn and I have an assignment in New York with the Gargoyles," Andel offered but didn't embellish. Hearing her name, Evelyn turned an ear to the group.

"Oh! Gargoyles are awesome!" Douglas' eyes widened in awe. "I mean, I've heard they are. They saved Zora from those fairies"—Zora's eyes darted to Douglas, but he continued unhindered—"and they're some of the oldest immortals on Earth."

"Is that so?" Evelyn zoned in on Douglas.

"Yes. Some of the Gargoyles in Asia have been around longer than our Elders."

Andel folded his arms over his chest, settling in for Evelyn's inquisition. She wouldn't stop until she drained Douglas of everything he knew or a dessert appeared.

"What else do you know about them?" Evelyn asked, prodding Douglas for more information.

Zora brought her hand up to her forehead and rubbed her temples. She'd been saved by Gargoyles, but talking about them probably brought back some bad memories. Andel didn't hate Zora; in fact, he found her to be kind. Her facade of perfection and provocative behavior were a show. But he'd learned not to encourage her actions.

"Hmm... They mostly take their stone form at night to fight off the Nox. That's when most attacks on mortals take place, and the Gargoyles are the first line of defense. It's also been said that each Gargoyle is given the opportunity to live as a human for one lifespan. But, then they're stuck being a Gargoyle for the rest of eternity. I've only heard rumors, though. I bet Zora could tell us if any of them are true."

Zora sucked in air and looked up from Douglas to Evelyn. Andel moved toward Evelyn, anticipating another question. He had always given information as needed, but Douglas was like handing Evelyn a supernatural encyclopedia. Now between the two women, Zora looked him up and down, similar to the way Evelyn checked out a piece of chocolate cake before taking a bite.

Zora had ignored Douglas' attempt to invite her into the conversation. Instead, the foreign beauty folded her arms across her chest and hesitated. "It wasn't a big deal. And it's over now."

"Oh! Come on, Zora. It's such a great story. Andel would probably love to hear it, too," Douglas appealed to them both, especially by leaving Evelyn out.

"Actually, Evelyn and I need to do some training," Andel interrupted. "Maybe another time." He didn't leave his statement open and surprised himself when he placed his hand on Evelyn's lower back. It wasn't exactly a shove, but he applied pressure, moving them quickly around Zora and Douglas.

Zora's slack jaw and Evelyn's tense shoulders indicated they were just as surprised as Andel. He hadn't intended to come across so boldly, but he was saving Douglas as much as Zora. That guy could be enthusiastic to a fault.

"Bye! Nice to meet you both!" Evelyn shouted over her shoulder and elbowed Andel in the side.

"Do not oversell it," Andel smirked but continued his brisk pace.

"You're right. I should have just let that one go," Evelyn agreed. "But meeting Douglas really wasn't that bad. Although, your little Cupid love triangle is pretty messed up. Poor Douglas probably follows Zora around the heavens all the time, and she would do the same for you if you'd let her."

Andel chuckled as he let his hand fall to his side. "I believe him following her has something to do with her protection detail."

"He doesn't seem like the protection-detail type."

"Douglas is a very capable Cupid, regardless of how he looks. I would fight beside him any day."

"That's saying something. But he didn't do a very good job of *protecting us* from Zora," Evelyn smirked, but Andel's face remained stoic, as usual. Her sarcasm hadn't been well received by Andel in the past. "That was supposed to be funny.… Never mind."

"Oh." Andel's lips spread into a smile. "I believe Zora is his weak spot."

"Yes, she is. So, what's the story there, because it's obvious she totally has the hots for you."

Andel's smile shriveled. "Zora is very forward, and that quality is lost on me." From information to emotions, Andel very rarely let go of either.

"It's too bad she doesn't return Douglas' affection. That guy is head over heels for her."

"It will never happen. And, even if it did, it would be frowned upon." Andel and Evelyn walked down the heavenly street toward their living quarters. Andel had always hated that Cupids couldn't transcend in the heavens like they could on Earth, but then he'd never get to enjoy watching Evelyn's knees wobble as they walked on clouds.

As they approached the dormitory, Evelyn asked, "Frowned upon? That sounds appalling." She placed a hand over her frown feigning horror.

"It is understood that fraternizing with other Cupids can only lead to tragedy. It is the same with all immortals, that is, until you came along." Andel opened the front door and waved her inside, but stopped in a small common area and crossed his arms. "Loving forever takes on a whole new meaning when put into the context of an eternity. Supernaturals are not perfect. While mortals have us to assist them, immortals are on their own to make it work. Needless to say, after a century or so, it gets old. Lux have learned to avoid relationships, but Nox find lust an adequate substitution."

Evelyn slipped over the cushioned arm of an overstuffed chair, making herself at home. "I get why other immortals might struggle with everlasting love, but what could be so disastrous for Cupids? We should understand love more than the others. Heck, we dish it out! Wouldn't it be a beautiful thing for two Cupids to find love with each other?"

"No," Andel answered without hesitation. His jaw tightened, but he stood immovable.

The air around Andel grew cold, and that should've been impossible since it was the heavens. The realm replicated the perfect sunny day, perfect temperature, and even the perfect smell of spring. The light floral notes with hints of rain and clean cotton brightened everyone's senses.

"Ookaay…" Evelyn twisted and curled her knees up to her chest.

"You are so new to our way of…life, for a lack of terminology. Until you came along, immortals did not have a hope for eternal love. Some try, but knowing you will live forever tends to change your perspective of love."

"Perspective? What other view of love is there?"

"Immortals fear love. In your lifetime, you experienced one of the strongest kinds of love. Once you died, you struggled to let that love go. Can you imagine living a lifetime or several lifetimes with that love and losing it?"

"Zora didn't seem to be avoiding a relationship with you." Evelyn's eyebrows bounced up and down. "So, are you saying that Cupids don't have long-term relationships or that they don't have relationships at all?"

"Yes." Andel nodded.

"Not funny."

"I am not trying to be funny. Cupids—all the Lux immortals—have a choice, but we don't get caught up in love. There are too many consequences."

"But you have booty calls."

"Yes—I mean, no. *I* do not have meaningless relationships, but there are Cupids who do." Andel's eyebrows threatened to fold over his green eyes. He'd been wanting to clear something up, so he walked over to stand in front of Evelyn. It took her off guard when he sat on the coffee table at the center of the room. "Now, we should discuss a few things before we get our assignments."

Evelyn pulled herself up and out of the cushions, perching at the edge of her seat. She and Andel sat knee to knee. "Assignments? As in, we have two couples to pierce?"

A passing Cupid stopped and stared at them from the entryway. When Andel turned to see who had caught her attention, a short, stout man scurried out of view.

"It makes sense. You are a Cupid now, and your targets will be different than mine," Andel said in a whisper. He leaned close to keep their conversation private.

"Yeah, I guess so." Evelyn placed her hands on her knees and lifted her chin to meet Andel's eyes. "Don't get me wrong, I don't want more Cupids to get hurt, so I'll play along. But it should be on record that I'd rather follow my gut than pierce a couple I've been assigned."

Andel started to place a hand over Evelyn's but patted it and stood up instead. Maybe it wasn't the best time to bring up the notion he'd been wrestling with. Moving toward the hallway, he hoped Evelyn would follow but noticed she hesitated.

"What else is bothering you?" he asked.

Evelyn's face scrunched up, trying to puzzle her words together. Probably to keep from ticking Andel off. She'd always been honest with him but lacked a filter. Her eyes darted from his tattooed arm to his face. He waited for her.

"I, well…I don't want you to get another score on your fletching. You'll be one step closer to riding off into the sunset, and I'll be stuck trying to hold my own here." The words tumbled out, like wet noodles onto a plate.

"I made a promise to you, Evelyn. I told you I would help you find out why your powers are different, and I will." Andel took a step toward her and reached for her hand. "I do not make promises lightly."

"Okay." Evelyn took Andel's hand, and he pulled her up out of the chair. "What should I pack?"

"I hear January in New York City can get chilly," Neomi's worn voice called from the front door. "Evelyn, we don't have time for you to pack. Another Cupid has been abducted, and we've received a ransom note."

Evelyn paled, and Andel knew she was picturing some Cupid being tortured. Her face went blank, slack, but only for a few seconds. Slowly her jaw clenched, her lips straightened, and her eyes focused on Neomi.

"When do we leave?" Evelyn asked Neomi, but Andel knew what was coming before it happened. Neomi had a mischievous glimmer in her eyes.

Poof.

Chapter 5

Evelyn, Andel, and Neomi appeared in the doorway of a New York City penthouse.

"Wha—" Evelyn's lack of exposure to the world, let alone the privileges of the upper class, left her lips slightly parted and her eyes wide. She didn't want to blink and have everything before her disappear.

All but one of the walls were bright white, and sharp columns stretched from floor to ceiling systematically. The last wall spanned the entire length of the apartment, and windows filled the complete two-story space from floor to ceiling. Afternoon light poured into the room, warming it and making the modern furniture more inviting. A black sofa and chairs invited them to sit at the center of the room, and around them, contemporary art and tall lamps complimented the minimal decor. Small pops of color grabbed Evelyn's attention, including a lime-green mixer in the kitchen at the other end of the open concept quarters.

"You have until nightfall before you need to be at the Cathedral," Neomi stated as Evelyn began exploring the space, eyes still wide. "Is there anything else I can do for you before I transcend back? Anything at all?" She moved into the living room, hoping to make herself comfortable.

"Wait a churro minute," Evelyn exclaimed. "You're leaving us here? Like, we're staying here?"

Neomi grinned at the heavenly interference into Evelyn's vocabulary. Neomi would take that as a yes.

"Just how long has it been?" Andel asked, following her into the room. Neomi stepped over to the windows, and Evelyn was eager to see the other rooms. "I am sure Evelyn has plenty of questions in her queue."

"I'm sure Andel can fill me in," Evelyn said and waved absently, popping out of a bedroom she'd disappeared into. She would let Andel have that room for sure. It felt more masculine, and there was an armoire filled with bows and arrows. Plus, the queen-sized bed couldn't make up for the tiny excuse for a bathroom.

Ahem. Andel's subtlety was lost on her.

Evelyn ignored them and beelined into the kitchen. She may not have had to eat to survive, but that didn't mean she wouldn't bake a chocolate cake or chocolate chip cookies the first chance she got. At least now, the calories wouldn't have to be balanced with hours on the treadmill. Before she could inspect the double ovens, she noticed Andel and Neomi conversing.

"I haven't been here for over a century." Neomi sat down in a chair that faced the windows. She peered out into the city letting the full view sink in.

"New York? Heck, I've never been here ever," Evelyn interrupted. "I think I'll try and poof to the top of the Empire State Building later."

"No, dear. It's been about 108 years since I've walked this Earth. Time flies, I think the saying goes."

"Oh." Evelyn sat down next to Andel on the couch. "Is that what you really want your immortality to be?"

She intended the question for Neomi, but the Elder and Andel exchanged a look that made Evelyn wonder if she should've pointed the question at Andel. Neomi had chosen to accept her role as a Cupid long before Andel was born. Her eyes sparkled with wonder at the city below them, and her face appeared as timeless as the Empire State Building.

"As a Cupid, I have felt the exhilaration of first love innumerable times. I've witnessed the greatest sacrifices, including the both of yours." Neomi swiveled in her chair to face Andel and Evelyn. "Wars have been waged, both lost and won for love. A boy has the potential to be made into a great man when fostered by love, and a girl flourishes into an exceptional woman with the security of love. I could act on love's behalf for an eternity."

Evelyn joined Neomi, watching for Andel's response. Both admired his handsome face as well as wondered if he would answer Evelyn's question. Neomi treated Andel more like a son or grandson.

"What?" he asked the two women as he ran a hand through the stubble along his jaw. "I would rather not say, yet." Andel looked to the floor and rubbed the back of his neck.

"If it's to save my feelings, please don't. I'd rather know now before we step out there and start this mission." Evelyn thought she did want to know. She hadn't had much time to consider what it would be like if Andel struck a few more couples and accepted a position as an Elder, but she'd like to start prepping herself for the change. She'd be ticked, but prepared.

"I believe he is sparing my feelings, Evelyn," Neomi interjected. She stood and began pacing in front of the window. Evelyn had witnessed Andel think through a situation the same way. "Andel, you know it better than anyone, once your fletching is filled with scores you must make a decision, but take your time. I mentored you long ago, I'm not here to baby you now. During the next four assignments, an alternative might present itself."

Neomi's cryptic advice stirred a plethora of questions in Evelyn's mind, but before she could open her mouth, Neomi had transcended.

"Is she gone?" Andel inquired with his hands, palming his head on either side like a basketball.

"Yep." Evelyn patted his leg and jumped up. "Do you need something for that? Like some Tylenol or something?"

"No, I do not have a headache." Andel looked up at Evelyn, and his eyes were wet and red-rimmed. He'd teared up.

"Are you okay?" Evelyn sat back down and placed a hand on his back, unsure of what else to do. Andel had only opened up emotionally once before. "I can make chocolate chip cookies. If you eat them while they're still warm, they can make anything better."

Andel grinned. "That sounds nice."

Evelyn didn't push Andel to talk about it. The future could be as difficult to think about as the past. Instead, she made him go out in the cold, wintery weather to the market where they purchased cookie supplies. Wiggling her nose to have sugar, chocolate, and a baking sheet appear would have been the most epic immortal super power in Evelyn's opinion. But the diversion of shopping provided another form of therapy for them both.

Twenty minutes later, back at the apartment, Andel seemed thankful for the distraction. Sitting on the couch dwelling on the implications of Neomi's words would have driven him nuts. He had four couples to pierce with love before his covenant with the Cupids was fulfilled. Evelyn wasn't sure what his plans were, but Neomi left him with another riddle to work out. He needed a break from convoluted teases and imminent doom. Neomi was probably trying to hint at something helpful, but it was all too much for Evelyn to try and work through while measuring ingredients.

As their sweet treats baked, Evelyn found her closet had been filled with her personal gear and belongings from the Cupid dormitory. She and Andel regrouped in the living room, where two folders sat waiting on the coffee table. While perusing the files, they ate a dozen warm cookies.

They'd be meeting their marks soon. Thinking of the Penthouse and dossiers as work almost soured the perfect sweetness of her warm cookie. Almost.

Evelyn had never used a matchmaker, but she felt like she'd become one overnight. The couple she'd been charged with had never met. The information on the young woman, Sydney Mitchell, made up two-thirds of the stack of papers, but the Gargoyle's data reminded Evelyn of blacked-out documents you saw in the movies. This Gargoyle felt more like a ghost. If the Gargoyle, Roscoe Thomas, had left the blanks on purpose, Evelyn worried he wasn't all in. She and Andel would be piercing their couples with love-imbued arrows if all went according to plan, but she needed to meet Roscoe.

Andel cleared his throat to get Evelyn's attention. "We still have an hour or two before dark." He glanced down at his watch, and Evelyn was intrigued.

"Since when do you wear a watch?"

"Since I need to blend in at a museum."

"Umm… Aren't we supposed to be going to a cathedral?" Evelyn asked.

"Your assignment is at the cathedral, but mine is at MoMa."

Evelyn's hands clapped together, and her lips spread, revealing a toothy grin. "The Museum of Modern Art, MoMa? Can I please, pretty please with a cherry on top, go with you?"

"I guess." Andel didn't have the heart to turn her down. "But, I want to be clear about something."

Evelyn nodded for Andel to continue, scooting to the edge of her seat.

"This is *my* assignment. I will allow you to accompany me to the museum, and I will review procedures—all in an effort to educate you in the proper protocol. Can you handle that?"

"Yes, sir," Evelyn saluted.

"Take it easy, Bowden. We need to get back to planning." Andel casually waved Evelyn's perched hand down from her forehead.

Andel had never called her by her last name, but she kind of liked it. After a day like today, she needed something grounded and secure, and Andel served as an anchor for her. She beamed at him, confident that no other afterlife could be as awesome as getting to walk through museums in New York City. But they had two assignments to get ready for, and her's included meeting her first Gargoyle.

"You'll need a quick brief on my couple," Andel began. "Jane Platt is a thirty-two-year-old woman working at the Museum of Modern Art in Art Acquisitions for the Department of Painting and Sculpture." He jotted something down in a pocket-sized notebook Evelyn hadn't seen before. "There is a delivery company the museum works exclusively with, and Kendrick Tate is one of the drivers. He's a thirty-year-old man working on his Doctorate in Art History."

As Andel continued to write, Evelyn itched to ask him follow-up questions. Biting her lip, she leaned forward and tied one of her boots. After a few more seconds of silence, she fidgeted in her seat and fluffed a few cushions. When she couldn't handle staying silent anymore, Evelyn shot off the couch toward the kitchen for another cookie. It wasn't her case, and she didn't know where the line would be drawn between their two assignments.

Andel chuckled.

"Gah! I had a feeling you did that on purpose!" She pointed a cookie at him.

"I could not resist. Come back over here and tell me what you think we should do to arrange their first meeting."

"You want my input?"

"Sure." Andel stood, knowing it would be more logical to move closer to the cookies. "To be honest, there are a few things in Jane Platt's file that remind me of your mortal life."

He didn't offer any other insight, but Evelyn was relieved Andel had opened up the line of communication about their assignments. She'd feared she would have to handle the Gargoyle situation on her own, and that scared the crap out of her. Google would have proved useless for this kind of research. Evelyn hoped they could help each other.

"How about we talk while we walk?" Evelyn suggested. "I really want to see the city, and maybe it'll inspire us. You know, give us some perspective on where they live and work. Maybe even find some places we could shoot from when they're ready."

Andel simply nodded his approval, and the two bundled up into their jackets before leaving. The cold didn't really bother either of them, but the stares they'd received when walking to the store without coats to get cookie ingredients was enough to convince them they needed to work on blending in a tad more.

Once on the street, Evelyn couldn't stay focused. There was something to see at every turn. Her eyes scaled each building, appreciating the architecture. The loud sounds rang in her ears. The smell of rotting fruit made her eyes water as they passed an alleyway. People in muted gray and black coats shuffled around her and Andel.

"The penthouse is located at East 51ˢᵗ and 2ⁿᵈ Avenue." Andel nodded to the street signs at the corner. "As long as you remember the address, you will be able to find your way back. St. Patrick's Cathedral is four blocks this way, and MoMa is only two blocks further," Andel explained while pointing and ushering her through a crosswalk.

"Got it," Evelyn answered as she tried to locate the sun, seeing as it was still daytime, but it was hidden behind one of the highrises.

"We will scout out MoMa first. And, by scout, I mean take mental note of where Jane's office could be located as well as any security measures they take with deliveries."

"Okay, but how are we going to get a mature art enthusiast to fall in love with a delivery guy?"

"I'm glad you asked." Andel held out an arm for Evelyn to take. The sidewalks grew more crowded the further inland they walked. "Jane has recently ended a relationship with an older man. She does not know it, but Kendrick's love for life and learning is just what she needs. Kendrick is actually working as a delivery man for his uncle while he finishes his doctorate."

"I'm still not convinced it's a match made in Heaven." Evelyn waved her hand up and down in front of her. "Are we planning to go in like this? Or, will we be using a glamour?" She smiled, hoping for the latter.

Andel's power glided over her skin, cool and tingly like when the spray of a fizzy soda touches her upper lip. Evelyn knew she didn't look like herself any longer. Andel could have created the illusion of two celebrities walking down a New York City street, or they could appear to look like two Muppets.

"How do you feel about growing old together?"

Evelyn thought of what she and Andel would look like with an additional fifty years of wrinkles and gravity. They would look cute together as an old couple. She glanced over at Andel, and the glamoured age he'd projected only made him more handsome, in a John Stamos kind of way. A gust of wind blew past them, tinting her cheeks pink. Avoiding Andel's eyes, she caught sight of some beautiful, gothic architecture.

Approaching St. Patrick's Cathedral, Evelyn stretched her neck in every direction as to not miss anything. She peered up at the roofline, searching for Gargoyles. The turrets towered over them. Each spire reaching for the heavens was surrounded by stone statues. Evelyn couldn't imagine any of the winged beasts or monk-like characters coming to life.

"Do you know which one is Roscoe?" A small part of her didn't want to know.

"That would ruin the fun." Andel tugged on Evelyn's arm teasingly, and she smiled. He actually seemed like he was having fun, and the only other time she ever saw him with a smile on his face was when they were training.

Evelyn's feet stuttered repeatedly, begging her to stop and take the structure in, but that could have taken hours. She couldn't understand why Andel didn't feel the same urge to stop because he kept pulling her along like they were late for an appointment. As they passed a gated courtyard, Andel hesitated and looked over his shoulder.

Evelyn? Andel asked for permission to mentally speak to her. *I do not want to startle you, but I believe we are being followed. Stay close.*

Thinking of the worst case scenario, Evelyn asked, *Are you referring to those creeps that have been kidnapping Cupids?* Her pace picked up, forcing Andel to lengthen his stride.

Breathe Evelyn. No one knows you are the Cupid with red arrows. If someone is following us, it will only make them more suspicious if we hurry off somewhere. Currently, we look like happy, old tourists to everyone. Andel slowed, and Evelyn shortened her gait.

The two Cupids made their way to the front of the cathedral where a crowd gathered. Evelyn's mouth fell open in wonder. She froze. The gray structure was more than a church. It was divine; it called to her.

Andel struggled to move Evelyn, so he played up their tourist act and tugged her forward. "Darling, we will be taking a tour of the cathedral tomorrow. We still need to get to the museum, and you know how my knee gives out if I stand on it too long."

Evelyn blinked, and Andel moved into her line of sight. "Alright, dear." She played along and patted his bicep.

Slow and steady wins the race. Andel fought walking any faster than a turtle.

Reaching the next intersection, a red flashing hand taunted them as they waited for the light to turn green. They could have easily made it across if they weren't posing as seventy-year-old sightseers. More people surrounded them as they waited patiently. When the walking man lit up, Evelyn and Andel struggled to stay together. The oncoming walkers weaved between them, breaking their hold, but before they were pulled too far apart, they reached the opposite side of the street.

Do you think we're still being tailed? Evelyn looked around the swarm of people passing them by on the sidewalk. *And won't they be able to see through our glamour if they're supernatural?*

I do not think so. I mean, yes, they'll see through it, but to be sure they are not following us, we should slow down. If I recognize anyone, I may pull you into an alleyway and transcend us both back to the penthouse.

The first few times Evelyn and Andel had transcended anywhere, Evelyn wasn't fully a Cupid. Now she could poof anywhere she wanted in the blink of an eye. *I think I can handle it.* If she let him, Andel would *poof* them to their destination without warning, and it drove Evelyn crazy. Not having control of where you'd turn up felt falling off the bed after being shocked awake. She'd learned to look for his tells, and she found he had a bad habit of gritting his teeth before thinking them from one place to another.

So, instead of looking for a needle in a haystack, Evelyn focused on Andel. She wouldn't recognize an immortal among this many humans anyway. Andel had over two hundred years more experience than she did as a Cupid. After another block, he slowed to a stop in front of another gothic church, St. Thomas. Two giant wooden doors stood at the top of a small staircase.

Andel bounded up the stairs with his arm around Evelyn's waist. His muscles tensed, pulling her close into an embrace. He must have seen someone or something that looked suspicious. Evelyn tried to relax in his embrace. It was the safest place she could think to be. The longer he held on to her, the easier it became to compose herself.

"Just a few more seconds," Andel whispered in Evelyn's ear. Heat rose from her chest to her neck. The pink blotches were definitely not caused by a cool breeze. Before her ears could put her feelings on display, Andel released Evelyn. She sank an inch or two without him holding her close. Stepping back onto the busy sidewalk, Andel left Evelyn a moment to inhale. When she turned to get a better look at their surroundings, the Museum of Modern Art came into view across the street.

"Are they gone?" Evelyn asked as she took a step down toward Andel.

"I think so, but the best way to know is to stay in character and scope out MoMa." Andel reached for Evelyn's hand and pulled her to his side. Her heart leaped. She wasn't sure if the affectionate performance from Andel, the anticipation of walking through art-filled galleries, or the apprehension at meeting a Gargoyle soon was to blame.

At second thought, it could also have been due to the striking blond man approaching. He wore a tailored suit, blending into the mob of pedestrians. But his knowing smirk gave him away. Once the stranger locked eyes with Evelyn, they flashed red in warning.

Chapter 6

The world around them blurred while his features sharpened. The stranger's light hair and complexion contradicted his dark, penetrating eyes. His blond hair was longer on top and short on the sides, and he wore a dark blazer with gray pants. As he drew nearer, the stranger's eyes squinted, peering through the glamour Andel had orchestrated. She knew he *saw* them, not the cute, elderly tourists. Andel squeezed Evelyn's hand, and it brought her out of the hazy trance she'd fallen into.

Only a few feet away, the man winked at Andel. Evelyn felt the air around her cool, and the people around them began to spread out, unaware. The power the stranger wielded had created a bubble, and none of the pedestrians paid them any attention. In a blink, the man sidestepped and came face to face with Evelyn. She struggled to remain calm; everything in her told her to thrust her knee up and ask questions later. He stood a few inches taller than her, and while he had attempted to blend in, he hadn't succeeded.

Evelyn. Andel called to her.

The man's perfectly chiseled face screamed supernatural. He'd also moved with inhuman speed, but so did Andel. As the stranger reached for Evelyn, Andel pulled her by the hand behind him and around to his other side. For a millisecond, the two men came chest to chest.

Evelyn didn't know what supernatural race the stranger belonged to or how to break up the standoff. She debated yelling for help. Posing as a little old lady, she figured the attention she'd draw would distract the stranger, but if he'd cloaked them, it wouldn't do any good. Instead, she forced a mental threat to the stranger. *You don't want to go there, Buddy.*

The stranger's jaw clenched like he'd actually heard her. She hadn't known it would work. She wasn't even sure she'd intended it to work. The man's eyes flitted between the two Cupids, and as quickly as he unfolded from the crowd, he was lost amongst the New Yorkers who passed them.

"Are you okay?" Andel leaned over and asked as they rushed across another intersection. MoMa was a few steps away, and Evelyn preferred to get inside before officially freaking out. Looking up at the building, she hated that she couldn't take her time and enjoy the moment. The museum was a piece of art in its own right.

Can we just get inside? I need a second to process. Evelyn had questions, as always, but there were too many to get her brain wrapped around.

I thought walking through the city would be… Well, I should have known better. Andel squeezed Evelyn's hand. *We could cloak ourselves and stay invisible for a while or transcend back to the penthouse.*

It wouldn't matter much, would it? That guy could still see us even if we were glamoured. And if he's been following us long, he might already know where we're staying.

Evelyn tugged Andel in the direction of the entrance to the museum. Without more to go on, Evelyn wasn't sure if Andel would have any answers to offer. The stranger radiated magic and could have been any kind of Nox. He was going to take Evelyn, but her telepathy had spooked him. There was still so much about this world she didn't know about.

Reaching the doorway, Evelyn rediscovered the tedious nature of being human. They needed money for tickets, and if she'd carried a bag, it would have been searched by security. Andel reached for his back pocket, pulling out a brown leather wallet. The act surprised Evelyn as much as him wearing a watch. He purchased their tickets with a black card and escorted her through the entryway.

The galleries were buzzing, and Evelyn couldn't help but worry that another immortal might be watching them. She played it off by pretending to admire the first exhibit they came across. The pop art screamed at visitors as they entered. Not being her favorite style of modern art, she took everything in with her peripheral vision, focusing instead on a mother pushing a stroller then a young couple standing inches apart in front of an abstract painting. Their body language screamed first date, and their flirting buzzed along Evelyn's skin. She itched to summon her bow and arrow and pierce the couple.

"Stop, Evelyn." Andel softly tugged her hand.

She rolled her eyes at him. Evelyn wouldn't really shoot the couple. They weren't ready. They might never be ready. Cupids might be tempted by lust or desire, but acting on that fleeting feeling would tie them to those two people for the rest of their mortal lives. Striking a couple was only the beginning for Cupids. A successful shot bonded them to the hearts they pierced. As a heavenly warrior, Evelyn would be called on if their love was ever in jeopardy. She had only struck one couple with love, and she had a really good feeling about them.

"I'm enjoying this…uh"—she struggled to bring a sincere smile to her face as she searched for the title or description of the exhibit—"okay, I suck at seeing the value in this particular piece. It's the same picture in four different colors." She placed a hand over her mouth as a class of children rushed past them in amoeba-formation.

"It is not my favorite, either. How about we go upstairs to see some Monet's?" Andel tucked Evelyn's hand around his arm and walked toward the elevator. "I would offer to take the stairs, but I think we would draw unwanted attention. Can you imagine an elderly couple trying to climb those?" He pointed over to an open staircase teeming with visitors.

Two grandparents jogging up five stories would probably be noticed by humans and immortals alike. Evelyn needed to focus. She and Andel had a job to do while they were at the museum. Their disguise would be a great way to coax information from employees, but first Evelyn needed to settle her nerves. A ding startled her out of her headspace and back to the job at hand. As the elevator door slid open, Andel held it for Evelyn to step in. Once inside, and alone, Andel spoke freely.

"Do you know what happened out there? With the immortal? He had to be planning an attack but changed his mind at the last minute. Did you notice the way he looked at you just before disappearing?" Andel ran his hands through his hair and pulled at the back of his neck. "How did I end up being the one with all the questions?"

"I must be contagious."

Andel swept the back of his hand across his forehead. "I thought I might be coming down with something."

A soft buzz sounded as they passed the second floor. Evelyn chuckled at Andel's comeback. Sometimes, she thought if Captain America and Sheldon Cooper had a baby, the result would be Andel. But on rare occasions, he let himself relate to Evelyn more personally. He was more like the Ricky to her Lucy.

Evelyn bit her bottom lip, unsure how she should word what she wanted to say. "In all seriousness, I *thought* something at him." It sounded even more ridiculous coming out of her mouth than it had thinking it. Andel tilted his head to the side, and Evelyn felt the need to explain further. "You know, like when we mentally communicate? I just pushed a threatening thought his way, and he seemed to hear me."

"That would explain his leaving so quickly." Andel's eyebrows rose with his own surprise. "What did you tell him?"

"Nothing bad...I warned him. And it seemed my voice in his head was scary enough for him to hightail it out of there."

"The idea of you popping into my head uninvited"—Andel elbowed Evelyn and laughed, hoping to lighten the mood—"not that mentoring you is scary."

Evelyn pursed her lips.

"I mean...well, how about I stop before I get myself into trouble." Andel's shoulders slumped. He was smart to surrender before he dug the hole any deeper.

"I get what you mean." She smiled at him. "I don't think I could handle your contraction-snubbing voice in my head, either."

As the corner of Andel's mouth turned up, the number five illuminated. A ding alerted them as the elevator doors opened. This corridor felt less crowded. People had spread out around the gallery to enjoy the thoughtfully hung paintings around the gallery.

Impressionism was Evelyn's favorite style of modern art, and she'd dreamed of seeing work by Monet and Matisse in person. Death for most resulted in a light at the end of a tunnel, but Evelyn couldn't help but think that someday she might get the chance to walk through the Louvre in Paris, France. Being immortal had its perks.

"I know we have a job to do—"

"Don't say another word," Andel interrupted her. "We will take a few minutes so you can enjoy this."

"Did I ever tell you I took an art history class in college? It was an elective that I might have pursued further if I hadn't died." Evelyn clutched her chest, taking in a deep breath. The gallery hummed, and she felt exhilarated.

"*I'll* keep an eye out for anything that might give us an advantage with my assignment while you soak this all in."

Evelyn nodded her agreement but made sure not to snicker at Andel's attempt to sound casual. She would take any contractions she could get from him, even if he was only doing it to tease her.

Evelyn and Andel moved slowly around the room. Both enjoyed the artwork, but she noticed him monitoring a guard's shift change while she approached a sculpture. His work ethic normally would have made her feel guilty, but being surrounded by priceless art helped outweigh any regret.

Later, Andel paid special attention to employees approaching a solid door with a card reader hung next to it. They swiped their I.D.s, and a click of the lock allowed access. Andel wouldn't be able to rely solely on his glamour. He'd need one of those cards, or he'd have to poof to the other side.

Jane Platt's file had revealed she had accomplished more than any woman in her field at her age. Her passion for art had obviously surpassed any desire for a relationship. Andel taught Evelyn that not every mortal was destined for the love Cupids dealt out. Jane's ambitions outweighed her affections, so Evelyn wondered why the Elders had assigned Andel to her.

Evelyn had lived with the same passion and determination, but somehow she'd found her way to Tate. The thought of her first and only love didn't hurt as much anymore.

Wrapping her arm around Andel's, she pulled him with her to look at a Monet painting. "Are you sure about Jane? I mean, do you think she wants love in her life?"

"Everyone is created for companionship. Some people just have a harder time getting it right and keeping it right." Andel took a step closer to the painting.

"You know, I've been thinking…"

Andel inspected the brushstrokes that made up a pond covered in water lilies. Standing side by side, they could empathize with all the emotions around them, even each other's. It was a Cupid superpower Evelyn still struggled to manage. Andel was aware of Evelyn's thoughtful mood and had kept his punchline to himself.

"You're really good at this, but I can't help but wonder if there's more guilt involved than you'd like to admit," Evelyn continued. "You can spend an eternity trying to make up for whatever happened when you were mortal, but when you sacrificed yourself for your wife and kids, they knew you loved them. There's no way they could question your love after something like that happened."

Andel's feet shuffled under him. He'd shared with her the burden he felt to serve as a Cupid after he died. She'd dealt with similar emotions after giving her life for Tate. The covenant every Cupid must seal with an arrow is difficult, but Evelyn's had been extra complicated. If she hadn't pierced her first couple to become a Cupid, a dark force would have overrun New Orleans.

"I'd rather not—"

"You don't have to talk about it." Evelyn tugged Andel back toward the elevator. Passing her favorite painting, *Starry Night*, she murmured, "Simply brilliant."

They arrived at the elevator, and Andel had a grin pulling his lips taut. "I saw Oscar-Claude work long ago," he admitted. Pressing the down button, he shrugged, and his grin exploded into a wide smile.

"Oscar-Claude? You say his name like you were on a first name basis with him." Evelyn rolled her eyes.

"I was."

If he'd wanted, he could have whistled in her direction and knocked her over. He hadn't just seen Monet's painting before, he had watched him paint those paintings. When the elevator doors opened, the bodies piling out jostled Evelyn out of her amazement.

"Name-dropper," was all Evelyn said before stepping inside.

Evelyn had quickly become more than an apprentice. She was sure he hadn't had a real friend in centuries. There would come a day he would have to make a choice, and Evelyn worried she would be left to fight for love on her own.

Once Evelyn and Andel made it to the street, they both became hyper-aware. The streets were still filled with yellow-and-black taxis and the pedestrians glided along the sidewalk like it was a conveyer belt.

"Are you worried someone will follow us again?" Evelyn's asked.

"Our assignments are not going to change, but lucky for us, they are in very public places. The supernatural cannot risk exposure, so we will be safe out in the open. If we must, we can transcend discretely, and that will keep anyone from following us," Andel reassured.

Glancing in the reflection of a glass door, the Cupids were white-headed and bundled up in coats and scarves like everyone else. Evelyn actually wore a lighter jacket; in fact, the chill in the air made her skin come alive with each breeze, making the hair on her arms stand up. It wasn't exactly cold to her, but brisk. As Cupids, their physical limits as humans were strengthened. What once seemed inadequate now felt absolute: strength, endurance, sense of smell, eyesight, and more.

"What do I need to know before we meet this Gargoyle, Roscoe?" Evelyn looked up, searching for looming stone creatures.

"Gargoyles are like any immortal race. They have an eternity to live, but the restrictions make you wonder if it is worth it. Half of their time must be spent in their original, supernatural form. They are unbelievable warriors, but in their human form, they are vulnerable."

"That's some valuable info, but I think you need to go back to trying contractions. I think people are going to overhear you and think you're practicing lines for a Shakespearian play."

How about we have our Gargoyle talk this way?

Andel nodded. *What I mean is, Gargoyles live most of their existence interacting only with each other. While Gargoyles are able to live out part of their days and nights in human form, they're also granted one human lifetime to live out. Roscoe is centuries old. He was created, by an artist and his Muse, to protect St. Patrick's Cathedral; but over time the Nox have grown in number, and the Gargoyles have become our first defense. His position as a leader is an honor, and I know if he could choose, he'd remain a Gargoyle and attempt to keep Sydney in his immortal life. But don't misunderstand, I believe he will choose Sydney if he cannot have both.*

Evelyn nodded. *I'm actually intrigued to meet Roscoe now. Any guy who'd risk everything for the girl is a winner in my book. But, I still don't understand one thing, if he's immortal, will he die if he spends a lifetime with Sydney?*

No. He will lose his ability to transform into a human and spend an eternity as a stone dragon. The only way for a Gargoyle to die is in his human condition. Roscoe will be able to fight and lead after his lifetime with Sydney, but he'll never be able to walk amongst mortals again.

Andel's footsteps stuttered in front of a red hand blinking across the intersection. The crowd continued to move while horns honked and cabbies hollered.

Have you ever had the pleasure of meeting a Gargoyle? Evelyn asked.

"Yes."

And... Evelyn hoped staying in Andel's head would prompt him to embellish.

"And, it was an interesting experience." Andel looked everywhere but at Evelyn.

"P-shaw!" Evelyn slapped Andel's bicep. "I don't know if you've noticed, but all of this is interesting to me. Can you be more specific?"

Turning one last corner, Evelyn and Andel finally confronted the Gothic cathedral. Lights shone against the ornate structure, stretching up the haunting spires. Shadows spilled onto snarling beasts and contorted faces. Evelyn shuddered when she thought she saw a carved figure twitch on the cathedral's front door. If nothing else, this assignment was going to be a curious one.

"For the love of—" Evelyn groaned.

"Exactly."

Chapter 7

Andel guided Evelyn as she processed how massive the marble church was. The delicate and eerie architecture still amazed him. Churches had a tendency to make Cupids feel safe, and Evelyn had experience with the St. Louis Cathedral in New Orleans. It was only a few weeks ago that the two of them were trying to figure out a riddle in order to keep the underworld...well, under. Andel had made a habit of going to church wherever he was on assignment. The crosses, candles, and steeples created a safe haven.

"Is it true that evil creatures can't step into churches?" Evelyn impatiently tapped her foot on the grimy city sidewalk while waiting for permission to cross the street.

It amused Andel that she was exhibiting premature New Yorker tendencies. He reached down and held his hand a few inches away from Evelyn's hip to soothe the anxiousness consuming her. That trick had its benefits, but it also left Andel feeling awkward. When she looked down to find his hand hovering, he shoved it in his coat pocket.

"Over five million people step into that cathedral every year. A few of them are bound to be deemed evil by the powers that be," Andel answered and looked up at the cloud-covered sky.

"Let me rephrase the question. Can evil immortals pass through those sacred doors?" Evelyn pointed. "Ya know, like vampires or witches?"

"Anyone with a soul is welcome in the house of God, Evelyn. Whether good or evil, if there is a chance for salvation, they're permitted to enter. There are safeguards that protect us when we're inside."

"Safeguards?"

The crowd around Evelyn and Andel began to cross the street, and the Cupids moved seamlessly with them in front of the towering cathedral. They maneuvered around people stopping to take selfies. If it weren't for Evelyn's arm folded over Andel's, they would have been separated. It helped that Andel exercised a glamour that detoured passersby from paying too much attention to their elderly disguise.

"Watch." Andel pulled her up the first few steps with him to the bronze front doors. Andel's height felt unmatched until that moment. The entryway to the church was more than twice as tall as the heavenly warrior. The last glint of setting sun reflected along the top of the doors and darkness rolled over the city block. Lights fought the cold, murky evening for space, but the cathedral's glow was full of life. Marble statues inhaled, waking from a heavy sleep, and with an exhale, they sang. It wasn't the same song of lust or love she heard from couples, but it was magical. Evelyn gasped as the first carved creatures stepped off its ledge into the air.

Mortals carried on, oblivious, as the rest of the Gargoyles took flight.

A bird the size of a bicycle, a winged lizard stretched the length of a dining table, and a man with contorted features all flew into the city. Quasimodo had plenty of Gargoyle cousins join him in the night, and there were countless creatures Evelyn couldn't exactly define. One stone cat twisted in the air, revealing its bird-like backside. Instead of a long, thin, furry tail, a fan of feathers was revealed. Andel knew there had to be a mythological name for the animal, but he drew a blank. Each immortal had left an imprint of their statue behind.

"Whoa!" Evelyn darted into the cathedral's doorway.

"Shh… They're glamoured like you and me." Andel, ever the gentleman, sidestepped to allow a young couple to pass them. "They may appear scary to the human eye, but all supernatural creatures are aware of the Gargoyles' protective nature. Their race is old, like the Cupids, and they're fiercely loyal to each other and anyone they consider family."

Evelyn shuffled just far enough to look out over the street where a few Gargoyles began to descend. After landing in shadows, they'd take on a human form and step into the sidewalk's current. They mingled through the crowd without anyone the wiser. "I don't mind the loyal part." She pointed to one fierce creature that had recently taken the form of a well-dressed, handsome business man. "It's just weirding me out that he was a fish-dragon with bulging eyes, fangs, and a tail a few seconds ago."

Looking down at his watch, Andel's eyes widened. "It's time for you meet Roscoe. If he cannot put your mind at ease, no one can."

Andel followed Evelyn into the church and admired her attention to the ornate stained-glass windows. They would have to come back during the day to see sunlight streaming through them. Andel continued into the room, passing Evelyn, and the echo of his footsteps broke her concentration. She would be coming face to face with a Gargoyle any minute. Andel had explained that Gargoyles took on a human form, but he could tell Evelyn was worried she'd be meeting with a serpent-demon-stone-monster. As Cupids, they could look past a glamour, but Gargoyles didn't disguise themselves. They had two physical states to choose from.

Out of the corner of his eye, Andel noticed his suspender-clad friend making his way inside from a side door. Roscoe's smile widened when he recognized them. He stood about six feet tall, but his lanky limbs made him appear taller. A tuft of brown curly hair on top of his head threatened to topple over with each step he took. Once close enough, the two men embraced, patting each other's back.

"Roscoe, it is good to see you, old friend." Andel held the Gargoyle at arm's length and gave him a once over. Roscoe wore khaki pants; a white dress shirt, wrinkled under navy suspenders; and penny loafers. "How have you been?"

"Honestly, never better." Roscoe hooked his thumbs around his suspenders and stepped to the side to invite Evelyn into their conversation. "You must be Evelyn."

Evelyn had been taking in the copper coins in each of Roscoe's shoes. Andel would define the Gargoyle as handsome. But the way Evelyn smiled when she met his eyes lead Andel to believe Roscoe had something going for him.

"How's Cupid-life treating you?" Roscoe asked.

"Honestly, until this assignment, pretty sh-crappy." Evelyn rolled her eyes when Andel's lips twitched. He'd attempted to add conjunctions to his vocabulary and respected her for trying to remove some of her cuss-words-turned-confections. Andel knew it annoyed her that he thought it was so funny she spouted out a dessert every time she lost her temper. "The superpowers make up for it, though," she shrugged.

"And, by superpowers, you mean…" Roscoe's eyebrows lifted in curiosity. He, more than anyone, wanted to know about Evelyn's supernatural red arrows. If they really did what the Cupid Elders were claiming, their agreement with the Gargoyles would be solidified.

"You know, the super-speed, strength, hearing, endurance, agility," she rambled off.

"I'm aware of *those* abilities. Most of us"—Roscoe waved his hand to include all of them—"have *those*. The rest of us don't have the power to grant an immortal divine love."

"Divine?" Evelyn glanced at Andel. He'd never referred to their job as something so holy. Cupid love wasn't perfect, but it was as close to it as someone could get.

Roscoe rubbed his palms together and took a deep breath. "Let me cut to the chase. There's a parishioner that comes in and out of this cathedral named Sydney. She stops outside the church and studies us, all of the Gargoyles, and she prays." Roscoe made eye contact with Evelyn before moving on. "Her words are like a song to my soul. I want to invoke my human form and live every second of her life with her. The only problem is my job is a little more demanding than most Gargoyles." Roscoe's plea was sincere, but something bothered Andel.

"So you've never met her?" Andel broke the silence.

"I thought I was being dragged into this because you wanted love, but you already have it." Evelyn pointed a finger at Roscoe. "And you don't even *know* this woman?" Evelyn's question echoed through the church.

"I am in love, and I know her. She just doesn't know me," Roscoe said with a frown.

"Ew!" Evelyn exclaimed.

"Evelyn"—Andel reached up and took her hand—"we should move somewhere more private and at least give Roscoe a chance to explain."

Before Evelyn could tug her hand out of Andel's, he was leading them out the side door Roscoe had entered. Once outside, Andel placed his hand on each of their shoulders, and in a blink, they were back in their highrise apartment. Being surrounded by streamlined furniture and glass didn't offer the same peace as the church, but Evelyn was less likely to cause a scene in the private residence. Looking over the cityscape, she took a deep breath. Transcending was a perk of being a Cupid, but it literally took her breath away when she wasn't warned. Andel immediately regretted his mistake.

"That was awesome," Roscoe began. "I can only fly in Gargoyle form. I'm not complaining, but you'd be surprised how long it can take to get somewhere when the wind is blowing against you."

Evelyn quirked an eyebrow in Andel's direction and mentally screamed *Adieu*! He cringed and nodded, acknowledging the code word he had agreed to use before transcending Evelyn. She had the power to poof herself, and to say she got upset when Andel took liberties and transcended them both was an understatement.

I'm sorry.

Making his way to the couch, Andel asked, "Roscoe, how about you start from the beginning?"

"Sure buddy, let's see, from the beginning of our friendship?" Roscoe whipped his pointer finger between him and Andel. "Or, from my beginning?"

Evelyn huffed in irritation. "How about you start from the beginning that will most benefit me since you're willing to barter with the lives of all Cupids for my assistance."

Folding her arms over her torso, Evelyn crossed through the tension in the room to the kitchen. Andel had stocked the refrigerator, anticipating Evelyn would want something ninety percent sugar.

The scent of chocolate wafted into the living room from the open refrigerator. Evelyn grabbed a plate holding a cake covered with icing and snatched a fork out of one of the drawers. Grinning, she made her way back to the living room. She carefully maneuvered onto the floor and dug in.

Neither the awkward silence nor the befuddled stares from an ancient supernatural gave Evelyn pause. "What?" she asked with a mouth full of cake. "Did you want a fork, too?" Holding out her own fork toward Roscoe, he couldn't help but let out a laugh.

Evelyn gave Andel a toothy, sarcastic smile covered in sweet brown goo.

"I knew having cake at the apartment was a good idea," Andel said to Roscoe. "With Evelyn, I'd say digesting chocolate is a superpower."

"I don't think I've heard of that ability. I'd have remembered." Roscoe glanced down at Evelyn.

"Is that your way of saying you've been around for a while?" Evelyn asked.

"I've been around for a long time." Roscoe sat down in a sleek black chair across from the Cupids. A perfect, glittering New York City was framed behind him in the window-wall. "A Muse created me in Paris, late in the twelfth century."

Andel took mental notes of everything he thought Evelyn would ask about later. Hopefully, Roscoe's story would come full circle or contain context clues. Setting her plate on the floor next to her, Evelyn pulled her knees to her chest and gave Roscoe her full attention.

"The Muse was in love with a sculptor, and little did he know the dragon he carved would transform into a man for the next 800 years. Before the Muse moved on to her next charge, she explained to me that I wasn't the first Gargoyle, nor would I be the last of my kind. You see, a Muse has the power to enchant a statue, or gargoyle in my case, to live and breathe for an eternity. My Muse explained to me that if I ever found a love as powerful as her love for my artist I could choose to live a lifetime with that human."

Roscoe paused and swiveled his chair to face the city. He'd resided at St. Patrick's Cathedral for the last 200 years. The world had changed during those two centuries. Not simply growing from farmland to skyscrapers, but the people had transformed, too. And it was part of the Gargoyles' job to protect them.

"This world is night and day from when I was called to my mission." Roscoe stood up, unable to stay still for too long. "That's one reason I've requested your help."

"Really? Requested?" Evelyn shoved a forkful of cake in her mouth, but it didn't stop her. "If you love this woman, Sydney, why don't you just commit and drop the ultimatum?"

"Evelyn." Andel placed a hand on her shoulder to calm her.

"No! If you love her, then prove it! Fudge!" Evelyn picked her plate of cake up and waved her fork at Roscoe. "I took a bus in the face to prove my love, having to let go way too soon. So don't give me some melancholy tale about finally finding your true love and having to give her up to keep aliens from invading. You haven't even got the guts to introduce yourself to her."

Andel groaned at Evelyn's outburst, but instead of apologizing for her, he decided to go with it. "Roscoe, we need a little more background to fully understand your situation."

"Fine." Roscoe turned to face Evelyn. "If I succumb to my human form permanently, it will start a civil war among the Gargoyles. I must remain the leader of the North American legion, or our alliances will deteriorate. Our alliance with the Cupids is only in question because the Gargoyle Council can't, no, won't choose someone to take my place. Andel, you know better than most, this will lead to casualties, and not only immortal ones."

"I understand," Andel said.

"Will you help me?" Roscoe asked Evelyn specifically.

"Unlike Andel, I'm not sure I understand completely. I need to know you're not some pigheaded creep." Evelyn passed her plate of cake to Andel and stood up. "We've got to start somewhere, so where's Sydney?"

Roscoe shoved his hands in his pocket. "I can take you to meet her. She's a barista and works during the evenings."

"So you've been stalking her?" Evelyn asked, and Andel groaned. She took the cake back from Andel and shoved a bite into her mouth on the way to returning it to the refrigerator.

"Not really?" Roscoe shrugged. "It's not as bad as it seems, I promise. She wears a name tag, and that's how I learned her name. And I have to give her my name to write down my coffee order. So, in a way we've been introduced, right?"

"Wrong," Andel and Evelyn said simultaneously. Andel couldn't believe his ears. One of the fiercest warriors he knew turned out to be a chicken when it came to women.

The three immortals headed for the apartment's front door. It wasn't safe to try and transcend to a place he hadn't seen or been to before. Evelyn had only tried poofing in the heavens and, while absurd, she had a fear of bumping into someone or appearing inside a wall. Andel explained that it wasn't possible, but Evelyn was not the typical Cupid.

As they stepped onto the street, an ominous darkness crawled across Andel's skin. He noticed Evelyn shiver. The protection of the church and privacy of the apartment had been like a blanket of security, but moving out in the open was like ripping that blanket off. Andel considered conjuring his bow and arrow. While they couldn't hurt a human, his arrows had the ability to be used as a weapon against supernaturals. They didn't kill, but they slowed an attacker down.

Andel had a good sense of direction, but the looming buildings and heavy cloud cover blocked any view of the moon or constellations. A few blocks to the left, then another to the right, and Roscoe slowed. The avenue was lined with eateries and cafes, but Andel recognized the name of the coffee shop a few steps away, *Culture Espresso*.

Roscoe stopped at the window and locked eyes with a busy barista for a millisecond. She grinned but kept moving. She shouted orders and the names they belonged to. Roscoe gulped down a mouthful of air and reached out to open the door for Evelyn and Andel.

"I promise not to embarrass you," Evelyn smiled. Andel was relieved Sydney had recognized Roscoe, and he could tell by Evelyn's face that she was, too.

Walking toward the counter, the three immortals got in line. Evelyn became distracted by the glass-encased treats while Andel perused the menu made up of white plastic letters behind the register. Roscoe simply watched Sydney. The poor guy probably hadn't considered he might come across as creepy, and he must have come to the coffee shop a few evenings a week for Sydney to remember him.

As they stepped up to place their order, Sydney interrupted Roscoe, "The same?" she asked from behind a large silver box topped with coffee beans and blanketed in steam.

"Yes, thank you," Roscoe replied with a wave.

"What'll you two have?" the cashier asked Evelyn and Andel.

"I'll take one of those muffins," Evelyn pointed out. "And a caramel macchiato." She shifted to the side to let Andel order, but the cashier stopped her.

"That's not a muffin, it's a cupcake."

"Oh." Evelyn avoided eye contact with Andel.

She had to have known it was a cupcake, but ordering the dessert after eating cake at the apartment would give Andel more ammo to tease her with.

"I'll have steamed milk, please," Andel ordered.

"A latte?" the cashier asked while focused on the computer screen she tapped orders on.

"No, just milk, please."

The cashier looked up and grinned at Andel. Nodding, she placed the order. Cupids frequently had that effect on mortals. Either the love they carried or their heavenly presence made humans mimic lovesick fangirls. Next time they'd have to come in a less attractive glamour. Andel couldn't risk being a distraction to Sydney.

"What name can I put with this order?" The cashier winked and waited with her marker pressed against a cup.

"Evelyn," Evelyn answered from over Andel's shoulder, and she winked back at the cashier before walking over to sit with Roscoe at one of the tables.

Andel looked back and forth between Evelyn and the cashier as he pulled a twenty out of his wallet. He set the bill on the counter and followed Evelyn and Roscoe. Andel chalked up Evelyn's frustration to her being embarrassed about the cupcake order. She'd handled meeting her first Gargoyle better than he'd expected. Sweets had become her way of staying connected to her humanity, and if a cupcake helped her feel more comfortable, he'd order her two.

After two hundred years of being a Cupid, Andel often felt like he'd lost every connection to his humanity. And until he started training Evelyn, he hadn't remembered how much he missed it.

Chapter 8

Coffee and conversation with Roscoe had lasted more than an hour. Evelyn learned enough about the Gargoyle to know he needed more than an arrow to find true love with Sydney. Cupid arrows helped solidify a couple's love. The way Evelyn saw it, their process was similar to adding a side of ice cream to a slice of pie. Heavenly love added depth and texture to an already wonderful thing.

Roscoe had it in his head that if it was meant to be with Sydney, they could make his being a Gargoyle work. Evelyn could tell he really liked Sydney, and Evelyn even noticed Sydney make a few extra trips to their table to check on them. But Roscoe would need to learn how to date. Evelyn spent most of the next day making a list of dating dos and don'ts while Andel went to MoMa for more recon.

"Welcome ho-ome," Evelyn sang from the kitchen to greet Andel. "Did you get some good *Cupid*ing done today?"

"Cupiding?" Andel moved into the apartment and plopped onto the couch with an exhale.

"You know…get your Cupid on!" Evelyn walked into the living room and took aim as if she was about to shoot a plate, topped with a slice of pie, like it was an arrow. She handed the meringue-covered chocolate pie over to Andel. The white fluff reminded Evelyn of the heavens. Evelyn wondered when they'd be returning. The last time they were on assignment, they spent a month in New Orleans. She wouldn't mind getting to stay here even longer. She still had so much to see and do.

"Thanks."

"Whoa, wait a sec. Did you just say *thanks* instead of thank you?"

"Yes, why?" Andel scooped a fork full of desert into his mouth.

"Well, first off, you only started modernizing your speech yesterday. Second, you aren't lecturing me on my mortal sweet tooth. Are you feeling okay?" Evelyn pressed the back side of her hand to Andel's forehead and feigned being scalded before settling onto the rug.

Andel fidgeted in his seat and avoided looking at Evelyn. "My Cupiding seems to be a little off today." He rolled his eyes at the new term.

Evelyn sat, dumbfounded. After a few moments of debating with herself, she decided to use Andel's tactics against him. She'd wait him out until he gave her more details. Andel's will was older than Evelyn, heck it was older than the titanic. And she hoped that meant his will would sink before hers. They each finished their pie in silence, and Evelyn got up to clean her dish without a word. Halfway to the kitchen, Andel followed suit. Evelyn's fork clanged loudly in the sink, then her dish. Andel stepped up behind her and turned on the water. Jumping onto the opposite counter, Evelyn sat and watched Andel gently rinse both of their dishes. He turned the water off and faced her.

Stopping in front of her, he asked, "What are you thinking?"

Evelyn looked over her shoulder at the cabinet and glanced into the living room searching for who he was talking to. "Me? I'm trying to figure out what you meant by your '*Cupiding is off*.'"

Her fingers bounced in the air around her words, and instead of interrogating him, she waited, again. This time, the silence didn't last as long.

"My goal today was to introduce Jane and Kendrick." Andel rubbed the back of his neck. He made a habit of doing it when he was stressed. "It seems Jane will not acknowledge anyone outside her inner circle of work relationships during work hours. So, I glamoured myself as a co-worker to get her down to the docking area, but it was all in vain. By the time she was convinced to go, she was in a horrible mood. I couldn't chance introducing her to Kendrick because I knew it would leave a terrible first impression."

"Oh. Is that all?"

Andel scooted onto the counter across from Evelyn. His legs nearly touched the floor, dwarfing the kitchen. "That's all, but I should warn you about glamouring—"

Evelyn cut in before he started lecturing. "Are you asking for my advice right now or just venting?"

"To be honest, I think your familiarity with women in today's culture could be beneficial. And you did take that art history class in college." Andel stared at his dangling feet. He'd served as Evelyn's mentor for a while, and Evelyn never imagined he'd need her help. She was flattered he'd opened up to her.

"I did, but if I help you, I'm going to need to be on the inside. You know, undercover."

"Undercover doing what?" Andel looked up with narrowed eyes.

"Cupiding," she grinned.

"Can you be more specific?"

Evelyn slid off the counter and stood inches in front of Andel's knees.

"I'm going to befriend Jane and set her up with your guy."

"Oh," Andel frowned.

"Don't worry, you'll have a job, too." She tapped one of Andel's legs. "You'll have to get in good with Kendrick and convince him to go on a date with a friend of yours, a.k.a. Jane."

"I can do that." Andel slipped down from the counter, nearly bumping into Evelyn. A charge rippled between them, heating the air around them. The shock stilled Andel, and Evelyn took in the dark stubble along Andel's jaw. Slowly, a dimple appeared, fracturing Andel's typically serious demeanor.

"There are a few more hours until the museum closes. Do you want to get a head start and meet Jane now?" Andel asked.

Evelyn shifted back a few inches, giving herself room to breathe. The humid feeling in the kitchen had begun to evaporate, but Evelyn's cheeks still felt flush. Her heart swelled at the thought of Andel wrapping his arms around her. Was it because she wanted Andel to hold her or that she simply missed being held?

Shaking the question from her head, Evelyn answered, "It beats waiting around here for the sun to set. Roscoe wants some lessons on asking a girl out. So, I'll have to be back around seven."

Andel glanced down at his watch and smiled. "Adieu."

With the use of their code word, Evelyn knew they'd transcend, and in a fraction of a second, they stood across the street from the museum in a discreet alcove. Evelyn didn't have to worry about disguising too much of her appearance. She'd never been to New York City, and it wasn't likely she'd run into anyone she knew. She used her Cupid abilities to glamour a power suit. Evelyn rocked navy slacks and a white silk blouse, with nude heels to complete the ensemble.

To an immortal, who focused on seeing past the facade, Evelyn's glamour was useless. Underneath it all, she wore skinny jeans, boots, and a gray V-neck T-shirt. It wasn't Gucci, but she could move freely in it if trouble arose. Andel stood next to her, glamoured in the same uniform the crew wore at the museum's loading docks. Under his illusion, Andel sported dark jeans, a navy dress shirt, and brown ranger boots.

"You have an interview with Jane in about 15 minutes, and I'll meet you back here after work." Andel didn't wait for a reaction and darted across the street.

"Hey! How did you set up an interview if you didn't know I would help you?" Evelyn yelled after him.

Andel glanced over his shoulder with a grin and opened his thoughts. *I knew you'd offer.*

Evelyn wasn't sure if she should be offended or take his presumptions as a compliment. She couldn't poof into Jane's office, so she followed Andel across the street. The woman selling tickets into the museum had Evelyn's name on a visitor's list with a small difference. The badge for her read *Evelyn Hart*, and she needed it to bypass security. Knowing her interview was a few minutes away, Evelyn went straight to the elevator to arrive early. Even if she didn't qualify for the position she interviewed for, she'd try and make a good first impression.

Once she arrived on the administrative floor, Evelyn approached a door that looked more like an emergency exit. Swiping her badge over a security pad, she crossed over to the corporate side of the museum. An elevator stood along the wall to the left, and a secretary sat at her desk on the right with three chairs lining the far wall.

"Hi," Evelyn began. "I'm Evelyn B—Hart, here to see Jane Platt."

"Please, take a seat. Ms. Platt will be with you shortly." The secretary's nameplate read *Gloria Knight*. The woman's tightly-pulled-back braid and turtleneck, in addition to the sound of her nails clacking along her computer's keyboard, warded off any small talk.

A few moments later, the elevator dinged, and the door slid to the side, revealing Jane Platt. The secretary obviously avoided making eye contact. Evelyn hoped she could answer Jane's questions and get hired. None of what had transpired in the last thirty minutes felt like an Andel Lambros plan. For as long as she'd known Andel, he paid more attention to details and relayed those details to Evelyn. She would definitely be giving Andel a piece of her mind as soon as she got back to the apartment.

"Ms. Hart." Jane stepped in Evelyn's direction and held out her hand. After a temporary brain lapse, Evelyn stood to join her and shake her hand. Ms. anything sounded foreign to her. "Thank you for being prompt."

Jane's handshake was strong and sturdy. Her blue eyes darted over Evelyn's shoulder at Gloria, and without so much as a smile at the secretary, she turned around and moved back into the elevator. The simple black dress she wore reminded Evelyn of a dress an actress in the 1950s would wear—artistically conservative. The perfect tailoring revealed her trim physique, and Jane's red wavy hair was pulled up loosely, revealing intricate cutouts along her shoulders.

"Thank you, Gloria." Evelyn waved to the secretary as she stepped into the elevator, breaking through some of the tension. As the door slid shut, the secretary's fingers stuttered over her keyboard, but it was the only indication she'd heard Evelyn.

"Let's not waste any time, Ms. Hart," Jane began. "I was intrigued when our museum's director called to inform me of your desire to intern with me. Most of our internships are with our Director of Education. Tell me, what's inspired you to seek out a position in curating?" Evelyn breathed a sigh of relief. She could make something up.

"Well, Ms. Platt, I hope you'll call me Evelyn." Remaining so formal would hinder any possibility of getting personal and eventually convincing her to go out with Kendrick. They needed to get on a first name basis. "My studies have brought me to a place where I want to stretch my knowledge, not simply share it."

"Tell me more." Jane nodded as the elevator doors opened at the next floor. Glass boxes lined the hallway with businessmen and women sitting at their desks quietly.

"I wish to learn more about the ins and outs of such a prestigious museum. Specifically, the process of arranging exhibits." Evelyn had a feeling too many compliments would have the opposite effect on Jane, so she decided to keep her answers as close to the truth as possible. "And I had a feeling curating art would not only teach me some of the museum's business, but I would learn more about the art we're exhibiting than any tour guide could teach me."

Walking into one of the corner offices, Jane waved toward a chair in front of her desk. Evelyn sat, crossed her legs, and took in the space. If she stood at the giant window serving as the outer wall, she'd be able to see half of Manhattan.

"You make it sound more glamorous than it is." Jane opened a file folder, and Evelyn's enhanced immortal senses allow her to see her own name written on the tab. Andel had gone to more trouble than she'd suspected if she had a file.

"If I do agree to take you on, Evelyn, you'll need to be prepared for the mounds of paperwork and red tape we are required to work through. I would feel obligated to expose you to the reality of it all."

Evelyn relaxed as she felt the tension in the room melt away. She didn't have to know everything about this position because the job would be to learn the position. The real work would be building trust with Jane. "Ms. Platt, I wouldn't expect any less. It'll be the daily grind of work that I hope to learn from most."

With a smile, Jane closed Evelyn's folder, "Please, call me Jane."

Chapter 9

After her meeting with Jane, Evelyn transcended into the middle of her New York apartment. Andel and three ancient creatures surrounded her. Each Gargoyle had transformed into a mortal, and Evelyn didn't try to guess which grotesque faces they wore on the roof of the cathedral. Roscoe sat on the couch facing an older-looking man with salt and pepper hair who paced in front of the window. The stalky Gargoyle's fingers snapped in the direction of a third dark, brooding man who'd suddenly frozen in place at Evelyn's arrival.

"Come on, Jude, focus." The older man clapped to get the attention he sought. His tortoiseshell glasses and manicured mustache disguised some of his wrinkles. "If Roscoe can defend Lux royalty from a hoard of Nox vamps, he can ask a mortal girl out."

Evelyn couldn't picture her new floppy-haired friend, Roscoe, fighting with anything but a litter of kittens. And she'd never heard of royalty amongst the Lux, but maybe the guy was exaggerating.

"It's fine, Leo," Roscoe offered. His voice sounded more commanding in the presence of these new Gargoyles.

Before Evelyn could think of a sarcastic welcome, Jude turned to face her. The contrast of his coffee-colored skin framing his light hazel eyes surprised Evelyn. He was exotic and beautiful, like a wild animal. He crossed his arms over his chest and gave her a once over. "So, you must be the one giving my best friend, and commander, false hope."

Evelyn had only ever met one other character as imposing as Jude. Andel. As Jude moved closer to her, he stepped past Andel. The two men took up space, and not just because they were big in size, but because they moved with purpose. Another thing they had in common was that they looked like they were both in their early twenties, but they exuded an ancient air of condescension. Andel obviously knew Jude, and if he allowed Jude to move closer to her, she wouldn't have any reason to fear the Gargoyle.

"Jude, do not underestimate her," Andel warned. Passing Evelyn by, Jude made himself at home in the kitchen. He rummaged through cabinets and drawers, pulling out a plate and fork. As Jude reached for the refrigerator door, Evelyn's insides burned with irritation.

Feeling the need to warn him on more than one front, Evelyn followed. "Hi-ya there, Jude." She plastered her best fake smile across her face. "It's a pleasure to meet you, too."

Jude pulled out a decadent indulgence, fudge, and cut a sliver. After placing it on the dish, he made himself comfortable on the arm of the couch next to Roscoe.

Evelyn pushed away the desire to get a piece of fudge for herself and began pacing. Who did Jude think he was? And why he was there pushing her buttons? She couldn't pinpoint where he might be from by his accent, and it didn't help that he looked like he could be from anywhere and any time. Jude's narrow, hazel eyes exuded cunning. His jet-black hair and black suit made him appear mysterious.

Evelyn forced herself to be still as she sat on the rug at the center of the room. She was surrounded.

"Um, I'm Leo." The older man waved to Evelyn, chopping through the tension building in the room.

"What's your plan?" Jude interrupted with a mouth full of fudge.

"What's your deal?" Evelyn pointed a finger Jude's direction.

"How about we start over," Leo interrupted. "I'm Leo, Roscoe's other, less pigheaded, best friend." He held out a hand to Evelyn, and she leaned forward to shake it. "I'm also the supportive friend."

"Nice to meet *you*, Leo."

Leo grinned, "You may have met your match, Jude."

"Let's leave the matching to the Cupids." Evelyn looked over at Andel for some backup, but he'd conveniently made himself comfortable in a chair at the edge of the room.

"In my two hundred years, I haven't met anyone as headstrong as Evelyn," Andel directed to Jude.

Roscoe moved to sit down next to Evelyn on the floor. "I'm sure that was a compliment," the gargoyle murmured.

"Oh, I speak Andel, and I know exactly what that meant." Evelyn had taken Andel's words as support, but recognized the warning for Jude. She wasn't sure she needed the help, but she was thankful for it. "Now, in regard to tonight's lesson, I was hoping we could work out a little bargain."

"What are you thinking?" Roscoe asked.

"Bargain?" Jude frowned. "The deal has already been struck. The Gargoyles continue to save your kind if you help Roscoe."

"Calm down, Jude." Leo patted the cushion next to him on the couch. "Sit down, and let's hear the girl out."

Jude slid over the armrest onto the couch with a huff, but as soon as he'd conceded, Evelyn felt self-conscious. Three Gargoyles and a Cupid waiting for her to haggle for information. She hadn't run the idea by Andel because she knew he'd try to lecture her out of it.

"Okay, well, the Elders agreed to send me here based on the terms you so eloquently articulated, but I consented in hopes of getting intel."

"Evelyn," Andel warned.

She ignored him and went on, "I'm here because I'm different, and I can help immortals. I want to help the Lux, but what I also want to know is *why* I'm different."

Before she could haggle, she felt a mental knock from Andel. His thoughts pressed along her brow until she let them in. *This is not a good time, Evelyn. I don't believe Jude will react positively. Please, heed my warning.*

Evelyn considered Andel's advice and decided to compromise and point her question at Roscoe alone. "I understand that you're hoping my arrow will allow you to remain an immortal so you can stand with the Gargoyles and also be with Sydney."

Roscoe nodded for her to continue.

"I want to help you, but I'm hoping you might feel compelled to help me, too." Evelyn left her unasked question in the air between them. By not asking outright, Jude wouldn't have any reason to argue, and Roscoe's heart would lead him to the answer for her.

"How about you teach me how to be suave so I can get a date with Sydney, then I'll tell you what I know."

"Deal." Evelyn stood and reached a hand out to Roscoe to help him up. "But you're never allowed to say *suave* again. I should clarify, my job as a Cupid is to solidify the love between you and Sydney. We have some serious work to do before we get there."

With her hand in his, he said, "I should warn you, I don't know much, if anything, about dating or women. And why can't I say *suave?*"

She grimaced at the word. "It's the name of soap and ages you fifty years. No offense, Leo."

"Hey! I resemble that." Leo acted affronted, but couldn't help grinning at the laughter that erupted from Roscoe. "I can get away with posing as a forty-five-year-old on a good night."

"Yeah, because it's so dark." The corner of Jude's mouth lifted.

Evelyn stood and made her way to Roscoe; his body froze at her proximity. She stood mere inches away, and his unease hinted at the amount of work ahead of them.

"Pretend I'm Sydney," Evelyn began the lesson. "How would you ask me out?"

"Wait. You want to do this in front of them?" Roscoe asked.

"I just want to see what I have to work with, *Mr. Suave.*"

Roscoe swallowed down his nerves and shoved both hands into his pockets. Evelyn felt for the guy. To him, asking a girl out was more difficult than slaying multiple Nox all at once.

"You can do this, Roscoe. Keep it simple," Evelyn encouraged him.

Removing his hands from his pockets, Roscoe wiped his palms on his pants. "Okay, uh. Hey, Sydney!" His lips pulled tight in an attempt to smile, but the Evelyn was getting a *God-help-me* vibe. "I was, uh, wondering if you're doing anything tomorrow night?"

Evelyn fell into character and smiled back at Roscoe. "I'm working. Why?" She twirled one of her fingers through her hair.

"Oh. Uh. What about the next night?" Roscoe rocked back on his heels, and a mass of his hair flopped down over his eyes. "I suck at this."

"Hold on." Evelyn stopped him. "You're adorable in an awkward way, and if you ask the right questions, I think Sydney will go out with you." Evelyn patted him on the shoulder.

"Really?"

"She totally smiled at you last night at the coffee shop."

"She smiles at everyone," Jude mumbled. "It's her job."

Evelyn ignored the slight. "Roscoe, your problem is you're nervous and don't know her work schedule. Sit."

Roscoe fell into the couch beside Leo. This would be more difficult with an audience, but since Sydney worked in a coffee shop, there would be no escaping the public eye. She needed Roscoe to let go of his anxiety.

Glancing at Leo, Evelyn had an idea. He may have looked older, but she had always thought Clooney was attractive. Evelyn needed Leo's light-heartedness to prove a point.

"Leo, would you join me at the front of the class?" Evelyn teased.

Looking to Roscoe, Leo waited for his friend's approval. "Don't look at me. You have to decide whether to take your life into your own hands."

"I don't bite, guys." Evelyn snatched Leo's hand. "You and I are going to show Roscoe how it's done. We don't want him having a panic attack before he even gets a chance to ask the real Sydney out."

Once at his feet, Evelyn released Leo's hand. "Am I supposed to be getting into character?" He ran his fingers over his manicured mustache.

"Oh, no. I want you to be you. Let's give Roscoe an example of what a casual invitation to go out looks like. Can you handle it?"

"I think so," Leo winked. "But remember, this is merely an exercise. I can't risk you falling for me."

"Of course, I'll try to keep it professional." Evelyn pressed one hand into a back pocket of her jeans and strained to keep a straight face.

Leo took the following silence to be his cue.

"Hi Sydney," he greeted.

"Hi."

"I'm Roscoe."

"I know." Evelyn smiled at Leo. "I write your name on your cup every time you come in."

"Well, I'm going to take it as a good sign that you remembered my name," Leo flirted and ran his hand through his white hair. "I was hoping I could take you out to dinner on your next night off."

"I'm actually off this Friday night." Evelyn twisted a few strands of hair around her finger. "But I barely know you."

Leo took a second to compose his response, "You'll know me better if you join me for a cup of coffee on your next break. I'll be sitting right over there." Grinning, he pointed to the spot on the couch between Jude and Roscoe.

"Okay, sounds good." Evelyn laid her hand on the outside of Leo's arm. "See you in a few minutes."

In her peripheral vision, Evelyn noticed Andel shift in his chair. She dropped her hand back to her side and turned to Roscoe. Next to him, Jude rolled his eyes at the display.

"You make that look so easy," Roscoe complained. "There's no way I can come across that confident."

"You can, and you will—even if we have to practice a thousand times." Evelyn sat down on the floor. "It's your turn, but let's try something different this time. I'll be you and you pretend to be Sydney."

"Why can't you just pierce them with the arrow?" Jude nudged Roscoe with his elbow. "She'll fall madly in love with him, and the poor guy won't have to worry about being rejected."

Andel stood, taking offense to Jude's insinuation. "Cupids don't work that way, and you know it."

Jude straightened as all the eyes in the room fell on him. "I apologize."

"We know how serious your jobs are. It's just hard to keep that in mind with a bunch of chubby, naked babies posing as Cupids on Earth," Roscoe joked. "In all seriousness, we know you guys play into what we all do: help and protect mortals. We physically fight Nox immortals who think humanity is their plaything, and you guys take on the spiritual and emotional darkness."

"That's not entirely true," Andel said.

"You are our brother in arms, Andel." Roscoe placed a fist over his heart. "There are not many Lux strong enough to fight by our side."

"Are you sure you're the commander of a legion of Gargoyles?" Evelyn asked, and all the men in the room squirmed at her question. "I want to hear you take Sydney that seriously. If you really care for her, you'll fight for her."

"You're right."

Evelyn could feel Roscoe's apprehension fade. She may have had selfish motives, but if Roscoe could get the nerve up to ask Sydney out, he'd get an answer that would change his immortal life. Evelyn had a good feeling about Sydney and Roscoe, but if he screwed this up she may never learn anything about why she was different.

"Let's practice a few times together, so you can get more comfortable. When you're ready, we'll go to the coffee shop. Just think, if you ask Sydney out tonight, we can work on dos and don'ts on a first date tomorrow."

Roscoe grimaced but squared his shoulders. He was ready to fight.

Chapter 10

Depending on your view of the glass, it could be considered half full or half empty. Wednesday's workday was almost at an end. Since Evelyn worked at MoMa in New York City, surrounded by world renowned art, she saw the glass as being half full.

Walking alongside Jane, weaving through crowded galleries, Evelyn listened to her explain how the human psyche interpreted different exhibits. Evelyn soaked in her lecture like sunlight. She welcomed the topics of color, texture, and style as opposed to the duty of a Cupid. Andel had a way of communicating the most beautiful emotion humankind exhibited in an unfeeling, professional tone. But Jane exuded passion for art. She loved her work.

Jane came alive in the galleries. Whether the art struggled to be recognized or the sculptures made Evelyn blush, she felt an echo of the same life Jane had in all the pieces they reviewed. Evelyn quickly decided

Jane didn't need to meet Kendrick down at the delivery docks, he needed to see her in her element.

After Roscoe left to ask Sydney out the previous night, Andel went out with Leo and Jude to patrol the city. Evelyn borrowed Andel's file on Jane and Kendrick for some light reading before she fell asleep. Andel teased Evelyn about the unnecessary hours she curled up in bed each night, but it was another one of those ties to her mortal life she couldn't let go of yet.

As her eyelids grew heavy, Evelyn skimmed over Kendrick's privileged childhood and ivy league education. He didn't have to work as a delivery man. It was his family's business, an internationally renowned business. Evelyn had hoped to send Andel off with the task of figuring out why Kendrick didn't seek out a more managerial position, but he'd left before she woke up or never came home.

Evelyn gawked at more Monet paintings and realized Jane had stopped talking. She'd gone on and on for hours only discussing what lay within the walls of the museum. Evelyn wondered out loud, "Is there anything else in the world you're as passionate about?"

Jane's head tilted to the side. "No."

"Oh." Evelyn frowned. "Not even family? Or friends?"

"No." Jane shrugged her shoulders, then straightened her jacket. She went from relaxed to rigid in a blink. "You'll find, in a position as taxing as this one, that family is not as forgiving as one might hope. When you miss family reunions and relatives' milestones, they tend to cope by ignoring the matter altogether. And don't even get me started on friends."

"Well, if you ever want to hang out—outside the museum—you're always welcome to come out with me and my friends." Evelyn tried to read Jane's expression, but her mouth didn't give, neither twitching up or down. "I actually have one friend I think you'd really like."

The words hung in the air between them for what felt like forever. Evelyn soon regretted her last, and very obvious, point. She avoided eye contact and let herself become entranced by the view of a cliff painted in pastels.

"I appreciate the invitation, but I'm too busy." Jane walked away, disappearing behind the administrative office door. Evelyn felt the need to give Jane a little space. She could sit on a bench in the Collection Galleries and pull her foot out of her mouth. Evelyn knew her attempt to set up Jane might have cracked the trust she'd spent the day building.

Focusing on the art in the room, Evelyn noticed the hum she sensed slowly grew into a song that resonated with her. It wasn't the same melody a couple in love emitted, but one painting hummed louder than the rest. Her feet lead her to The Starry Night, painted by Vincent van Gogh. The piece was her favorite in the room. It had always been a favorite of hers as a mortal, but when she saw the swirling night sky with Andel a few nights before, she felt a connection to it.

"Are you planning to head to the loft soon?" Andel's voice startled Evelyn.

"At five, why?"

He looked down at his watch like a normal guy. "It's six."

Evelyn forced herself to look away from the painting. She realized the natural light in the room had changed, shifted. It was getting darker outside, and while the museum continued to buzz with visitors, there were fewer of them. Evelyn didn't hear any of the giggling or squealing that normally accompanied the children who came in waves throughout the day.

"If it's six o'clock, then I've been standing here for over an hour. What the crap happened?"

"Shh…" a patron shushed Evelyn from across the room.

"Are you feeling okay?" Andel stepped closer to her.

"I think so." She pressed the back of her hand to her forehead, then her cheek. "I didn't realize so much of the art would sing to me. This one is the loudest." She pointed to the wall. "It's so beautiful. Almost as entrancing as when I pass a couple in love."

"The painting sings to you?"

"It's more like a hum or a heartbeat, but yeah. Don't you hear it? Or feel it? Because it kinda vibrates in my chest."

Rubbing his hand across his own forehead, Andel answered, "No."

Evelyn guessed he wasn't checking for a fever, not that either of them could ever get sick.

Evelyn's arms flew out wide, and after being glared at by a passerby, she whispered, "What's wrong with me?"

"Do you really want me to answer that?" Andel wrapped an arm around her shoulders. "Take a deep breath."

Evelyn leaned her head on Andel's shoulder. "What do you think it means?"

"I don't have a clue. It's one more thing for us to look into *after* you pierce Roscoe and Sydney. I'll make sure we do. But we have one problem we need to address tonight if we hope to make all that happen."

Evelyn waited for Andel to continue, but something made him hesitant. "Just say it."

Andel closed his eyes. "Roscoe is struggling to get the nerve up to ask Sydney out."

"You mean, he didn't ask her out last night?" Her head fell into her hands. "I bet this is Jude's fault."

"He was with me all night. I think this has more to do with Roscoe's fear of ruining this before it begins. It's a big deal for a Gargoyle to want to settle down. I've never once met one who's made this choice."

"Well, maybe our two couples' progress is more aligned than I thought. I might have set us back a few days with Jane. She got spooked when I mentioned introducing her to a friend." Evelyn looked up through her lashes at Andel.

Andel kept any thoughts he had on the matter to himself, and Evelyn felt a little guilty. She wouldn't let their setbacks get her down. "We can do this. I'm not about to give the Elders a reason to second guess letting us work together."

Evelyn reached for Andel's hand on her shoulder and patted it.

Everything will work out, Evelyn, he thought while looking over her shoulder. *Don't look now, but you may have a chance to fix whatever happened with Jane.*

"Evelyn, I'll see you tomorrow. Have a good night." Jane waved in Evelyn and Andel's direction.

"Jane." Evelyn stepped out from under Andel's arm to stop her. "I'd like you to meet Andel."

Jane stopped. "A pleasure, Andel." As Andel approached Jane reached out to shake his hand. "I hope you're enjoying the museum."

"I am. I studied fine arts a few years ago in Europe."

"Really?" Jane asked. "That must have been exciting."

"It wasn't as long a trip as I would have liked, but I found my time there enlightening. You know, you should join us for dinner sometime." Andel slipped his hand into Evelyn's. "I have a friend whose family has collected some Van Gogh, Renoir, Monet, a handful of Rembrandts. He might be convinced to loan the collection to an establishment like the MoMa. Of course, it would take some teamwork to convince him."

Jane's eyes widened, giving away her interest. "Sounds intriguing. Why don't you send details with Evelyn tomorrow, and I'll see if I can make it work?"

"Perfect." Evelyn looked from Jane to Andel and squeezed his hand.

Jane started for the elevator then paused and turned back. "Evelyn, don't forget your bag is still upstairs."

"Thank you, I'll make sure to grab it."

While the sound of Jane's heels echoed through the gallery, Evelyn released Andel's hand and spun in a circle with glee. Andel had successfully figured out a way to get Kendrick and Jane on a level playing field. The pressure to get Roscoe on a date with Sydney was building, but she would make sure he asked her out tonight.

Evelyn nodded to Andel for permission to telepathically send him a message. He nodded in acceptance, and she thought, *After she's out of sight, you can go upstairs with me and we can poof to the apartment.*

How about I cloak myself? I don't want to get you in trouble or get caught on video. Andel nodded to the mounted camera in the corner.

Evelyn would still be able to see him the same way she could see through a glamour. She'd learned that cloaking was just another version of glamor. Instead of thinking of a great outfit or the color she wanted her hair to be, she focused on her surroundings. How it actually worked confounded her.

Sounds like a plan. Evelyn made her way to the administration door, slid her card through the reader, and went in. *By the way, thanks for getting Jane to agree to meet Kendrick. At least that's what I think you just did?*

The secretary's desk sat empty. Gloria had probably left for the day.

We should not get too excited. It will be business for Jane, and we need to come up with a plan to make it casual, too.

Let's tackle one problem at a time. Evelyn rubbed her chin, trying to think of a way to encourage Roscoe.

You should push the button for the elevator. Andel reminded Evelyn.

The button lit up when she pushed it, and the elevator immediately dinged. *So, what do you think we should do about Roscoe?* Evelyn stepped into the metal box.

Are you asking for my advice?

With a push from Evelyn, another button lit up, and the door slid shut. *You've known him longer.*

Once the elevator began moving, Evelyn noticed Andel stiffen and shift his weight from his heels to his toes. "What's the matter?"

You might not want to talk to yourself on camera. It's frowned upon unless white jackets with lots of buckles are in style.

A little defensive aren't we? I may not be the one that needs a padded cell. Are you nervous about being in this tiny metal box?

Andel stopped rocking and crossed his arms over his chest. *I feel like a sardine in a can.*

The elevator announced their arrival on the administrative floor, and Andel didn't wait for Evelyn to step out first.

You do remember you're immortal, right?

It's not a fear of dying I suffer from. Andel took a deep breath. *I fear being stuck in that tin can, alive, forever.* He pointed back at the elevator.

But you can transcend.

I know. He slipped his hands in his pockets. *I didn't say it was a rational fear.*

You're claustrophobic. Evelyn led Andel down the hallway. *Fear is nothing to be ashamed of, but I'd think you'd want to overcome it.*

How about we fix Roscoe tonight? Then we fix Jane, Andel thought. *And you can fix me when it's all said and done.*

Evelyn moved into Jane's office with Andel close behind. They were out of the security camera's view. After grabbing her bag, they left the museum through an employee exit. Once they were able to hide in the shadows, the two Cupids *poofed* to their apartment.

Chapter 11

After a lengthy debate, Andel decided to go along with Evelyn's plan to help Roscoe ask Sydney out. He couldn't predict how it would turn out, but at least Evelyn hadn't arranged a flash mob. The subtlety of Roscoe's practiced invitation, if he followed through, would appeal to any woman. Evelyn had promised Roscoe the personal touch would catch Sydney's attention.

"I'm not sure this is going to work," Roscoe complained as Andel and Evelyn followed him into the coffee shop.

"It will," Evelyn encouraged, again.

"I guess you'd know; you are a woman." Roscoe ran a hand through his wild curls. "I mean, you're definitely a woman, but what I meant—"

Patting him on the shoulder, Andel stopped Roscoe before he could make it worse. "She knows what you meant, and because she's a woman, I would stop talking. Now."

"What's that supposed to mean?" Evelyn quirked an eyebrow in Andel's direction, leaving him wondering why he even tried.

The coffee shop wasn't as busy as the last time they'd accompanied Roscoe. The trio didn't have to fight a crowd to the counter, so they quickly placed their order. Andel noticed Sydney behind the espresso machine hard at work. At the sound of Roscoe's voice ordering his drink, she looked over and smiled in their direction.

Sydney's brown curly hair begged to be released from the bandana she'd tied haphazardly over it. Her baggy overalls and freckled face made her look young. Andel and Roscoe didn't look much older, but being immortal made Andel feel ancient. He couldn't help but wonder how Roscoe thought a relationship with a twenty-three-year-old mortal would work. Roscoe wouldn't have any trouble keeping up, but the world had evolved and changed. Relationships were different than Andel remembered, but not in a bad way.

Andel grew up in a small farming community in Greece two hundred years ago. He had never dated a woman. In fact, his marriage had been arranged before he left for war. Evelyn reminded Andel of the youth he felt obligated to bypass. He'd never resented the decision, but her passion for living constantly reminded him he wasn't dead.

As they waited for their coffee, Evelyn pulled a marker out of her pocket and shoved it into Roscoe's hand. He hesitated, but Evelyn wouldn't allow him to back out again.

"You've got this," she said.

As soon as Roscoe's name echoed through the room, he would follow the plan or chance losing Evelyn's help. She hadn't laid out an ultimatum, but Andel had a feeling she'd lose her patience sooner than later.

Andel picked up his hot tea when they reached the end of the bar and Evelyn accepted her cappuccino with a grin. Sydney handed Roscoe his dark roast personally, but the next move fell to Roscoe.

"Thank you," Roscoe turned away and scribbled a note on his cup. After taking a sip, he swung back around to the counter. "I think I got the wrong drink."

Just as Evelyn planned, Sydney took Roscoe's cup. With a frown, she inspected the order written on its side. Her brows scrunched together, and she tilted her head. *Can I take you out for dinner?* As Roscoe's handwriting unfurled, Sydney's face relaxed, and she smiled.

"If this isn't your cup, then who am I going to say yes to?" Sydney teased, holding the coffee cup close to scribble a note of her own.

"How about I taste it one more time? I might have been mistaken." Roscoe reached for the cup, and once it was in his hands, he took a sip. "This is definitely my coffee."

"In that case, my next night off is Friday. Does that work?"

"It does. Want to meet me in front of St. Patrick's Cathedral at seven?" Roscoe asked.

"Perfect." Sydney's smile couldn't have been any wider.

Roscoe made his way to the table Andel and Evelyn occupied. They'd both watched with satisfied grins and didn't bother to hide them. Their heightened hearing had allowed them to eavesdrop, too.

Roscoe beamed. "I can't believe it was that easy."

"Ye of little faith," Evelyn quoted. "So, what does her note say?"

"Oh yeah." Roscoe searched the cup and found a group of curling numbers. "It's a phone number."

Evelyn's eyes widened. "That's good."

"She likes you," Andel said. "If you don't see it, then you'll be your own worst enemy."

"I hate to break it to you, but sitting here all night staring at her like a stalker is probably the fastest way to get your date canceled." Evelyn's chair scraped against the floor as she stood up. "You should swing by tomorrow for coffee and let Sydney know you're looking forward to Friday, though."

"Okay, I can do that."

"Yes, you can." Andel patted Roscoe on the shoulder as they stood and trailed Evelyn between tables and chairs to the exit. "Have you thought about where you'll take her on your date?"

After Roscoe sipped his coffee, he coughed, clearing his throat. "Uh, I have an idea, but is there any way I can run the details by you guys tomorrow? Then we can get to that crash course on dos and don'ts."

"Yes, definitely," Evelyn answered and looked to Andel. "I'll need a little help."

Andel couldn't imagine what Evelyn had in store, but he nodded his consent. Evelyn's assignment was beginning to move along, and tomorrow, Andel would work out the details for Kendrick and Jane's first meeting. If everything went according to the Elders' plans, Andel would only be three missions away from fulfilling his covenant. After two hundred years, things were just beginning to get interesting with Evelyn around.

"Let's celebrate!" Roscoe suggested as they walked down a gray New York City block. "I'll round the boys up, and we'll meet you in Columbus Circle, outside Central Park."

Andel looked over to Evelyn, worried more for Jude if he showed up. "I am not sure…"

"Come on," Evelyn encouraged. "I haven't been there yet."

If anything could distract Evelyn from Jude's negativity, it was Central Park. Plus, Leo would be there to keep things light, but then there were the Nox. Encountering another supernatural race could get tricky with the spreading rumors about Evelyn. "I would feel better if we went during the day."

"But I'm helping you during the day with Jane," Evelyn reasoned. "I know you're worried, but I'll have you and three Gargoyles there to protect me." She turned to walk backward, facing him, and pressed her hands together. "Please!"

"Fine," Andel sighed. "But you must be willing to transcend without our code word, because if there's any sign of danger I will not wait for your permission to keep you safe."

"Deal."

Chapter 12

In a snap, Evelyn and Andel stood in front of a stone platform topped by a gold woman and her sea-chariot. Cars zoomed past on the roundabout behind them. Lights shone around Columbus Circle, but Central Park loomed behind the monument, waiting for them to enter.

Before developing the ability to see as well at night as she did during the day, the darkness would have scared Evelyn away. The ability had come with the Cupid-package. She and Andel walked away from the gray city into lush flora. With the change of their surroundings, Evelyn also felt her disposition transition from bustling to serene. The several shades of plant life reminded her how much she loved the color green.

"I feel like Dorothy setting out on the yellow brick road." Evelyn locked arms with Andel. "Please, tell me you know who Dorothy is." She looked up at him, and he smiled.

"I may not enjoy the cinema in today's culture, but that doesn't mean I haven't been to the movies." Andel tugged Evelyn's arm, pulling her further into the park. "We should probably get going. I have a feeling

Roscoe and the guys will be in Gargoyle form, and you don't want to miss the spectacle they make when showing off."

The Cupids darted across one crosswalk, then another. Street lamps lined the walkways, and Evelyn let herself get lost in time. She considered all the people who'd walked along the same paths. The same trees branches woven into a canopy overhead.

A couple walked by, in the opposite direction, with hands knotted together. Neither of them acknowledged Evelyn or Andel, and Evelyn had a feeling she knew why. Their soft melody whispered to her. They were in love.

"Are we cloaked?"

Andel answered, "It is safer this way. Once I catch sight of the Gargoyles I'll remove it, but until then, we cannot risk any immortals knowing you're here."

"Glamour? Can't Nox or any immortal see through it?" A crack sounded from under Evelyn's foot. She'd stepped on a small branch.

"I'd rather us not be seen by anyone."

"It's not like anyone wants me dead. They just want me to shoot them with my red arrows, and if any Nox attacks, I'll be happy to aim straight for the heart." Evelyn summoned her quiver mentally, and it appeared strapped to her back. "If I accidentally miss by an inch it'll only sting a little, right?"

"I have no idea what *your* arrows would do to a target if you missed the heart, but mine can cause an immortal some long-term damage and kill a human."

"Ookaay..." Evelyn slowed down as they walked around a deserted play area. "That took a dark turn." Dismissing her arrows, they disappeared.

"I am glad that conjuring your weapons has become second nature to you. In case there's an attack, I'm confident in your ability to defend yourself."

"Thank you, I think." Evelyn didn't think he meant he was confident she'd miss the heart and hoped he genuinely trusted her aim.

A cry rang out from above the trees as Andel lead Evelyn into an open meadow. The sky was clear, but the bright city surrounding Central Park made it difficult to see the stars.

Andel pointed above them at a dark figure soaring across the sky. Evelyn looked along his tone arm, up past his finger, and followed one, two, three immortals flying above them. The creatures became clearer and larger the closer they flew. The first gray beast stretched out the longest. His outstretched neck and tail were covered in protective scales, while the dragon's horns and talons threatened danger.

"Roscoe," Andel greeted as the beast landed first.

Evelyn did her best not to look too surprised, but her mouth hanging open might have given her away. She'd seen the other Gargoyles transform her first night at the cathedral, but had no idea Roscoe's true form would be the size of a pickup truck. No wonder he served as the Commander of the North American Legion of Gargoyles. As soon as Evelyn picked up her mouth to greet Roscoe, the two other Gargoyles landed. A stone lion and a dark, large bird touched down between the dragon and Andel.

The three beasts had their own songs, like the inspired artwork at the museum. Each lilting sound harmonized with the others softly.

"Leo and Jude," Evelyn was intrigued to see such regal creatures. "How is it that neither of you is one of those horned, demon looking statues typically found on old churches?"

The lion's mouth opened, but instead of a roar Leo's voice answered, "Those grotesques defend the Lux as well as any, but they tend to hang out in units. Think of Gargoyles as an army. Our unit may be smaller in number, but the three of us make up for it in size."

Evelyn felt like she was in Narnia, except this talking lion had wings and could turn into a hipster-middle-aged human who flirted with her. And that's just what he did. In a swirl of silver magic, Leo appeared, waggling his eyebrows at her. Behind him, Jude and Roscoe transitioned, too.

"What kind of bird are you, Jude?" Evelyn looked past Leo, ignoring his teasing.

"He's more complicated than that." Roscoe chimed in and swung his hand out, hitting Jude in the chest. The swat was accompanied with an arched brow directed at Jude.

"I think she can handle it, and I think I can manage explaining myself." Jude stepped forward and held his arm out for Evelyn to take.

The gesture was opposite to the bristly, stubborn Gargoyle who'd sat in her living room the other night, but she cautiously took his arm anyway. Jude led her over a grassy knoll to a paved path while the others trailed behind.

"I'm the obelisk." Jude pointed to the north of the park. "Created over three thousand years ago in Egypt, I can take the form of any animal still etched on its sides."

"You mean Cleopatra's Needle?"

"Yes, that's one of many names I've been given. The four sides of my statue are lined with hieroglyphics etched by an inspired poet. Some of the art has eroded, and as the images disappear, I'm unable to take their form. Currently, I can transform into several types of birds and lummox. But, I figured if I flew in as a bull, you'd have some snarky comment ready."

Evelyn laughed, knowing he was right. "Whatever animal you choose, does your stone always look different than Leo and Roscoe's? Or is it because you're older than they are?"

It was Leo's turn to laugh as he walked up to Evelyn on the opposite side of Jude. Jude's muscles tensed, and he shook his head from side to side. Leo wouldn't be letting him live that observation down for weeks.

Evelyn relaxed while surrounded by her new friends, but a tingling sensation ran up her spine as they walked past a line of trees. She could have sworn she heard someone in the endless darkness mutter to her. It was probably a couple meandering through the park. None of them felt the chill in the air, but a biting breeze blew through Evelyn's hair. She heard what she thought was her name whispered in the wind.

"I'm ancient," Jude clarified. "And I'm as strong as any marble or stone Gargoyle." He looked from Leo to Roscoe. "Don't let the lighter shade of my granite or the darker trace of my magic fool you. The same magic that inspired me thousands of years ago also created this *little* guy." Jude patted Leo on the shoulder.

"Pfff…" Leo waved off Jude's slight, and even without claws, the gesture reminded Evelyn of a cat pawing its toy. "Evelyn, don't listen to him. We may be bound to a certain size as statues, but in battle, we're measured by our ability as warriors. I didn't become second in command by accident."

Roscoe cleared his throat from behind them. "Gentlemen, you may think your words can do our race justice, but I'd rather prove to Evelyn what we can do. Let's show her why her Elders were so eager to solidify our alliance."

"Game on!" Leo roared.

With a snarl, Roscoe ran out into the dense wildwood. His dragon form burst through the tops of the trees, and as he ascended, his stony-gray color blended in with the sky. Evelyn lost sight of him.

Leo and Andel followed her line of sight, but Jude kept his eyes on Evelyn. She felt his gaze and smiled as the dragon swooped down over her head from behind. A screech echoed all around them, and the gust of air Roscoe's wings created lifted Evelyn's hair up off her shoulders and over her face. Her breath caught in her throat at the magnificence of the dragon.

"Whoa," Evelyn exhaled.

"Are you kidding me? He only gets a lame *whoa* for that?" Leo ran forward to the line of trees. "Andel, is this girl always so tough to impress?"

A burst of laughter erupted from Andel.

"Don't you dare answer that." Evelyn pointed at Andel. Turning to Leo, she asked, "You think you can do better?"

"I know I can." Leo didn't use the cover of night to transform, changing in front of Evelyn's eyes instead. His clothes, glasses, and white hair dissolved behind shimmering power into a gray marble lion. He was the size of a smart car. Bounding several feet down the paved path, his wings unfurled from his back. He took off, joining Roscoe in the sky.

"I think that was an invitation to target practice." Andel winked at Evelyn and nodded to Jude before running into the foliage.

"What?" Evelyn yelled after him. "Jude, aren't you going to stop him?"

"Take a second and think about it, Evelyn," Jude calmed Evelyn with a reassuring pat on her arm. "We're all Lux, and while Andel's sword could do some damage to a Gargoyle's facade, his arrows can't penetrate our stone. Now, yours on the other hand…"

"Wait." Evelyn faced Andel. "You have a sword?"

The overload of information outweighed any worry Evelyn had, and she watched as Andel summoned his bow and arrows. A second later, he aimed for the sky, and she heard a clack as one of Andel's arrows bounced off of Roscoe's scaly, marble exterior. These guys had become friends or as close as immortals could be. They knew each other's abilities and weaknesses, and they fought together. A pang of envy hit Evelyn in her gut. She had no clue what she was capable of, but maybe

Jude knew something that could help her. In his three thousand years of existence, he must have heard of or encountered someone like her.

"Jude, can I ask you something?"

Anticipating her inquiry, he answered, "You can, but it doesn't mean I'll answer."

"That's fair." Evelyn folded her arms over her chest, unsure if it was the winter weather or Jude freezing her out that caused it. "Have you ever met anyone like me?"

Jude shifted his weight away from her while he decided what to say. The sound of Leo roaring above broke some of the tension and gave Evelyn something to focus on.

"I have, Evelyn, but I can't talk about it. Ever. So don't ask me again."

Evelyn's stomach sank. "But—"

"I can't." Jude emitted the same disappointment she felt. Whatever he knew about her kind, he wouldn't, or couldn't face. Maybe he'd tried to get help from a Cupid like her, and it hadn't worked. She feared that was why Jude fought so hard to deter his friend.

As if he'd known she was calculating her next question, he avoided it with the perfect exit strategy. Onyx magic sparkled around Jude as he spread his arms out and transformed into a six-foot hawk.

He was beautiful.

She watched as he darted forward and his wings carried him into the night.

Clack, clack.

Andel had hit his targets, and Evelyn wished there was a way to test her arrows on the stone supernaturals. Her muscles ached to run a gauntlet, and her pride itched to prove her skill.

Clack. Jude let out a squawk.

Crack. The sound of a branch breaking underfoot alerted Evelyn that someone was near. She immediately glamoured herself so she couldn't be seen by mortals, but if an immortal was in the vicinity, they'd see right through it. It could have also been Andel circling back around.

Evelyn pressed her thoughts out to her fellow Cupid. *Andel. Can you hear me?*

Yes.

You wouldn't be close by, would you? Evelyn instinctively summoned her bow and arrows. They materialized in her hands, and she swung the full quiver over her shoulder.

No, but I'm headed your way now.

Hurry. Evelyn drew and shelved one of her arrows, pointing it in the direction of the wooded area she'd heard the noise come from.

Quickly dismissing the urge to try and reach out to one of the Gargoyles mentally, Evelyn wondered if she could even penetrate their minds. Thinking she might have accidentally communicated with whoever stalked her, she waited to see who would show themselves first, Andel or the immortal watching her. Evelyn knelt down. Nestling her knee in the grass would help steady her shot and give her a better shot at the intruder's legs. She didn't want to kill anyone, she only needed to stop them.

Chapter 13

"Don't shoot." Andel pushed aside a branch and stepped out into the open. "What has you so spooked?"

Evelyn turned her back to Andel, not wanting him to see just how unnerved she was. "I just thought I heard something. I'm fine."

Andel didn't believe her, but he had no reason to press the matter. He hadn't seen or heard anything. "Okay, then, how about you try." He held out his bow to her.

Evelyn froze. When Andel caught up, her eyes were wide and her mouth hung open.

"If you're worried you'll hurt someone, aim for Jude."

Andel laughed at his own joke, but Evelyn's face morphed from stunned to sad. Her mouth turned down and her chin fell. "I guess you heard, then? Because I know you really wouldn't want me to endanger anyone."

"I might have unintentionally picked up on your conversation." Andel shrugged his shoulders. "You might want to give the guy a little time."

"So, you know what he was talking about?"

"No. I know Jude," Andel clarified. "I have a feeling he'll open up eventually."

"Really?"

Andel held out his bow again. "Really. Now take this."

"What am I supposed to do with it?"

"You know." He nodded up toward the circling Gargoyles.

"I can't," Evelyn began. "If I aim a red arrow—"

"That's the thing, I don't think your arrow will turn red if you're aiming at them. Just try, and if I see your arrow begin to change, I will stop you from shooting."

Andel hadn't planned to test her arrows, but it was better to do it now when he could stop her. In the past, each time her arrow had turned red, she'd been in the vicinity of love. Andel reached back over his shoulder and retrieved a golden arrow. He handed it to her, and once in her grip, he expected it to shift to a glittering red. When it didn't, he nodded for her to take aim.

"Are you sure about this?" she asked.

"Honestly, not really." Andel took a step closer to Evelyn and placed a finger under the arrowhead, pushing it to point up.

Evelyn pulled the string of the bow taught and paused. They both watched for the arrow to change. She caught Jude in her sight and aimed. The arrow remained gold.

A stiff breeze made Evelyn pause. The stone falcon flew in a figure eight pattern, and it would be easy for her to line up her shot again. Out of the corner of his eye, Andel noticed a couple making their way out into the open on one of the paths at the far end of the meadow.

Andel wasn't sure what would happen; if the couple got too close and Evelyn sensed their love, she might feel drawn to aim for them. But before he could warn her of their approach, she released the arrow at her flying target.

Clack.

Just as Andel had predicted, Evelyn's power didn't turn the arrow red this time. Her supernatural target wasn't near someone he loved.

Chapter 14

Thursday afternoon, Evelyn found herself hypnotized by the light refracting through the museum windows. She lost focus of the errand Jane had sent her on and thought of how Andel had tested her power, and her arrows, the night before. The results had brought some relief in addition to an answer. But there were always more questions.

Andel *poofed* the two of them back to their apartment after they checked Jude for any marks. When she asked about trying the shot again, Andel groaned something about fairies and twelve o'clock then suggested they get back to the apartment.

"Are you Evelyn?" Meg, by the name on her badge, asked.

"Yes."

"I think this is for you." Mag handed her a manila folder so full it had been held together with giant binder clips. "When you didn't show up right away, my boss sent me up."

"I'm sorry, I got a little preoccupied." Evelyn grinned and pointed toward one of the galleries.

"It's an easy place to get distracted. Even giving tours several times a week, I find myself enamored with certain pieces."

"Well, thank you. I really appreciate it." Evelyn held up the folder. "I better head back upstairs."

Passing a class of elementary-aged students dressed in navy and white uniforms, Evelyn decided to take the stairs marked as an emergency fire escape. Visitors didn't know they could be used like the main staircase, and Evelyn noticed the employees didn't share that tip on the tours. On busy weekdays, Evelyn found out the hard way that elevators entertain eight-year-olds more than Van Gogh. Some of the girls from the group pointed at a modern piece on the main floor and giggled.

As Evelyn pushed the stairway door open, she nearly trampled a tall slender woman. "Oh. Please excuse me. I should have been more careful."

"That's alright." Gracefully, the woman's statuesque figure stepped back into the stairwell to let Evelyn pass. She straightened her black couture bag on her shoulder while she waited.

Evelyn held the door open. "Are you heading out this way?"

"No, I'm actually looking for someone."

"Maybe I can help you?" Evelyn let the door click shut behind her.

The woman's purple lips curled into a smile. "Oh, you're Evelyn." She pointed at Evelyn's badge "I'm actually here for you. Your arrows used to be more specific."

"Arrows?" Evelyn swallowed down her unease. "I don't know what you're talking about. How about you come to the front desk with me, and we can talk." She reached for the door's handle.

Getting the stranger outside would be best, but maybe Evelyn could telepathically reach out to Andel. She might need backup. It would be ignorant to manifest her arrows since that's what the woman wanted.

Evelyn couldn't risk putting them in her vicinity. Each immortal race had a variety of supernatural abilities, and there was no telling what this stranger could do. But she had to be an immortal because her beauty rivaled perfection.

"I'd rather stay here. Your Cupid friend is nice to look at, but he comes across as the type who acts firsts and asks after."

"You're right about that." Evelyn attempted to open her thoughts to Andel, but the woman raised her hand, and her fingers twisted together in the air. *Andel?*

"Nice try, but I need to speak to you. Alone." The woman's hand remained raised in the space between them. "My name is Kalan, and I'm from the fairy realm. I've sought you out on behalf of my queen, Rhyan."

Evelyn tilted her head at Kalan's words and found herself mesmerized by Kalan's flawless skin and crystal-blue eyes. In the back of her mind, Evelyn knew there had to be more to this immortal world she existed in. The Cupids should have made learning about different supernatural races an advanced course. It would have been helpful before running into a fairy in a confining stairwell. Without much to go on, Evelyn's only references about fairies came from British Literature, and she hoped Kalan didn't have any Shakespearean plans.

"So, why do you want *my* arrows?" Evelyn asked, hoping to buy some time and come up with a plan. "And what makes you think I'd be willing to hand them over. I don't even know you."

Cupid arrows were all the same, and technically it was Evelyn aiming them at immortals in love that turned them red. She'd never thought about the arrows retaining their properties without her. She understood as much about her abilities as she did the fairies', or Gargoyles', or whatever else existed in her new world.

"My kind needs *your* arrows for protection," Kalan explained. "We used our last red Cupid's arrow last Fall to fight off a Forsaken."

Evelyn's nose scrunched up. "A Forsaken?"

"Troll."

"A troll?" Evelyn asked.

Kalan rolled her eyes, but her hand didn't budge. Evelyn had to figure out a way to alert Andel about the intruder.

"What makes me so special?" Evelyn stepped away from Kalan, putting some space between them. "You could have cornered any other Cupid just as easily."

Kalan laughed at her words. The shrill sound bounced off the concrete walls around them, and Evelyn ground her teeth together. Obviously, this fairy knew more than she'd have liked, but playing dumb would help her avoid offering too much information about her red arrows.

Kalan's flagrant amusement suddenly fell silent, and her eyes dilated. Her black pupils bled through her lucent irises and covered the whites of her eyes. Evelyn tried to swallow this new bout of fear, but the dry terror got caught in the back of her throat. Maybe Evelyn could distract Kalan and transcend out of the stairwell?

"Don't play dumb with me. We know you're the one we're looking for…just like we knew how to find the ones before you."

At the mention of others before her, Evelyn's fear wavered, and her curiosity grew. Not only were there others like her, but the fairies knew how to find them. Getting away seemed less important than finding out more about the immortal she'd become. Evelyn remained tight-lipped, hoping to coax more from Kalan.

"We're prepared to negotiate an exchange, not that we didn't try with your leaders. There are always wishes that can be granted or dreams we can make come true." Kalan smiled, but with her eyes blacked out, she looked tortured instead of pleased. "Your kind may frown upon such indulgences in the heavens, but don't let them fool you. We've been making deals with Cupids longer than your Elder, Sheng, has existed."

"Wait." Evelyn pressed a hand to her head. "I wouldn't put it past you to try and confuse me with your version of the truth. Let's keep this conversation simple. I won't promise you anything until after I've spoken to Andel."

Kalan stepped back, and her shoulders relaxed. "You're smarter than most of your kind." As she crossed her arms in front of her, her eyes cleared. She gave Evelyn a once-over, taking in her practical black flats and classic white blouse. "Alright, at least tell me what you might like in exchange, so I can begin the negotiations with Queen Rhyan."

"Nope. I'm not going to fall for that." Evelyn shook her head. "There are too many unanswered questions, like why are you killing trolls? Not to mention, why do you need *my* arrows for the job? I don't think I can trust you."

"You will." Kalan winked. "I'll be back, soon."

The door opened a few flights above them, and two voices echoed in a familiar tone. Evelyn stepped over to the center of the staircase and peered up to find Andel and Jane. As if he'd sensed her—or the fairy—Andel looked over the handrail, finding Evelyn in a similar position. She hadn't expected him to be at the museum today, at least not without a glamour. Earlier that morning, Andel explained that once he confirmed a time for their dinner meeting with Kendrick, he'd let Evelyn know.

"Evelyn?" Jane's head peeked over next to Andel. "Where have you been?"

"I have your paperwork here." Evelyn waved the folder in the air. "I got stopped on the way helping a visitor."

Jane's heels clacked on the stairs as she began making her way down to Evelyn. Andel walked behind her, but his focus remained over the railing and on Evelyn. *A visitor?* he asked mentally.

Later. Evelyn put him off. They needed to focus on Andel's assignment for the time being.

"No matter," Jane waved. "Mr. Lambros came up to the office looking for you, and when you didn't return, we decided to come look for you."

"I must insist you call me Andel." As they took the last few steps to Evelyn, Andel tried to keep things casual with Jane.

"It seems that *Andel's* elusive collector-friend can meet over dinner tomorrow night." Jane smiled from Andel to Evelyn. "Does that work for you?"

At Jane's enthusiasm, Evelyn's stomach churned. She needed to be available for Roscoe. "Um, actually, I have a friend—"

"Evelyn," Andel interrupted. "I have already made arrangements with Roscoe and Sydney so we can accompany Jane and Mr. Reid."

I can explain if you'll let me. He added mentally, but Evelyn needed to process being confronted by Kalan before dealing with group date night. *Not now.*

Andel's eyebrows pulled together.

He had to have known she'd want to keep an eye on Roscoe and Sydney during their first date. Evelyn didn't think Andel put his own mission before hers on purpose, but after talking to Kalan, she couldn't help but think that her fellow Cupids would always be making plans and decisions for her.

Gritting her teeth, Evelyn held herself together so she wouldn't explode. "I guess Andel has it all worked out." Evelyn cut her eyes over to Andel. "Tomorrow night it is." She plastered a smile on her face for Jane and pushed the exit door open.

"Great!" Jane's elation was sincere as she took her envelope from Evelyn. "Why don't you leave a little early tonight. The day is almost over, and you've been a trooper running all over the museum for me."

"Thanks." She could use all the time she could get for Roscoe's dating lessons.

"Have a good night, you two." Jane turned back up the stairs with a bounce in her step.

As soon as the two Cupids heard the fifth-floor door close behind Jane, Evelyn let the door to the first-floor slip closed. Once they ensured their privacy, they transcended to their apartment. Evelyn poofed in front of the refrigerator, and Andel appeared already pacing behind the couch in the living room.

"Spill it."

Chapter 15

"Are you planning to give me the silent treatment all night?" Andel attempted to break through the wall of silence Evelyn had built.

She was sitting on the couch with a bowl of Moose Tracks. She didn't know who stocked the freezer with creamy deliciousness, and she didn't care. A fairy confronted her in the museum stairwell, and she knew she should confide in Andel. But all she could think about was how Andel planned his date night for Jane and Kendrick the same night she wanted to be available to help Roscoe and Sydney. How could he?

Andel didn't get what he'd done wrong, but the spoonful of vanilla and chocolate served as a tangible way for him to know something was up. Usually, she only needed to consume half the container before she opened up, but she had already begun scraping the bottom of the carton.

"Don't make this all about you." Evelyn shoved another spoonful of ice cream in her mouth. "Don' ge meh wrong, ih ith abou oo. Buh—" Swallowing down her bite, Evelyn squinted her eyes shut and placed a hand on her temple. "Brain freeze," she explained, standing and walking to the kitchen.

Andel's head tilted to one side as he watched her throw the empty cardboard container away. Roscoe would be showing up for his dating lesson soon, and Evelyn needed to compartmentalize so she didn't end up taking her frustration out on the Gargoyles.

"I'm sorry, Evelyn. Whatever I've done to upset you, please forgive me."

Her spoon clanged in the sink, "How about I'll forgive you if you tell me what you did wrong?" Evelyn made her way back to the couch, laying herself across the cushions like she needed therapy.

"I'm fairly sure you are upset I scheduled dinner with Jane and Kendrick during Roscoe's first date."

Keeping her composure, Evelyn looked Andel square in the eye and told him, "You're danish right, I'm upset."

Her pastry slip was proof enough of her anger, but she'd remained in control of her volume. Andel hadn't asked Evelyn what she wanted to do during Roscoe and Sydney's date. And after her surprise visit from Kalan, her nerves were fried. Evelyn wanted to be able to make the call for herself as far as where she'd be tomorrow night. She also wanted to decide for herself if she'd give the fairies her arrows. Maybe she'd keep her run-in with Kalan to herself for now.

"I'll call Jane now and cancel the dinner."

"You have her number?" Evelyn sat up and narrowed her eyes. She shook her head, clearing it. Why should Andel having Jane's number matter? "No. Don't cancel it. It was hard enough to convince her to come in the first place."

"Are you sure?"

Knock, knock.

"Yes," Evelyn grumbled as she went to answer the door. Roscoe's arrival would at least keep Andel from asking any more questions. She could tell he had picked up that something else was bothering her, but luckily, she had planned Roscoe's dating lessons for after work.

As Roscoe and Leo entered the apartment, Andel made himself scarce and took a seat in a chair at the edge of the room. Roscoe wore snappy attire, including a bowtie, while Leo had pushed the sleeves of his Henley up to his elbows. The two were complete opposites. Leo had made himself comfortable on the couch, and Roscoe stood at the window waiting for instructions.

"I'm glad you came, Leo. I may need your help tomorrow night." Evelyn stood next to Roscoe. "You'll be on awkward-moment patrol." She patted Roscoe's shoulder. "Now that I think about it, this will be perfect. You can circle overhead and stay out of sight, but if Roscoe needs help, you can run interference." Leo's eyes widened in excitement. "Not literally, but, you have super-hearing, right?"

Leo nodded.

"If you hear or see anything going wrong, you can come get me."

A grin spread over Leo's face. "Considering who we're talking about here," Leo waved in Roscoe's direction. "What constitutes *wrong*?"

"We'll work on identifying that as we go, so pay attention." Evelyn faced Roscoe and reached up, tucking a piece of his curly hair behind his ear, but Roscoe flinched.

"Relax." Evelyn stepped closer. "You're going to have to get used to being close to Sydney. If she's like every other girl on the planet, she'll want you to hold her hand and put your arm around her."

Evelyn let her arm brush against Roscoe's. He sucked in air but didn't budge. He froze. Evelyn couldn't let Roscoe fail. She had started to like him. She wanted him to find love. She wanted Sydney to find love, too, and if it happened to be with Roscoe, then, bonus. She'd do everything in her power to help them have the chance they deserved.

Roscoe relaxed his fists at his sides. "Okay, I'll work on that."

"Good." Evelyn ran her finger slowly down Roscoe's arm. "How about we start with the end of the date, then?"

Leo whistled, and in the corner of Evelyn's vision, she noticed Andel shift in his chair. She wasn't really going to do anything, but if Roscoe had really loosened up, he wouldn't curl up into the fetal position when they addressed a good night kiss.

"Why?" Roscoe created some space between him and Evelyn. "You should keep in mind, I'm very old fashioned."

"What do you think I'm going to teach you?" Evelyn's brows knitted together.

"I'm sorry. I'm just nervous, and honestly, I have no idea what to expect, so I'm expecting the worst."

"The worst?" Evelyn asked.

"Not the worst. I mean—" Roscoe backtracked. "You know what I mean."

"Leo," Evelyn turned to the Gargoyle sitting on the couch. "This is a good example of what an awkward emergency is."

"I'd rather grab some popcorn, but I guess I could find you instead." Leo kicked a foot over his knee, enjoying the show.

Roscoe straightened his bow tie. "Where will you be?"

"Not far," Evelyn reassured. "I'll be close enough for Leo to get me, but I doubt you'll even need me. I have a good feeling about this."

"A Cupid-Feeling?" Leo asked.

Evelyn did have a feeling. She had a lot of feelings, and they threatened to overwhelm her. So, she decided to shove them all down like a box full of sweaters. If she let the lid pop off, the material would swell and be exposed. "Let's just say, after tonight, you be ready for anything."

"Great." Roscoe shook out his hands at his sides. "My nerves are all over the place. How about you use Leo as your guinea pig and I observe?" Roscoe asked. "I've always been a better visual learner."

Leo grinned. Evelyn thought he was cute, but he was also way too flirtatious for her taste. He also appeared to be old enough to be her father. As much as fun as he'd been during their last tutorial, she needed Roscoe to get his feet wet.

"Let me," Andel interrupted before Evelyn could turn Leo down.

Evelyn's lips formed a small O in surprise. "Okay."

Roscoe quickly took a seat next to Leo in relief.

"Do you still want to start at the end of the date?" Andel asked with an arched brow.

"Why not?" Evelyn countered. She placed a finger on her chin in thought and faced Roscoe. "So, at the end of the date, you'll offer to walk Sydney home." She started to slip her hand into Andel's, and he recoiled, so she took a step away from him. "You'll know if Sydney wants to hold hands if she leaves it resting at her side while you walk. The key is to keep it casual."

"May I offer a suggestion?" Andel looked at Evelyn's hand. "If you're nervous, you could also take her hand as a means to pull her out of the way of other pedestrians." He quickly grabbed Evelyn's hand and pulled her next to him.

A flicker of passion sparked between them. Evelyn didn't know if Andel had felt it, but her thoughts started to grow foggy, and heat crept up her neck into her cheeks. She had to create some space between them.

"That's a good idea," Evelyn affirmed. "But if she doesn't want to hold your hand, she'll come up with an excuse to let go, like fixing her hair or tying her shoes."

Evelyn bent her knees, releasing Andel's hand to straighten the laces on one boot. Once they were no longer touching, she looked up and noticed Andel frowning.

"Don't worry man, Sydney likes you." Leo encouraged.

"She does, so when you're holding hands and get to her apartment you'll need a game plan." Evelyn stood up. "I'm guessing you'll decline an offer to go upstairs, so how about you end the evening by asking her on a second date. That way she'll know you're interested in her, that is if you're still interested in her." She met Roscoe's eyes. "A kiss wouldn't hurt, either."

"I agree with asking her out again, but I don't feel like you have to rush the physical part of your relationship," Andel offered, making eye contact with Evelyn.

"Man, at least give the girl a kiss on the cheek!" Leo disagreed. "You don't want her to think you're a monk."

"How about you decide when you get there?" Evelyn suggested.

Roscoe nodded his agreement. "Can we go over a list of appropriate topics for dinner conversation next?"

"Sure, but you might want to take notes." Evelyn bolted to her room to get a pen and paper before Roscoe could disagree. The further away she got from Andel, the more clearly she could think, but all she thought was that she wanted to be near him again.

Chapter 16

The next evening, Evelyn put as much distance between her and Andel as *in*humanly possible on the New York City sidewalk. She'd successfully not run into Andel at the museum the entire day. Evelyn had been wrestling her own conscience instead of confronting Andel, although he seemed eager to clear the air. She simply wanted to dismiss the feeling of attraction that had taken her off guard the night before in addition to avoid telling him about her encounter with Kalan. So, as they walked to their meeting with Jane and Kendrick, she allowed every pedestrian moving the opposite direction to serve as a barrier between them.

Evelyn reasoned with herself that she'd always considered Andel attractive. Every woman did. Their evolving relationship, from mentorship to friendship, had blurred any professional lines drawn and there were bound to be a few awkward, defining exchanges.

Evelyn hated the repercussions of having a misunderstanding with Andel because he'd be determined to confront the awkwardness and lecture it to death. Evelyn hoped to ignore the issue until it dissolved. She knew her plan wouldn't work because avoiding Andel resembled neglecting hunger pangs. No matter how hard she tried, he would always come back to remind her until she gave into the conversation that needed to be had.

A sour smell, like old milk, crept out of an alleyway the two Cupids passed, and Evelyn's nose turned up. She stood out like a tourist amongst the New Yorkers who passed by the rank odor without flinching. Even using their Cupid-cloaking power wouldn't block the stink. Andel had suggested earlier that the two not use their glamour while making the trek to dinner. Any supernatural in their vicinity would be able to see past their disguise and mark them as Cupids regardless.

This is getting ridiculous. Andel directed his thoughts over a teenager wearing a cobalt beanie who skimmed between them. Andel had attempted to get Evelyn talking via telepathy all the way to Bistecca Fiorentina. The Italian restaurant was a lengthy walk from MoMa, but Evelyn found it therapeutic. Mentally ignoring Andel, she got lost in the current of people around her.

As she and Andel came to the intersection at 46th and 8th, Evelyn realized they were getting close. She would have to set the awkwardness aside soon and play girlfriend-boyfriend with Andel. Impersonating an elderly couple last week didn't carry the same complications that had recently developed. Evelyn started to notice a change in their relationship the moment they started working together on their assignments here in the city. The authority he'd wielded as her mentor had served as a barrier, keeping them from getting too personal. Now, they were peers. Friends. And in her experience, friendship with a good looking guy had always ended up as something more.

Waiting for the light to change, as she stared out over the crowd bustling to their Broadway shows, Andel's hand slid over hers. *Kendrick and Jane will be meeting us around the corner. You need to stop avoiding me and act like you like me.*

"It's not that I don't like you. I mean, I like you fine, I'm just distracted."

"Really?"

The light changed and Evelyn pulled Andel forward. Her immortal strength made it easy, but to the average bystander, it looked more like a mother hauling her child behind her. "I don't want to talk about it."

"Just get it off your chest," Andel reasoned. "You'll feel better."

"You know very well I'd rather be checking up on Roscoe. He's never been on a date, and there's no telling what he'll bring up over dinner. They could be discussing the Depression or bowties."

"Roscoe will be fine. Sydney may love bowties, and a man that enamored never throws it away over dinner conversation." Andel tugged Evelyn to slow down. "Plus, Jane and I need your help far worse."

"She's not that bad. She's been hurt, not to mention stereotyped. If your man Kendrick is as good as you say, then he should be able to sweep Jane off her feet."

"True, but we're here, so instead of arguing about this, how about I promise to help you any way you need with Roscoe's second date?"

Evelyn had made the Gargoyle promise to ask Sydney out again, regardless of how he felt the first date went. Roscoe was in love, but it wasn't the same kind of love Evelyn had witnessed in her lifetime. As a human, she'd never really grasped time, but now she had an eternity. To love someone so much—as an immortal—and want to spend forever with them was a kind of love Evelyn might never feel. It made her second guess if she'd really loved her ex, Tate, as much as she'd thought.

"I'll take that deal, and there'll be no excuses."

"No excuses," Andel squeezed Evelyn's hand.

The pressure was on for Evelyn. While Andel's gesture seemed kind, she couldn't help but wonder if it was laced with anything more. Looking up from their hands, Kendrick stood twenty feet away. His presence put a halt to any more thoughts on the matter. Plastering a tight smile across her face, she squeezed Andel's hand back.

"Hi! Kendrick, this is Evelyn." Andel didn't let go of Evelyn's hand when he shook Kendrick's, making it impossible for her to greet him the same way.

"Hi"—Evelyn waved at Kendrick—"nice to meet you."

"You too," Kendrick slid his hands into his coat pockets. "I've heard a lot about you."

"You have?" Evelyn's eyebrow rose in Andel's direction. "Don't believe a word of it."

From across the street, Jane's voice called over a row of taxis,. "Evelyn, Andel!" She wore an emerald green coat, and her red hair bounced over her shoulders as she darted between yellow taxis.

"Jane, I'm so glad you made it." Evelyn attempted to let go of Andel's hand, and just as he obliged, his arm snaked around her waist.

"Jane, this is Kendrick Reid. Kendrick, this is Jane Platt," Andel made the formal introductions, and the two shook hands for a second longer than necessary. Evelyn thought their ruse might actually work.

So, you talked about me to Kendrick?

Evelyn, I needed to play up our relationship to make this dinner happen. And, you will be glad to know, I did not lie about anything.

Anything?

There may have been assumptions made by Kendrick, but they're harmless. Now, we have a job to do.

"This way." With Andel's arm still at her waist, he guided her down a set of stairs and through an old wooden door.

The maitre d' nodded to Andel and, without hesitation, walked them through a labyrinth of tables. Every chair was filled, and as Evelyn took in the dimly lit room, her super-Cupid-hearing picked up a familiar voice. Roscoe was in the room saying something about a cathedral. Looking around the restaurant, Evelyn found Roscoe sitting with Sydney at a table for two near the front window. The spot didn't read blatantly romantic, but the rustic ambiance felt cozy.

Did you know they'd be here?

Yes, but I didn't tell you so I could see that expression on your face.

Evelyn squeezed Andel's hand. She wanted to be mad at him but couldn't bring herself to make a scene. *You should have told me. We'd talked about him taking her somewhere more casual.*

Well, I pulled a few strings and got them a reservation after you conveniently had a meeting during lunch.

"Your table." The host's stark white sleeve waved over a large round table in the back corner of the room. Evelyn ducked under a black and white family picture and sat facing Roscoe and Sydney. Andel took the seat next to her, and Kendrick pulled Jane's seat out for her before taking his own.

Andel brought up art while ordering a bottle of wine. They discussed business during bruschetta. By salad, Jane and Kendrick were lost in asking each other questions, and not only about work. It wasn't until the great cheesecake-debate that the new couple acknowledged Evelyn and Andel still sat at the table. Drinks, appetizers, salad, soup, steak, and dessert, Evelyn thought the heavens should resemble Bistecca Florentina more.

During dinner, Evelyn had kept herself occupied with listening in on Roscoe and Sydney. He'd asked all the right questions, and she seemed just as interested in knowing about Roscoe. With some bending of the truth, he was able to talk about himself and skip dates and places. But he'd spent more time listening. Evelyn knew it had to be hard for Roscoe to avoid telling Sydney the whole truth, but she also knew it was necessary if he didn't want to scare Sydney off before she got to know him.

"Evelyn, sweetheart, please break the tie." Andel squeezed Evelyn's hand to get her attention. The gesture made her jump but brought her back to the task at hand.

"Tie?"

"Should cheesecake be served with chocolate or fruit?" Jane asked.

"If you have to ask me"—Evelyn looked from Jane to Andel—"then I'm not sure I can call either of you friends."

Andel laughed and shifted his arm around the back of Evelyn's chair. "I told you she might become hostile." He smiled at her. "Always chocolate, unless she can have both."

"I couldn't agree more." Jane nudged Kendrick.

Kendrick feigned being hurt and grabbed at his ribs. "Andel, I don't appreciate being left to fight this battle on my own. Do you even eat sugar? You don't look like you have an ounce of fat on you."

"I eat enough for the both of us," Evelyn answered.

As the waiter approached to take their dessert order, Evelyn noticed Roscoe stand and help Sydney with her chair. Evelyn itched to get up and follow, and Andel could tell she was struggling.

When her plate of rich, sweet cake arrived, her anxiety subsided for the few minutes it took to finish but returned while the group waited for their check. Andel refused to let Jane or Kendrick fight over who'd pay, so he folded several bills and pressed them into the waiter's hand.

"Keep the change." Andel leaned toward Evelyn, and she could feel his breath brush over her shoulder. After he shoved his wallet into his back pocket, he straightened. The moment ended before it began, and Andel refocused on his mission. "Would the two of you like to go for a walk?"

"That's a great idea. I need to walk off that cheesecake." Evelyn placed her hand over her stomach. She'd picked up on what Andel had in mind since they'd discussed a romantic stroll through Central Park as an idea for Roscoe to consider the night before.

Jane's eyes bounced from Andel to Evelyn to Kendrick. Evelyn knew she worried about seeming too enthusiastic. Every girl hated coming off as eager. Evelyn wished she'd thought of asking Kendrick first because it took encouragement to get Jane to agree to anything.

"Maybe we could go to Central Park," Evelyn began. "I haven't been able to see all of the artwork in the park, and I've heard certain pieces are better seen at night."

Jane shifted in her chair, placing a hand on Kendrick's arm. "It's true."

"I agree." Kendrick stood and held his hand out to help Jane to her feet. "If you haven't been, then it's our duty as natives to take you."

As Jane's hand slipped into Kendrick's, Evelyn felt, more than heard, a symphony resonate around her. Gritting her teeth, she fought the need to call for her bow and arrows. As she stood, Andel offered his arm.

Evelyn.

She shook off the foggy desire clouding her thoughts. *What's up?*

I simply wanted to make sure you weren't planning to use my assignment for target practice.

Andel didn't normally joke, so Evelyn looked up at him to see if she could determine how long the lecture would last. Instead of a stern brow and thin frown, Evelyn received a wink.

"Thank you," she chuckled.

"For what?"

"You know…thinking ahead, playing along, and making me laugh."

"You're welcome. Now, let's see if we can convince these two they're made for each other."

The four walked alongside the congested streets with Jane and Kendrick leading the way. Shadows weighed down the buildings and swallowed alcoves and alleyways. Honking cars served as warnings, and street lamps and flashing crosswalk signs provided safe pathways. Central Park didn't look any different from the last time they'd visited, still enchanting and marvelous. Of course, there weren't any Gargoyles flying overhead that Evelyn could see.

Andel slowed his gait, allowing Kendrick and Jane some privacy. "Tell me, would you think this is a good first date?"

"It's been nice, especially for those two." Evelyn waved her pointer finger at the couple walking ahead of them. "But my perfect date would be a lot less busy."

"What do you mean?"

"There are so many people, and the noise never ends here. I thought New Orleans never stopped, but I can barely hear myself think. A date is also supposed to be about the person you're with, and I'd want to be able to listen to them without the sound of traffic screaming in the background. Don't get me wrong, New York is a great place to visit, but I wouldn't want to live here forever."

Once surrounded by trees, the sounds of the city faded. The honks and hollers didn't fade completely, but the foliage muffled their echoes. Here, the pull of Jane and Kendrick's new relationship also felt distant. The buzz had probably been replaced by the reassuring calm Andel exuded.

"What about you?" Evelyn asked.

"What about me?"

"Your dream date. What would it be like?"

"Definitely not like anything your generation would expect."

"I'm going to try and not take that as an insult."

He patted her hand and tugged her closer. "No, I didn't mean it that way. In fact, I wouldn't know where to begin in this culture."

"Agreed. I was lucky to find someone normal." Evelyn cringed. The topic of her the guy she gave her mortal life for silenced her and Andel, and she couldn't help but think she consistently complicated her relationship with Andel. Juggling the newness of being an immortal, having to let go of Tate, and her need to figure out why she was so different had kept her so focused on herself that she hadn't been the greatest friend to Andel. He'd created a perfect first date for Jane and Kendrick, and he'd worked it out for her to check in on Roscoe and Sydney. He'd proven himself to be a great mentor and friend to Evelyn.

Andel could be trusted, and she felt horrible about keeping her run-in with the fairy, Kalan, to herself. Evelyn opened her mouth to explain the ordeal, but Andel stopped her. "You don't have to say anything more. This must be hard for you, and I'm sorry for putting you in such an uncomfortable position."

He thought she was going to bring up Tate? "Oh, Andel, I'm really not—"

"How about we get out of here and do some training?" he interrupted her.

"I'm not sure. What about Jane and Kendrick?"

"I have a good feeling about them. Plus, Leo can keep an eye on Roscoe."

"How will he know—"

Andel smiled, knowing he was gaining ground. "We can stop on the way. I happen to know where he's perched."

"You're probably right," Evelyn admitted with a grin of her own. She hadn't expected the night to take such an emotional turn, and target practice would release some of the angst that pulled her shoulders in tight. They asked Jane and Kendrick to excuse them. Andel explained that his dinner wasn't settling well, and before Evelyn knew it, she and

Andel had stepped behind a tree and transcended to Leo on top of Belvedere Castle.

They explained they were headed to training practice. Since both dates were going so well, it wouldn't hurt to let Leo watch over Roscoe. So, Evelyn allowed herself to let go, and Andel poofed them to Greece. It was Andel's private training grounds, and he'd brought her once before. For the next few hours, Evelyn allowed herself to take full advantage of the escape.

The Cupids darted through the forest outside Andel's hometown, aiming their arrows at targets scattered high and low in the trees. Andel had hung the wooden circles throughout the small island, and they didn't have to worry about mortals spotting them. The exercise created a sense of freedom.

It was the same kind of independence she felt when she aged out of the system.

She'd escaped the expectations and limitations of the social workers and foster families she'd been appointed. At eighteen, Evelyn's life had become her own. She moved out on her own, and while fear and doubt crippled most teenagers, Evelyn used those feelings to propel her forward.

She would do the same with her fear of the fairies and doubt in the Elders. The unknown would propel her to find the truth. She just didn't know if she'd have to set out on this journey alone or if Andel would stick with her.

Chapter 17

Sitting in the moonlight, Evelyn and Andel gasped for air. Andel had beaten Evelyn through the course of targets, but Evelyn didn't care. He'd had two hundred years of experience more than her. They both stretched out on a blanket of silver hewn grass that covered the edge of the island. Evelyn couldn't bring herself to sit at the edge of the Grecian cliff, but the salty, cool air still brushed over her hot skin. It was Evelyn's second time transcending to where Andel grew up, and she thought it must be the most beautiful place on earth. The waves below crashed against the rocky bluff, and a lush forest behind them covered the plateau.

Evelyn didn't want to think about not ever having a home again. The fact that he trusted this place with her was proof of his loyalty. She didn't have a way to prove herself to him, and it didn't seem to bother him. Too bad it bothered her. She'd learned the hardest way possible that home had nothing to do with a place and everything to do with where her heart resided.

Turning to Andel, Evelyn took in his profile. His straight nose and dark curls reminded her of the actors who played gladiators in blockbuster movies. Even in the dark, her Cupid-sight made it possible for her to see the stubble that lined his square jaw. He'd wrapped his arms around one knee, pulling it close to his chest. And his brows were furrowed.

"What's on your mind?"

Andel stared out over the sea before them. "The better question is what's been on your mind?"

"You first."

"Your immediate avoidance is only one of the many reasons I know something is bothering you. I cannot imagine what I've done wrong now, but I'm willing to hear you out."

"It's not you, Andel." Evelyn felt the need to come clean with him. Deciding whether she should help the fairies was her choice, but if Kalan was really coming back for an answer, she needed to have one. Andel turned to meet her gaze. "I've been trying to decide if I should tell you something that happened. On Thursday at the museum."

"Oh?"

"I want your advice, as a friend and as an immortal, but I don't want you to lecture me for an hour after the fact."

Andel chuckled, but he didn't say anything. He was there for Evelyn. So why did she feel like she had to take this on by herself? Feeling that way didn't make it true.

"A fairy," she finally spilled.

"In the stairwell?"

"How did you—"

"I knew something must have happened, but I didn't want to pry."

"How? How did you know?"

"To be honest, I didn't understand what was going on. I became suspicious after Jane and I ran into you, but when you went through a dozen chocolate covered donuts the next morning, I was sure something was wrong."

"Why didn't you say anything? Usually, you're all in my business about acting human."

Andel paused, searching Evelyn for any indication she could handle this subject. Exhaling, he admitted, "I thought you might be missing Tate." He looked up to the sky. "You'll need time to work through those feelings, and the last thing you want is me breathing down your neck. If I had known it was a fairy, my reaction would have been very different. I want you to feel like you can come to me…with anything."

"But I know I'm going to have to handle this kind of stuff on my own at some point."

"I was your mentor on your assignment in New Orleans. But now, I'd like to be your friend, whether we're working on an assignment together or not."

"I'm not just any normal Cupid, Andel."

"I know."

Evelyn waited for more, but nothing else came out of his mouth. This friend-version of Andel didn't try to fix everything, but sat quietly and listened. She worked through her encounter with Kalan in her mind before explaining to Andel. He wasn't as prejudiced as the Elders, so if the fairies were considered Nox, Andel still might hear her out about helping them. Evelyn had a feeling the supernatural world was made up of more than light and darkness.

"So, a fairy named Kalan stopped by MoMa for a chat…"

Chapter 18

"They cannot be trusted." Andel's logic grew more and more irritating with each attempt to convince him to help with the fairies.

By Saturday afternoon, she still hadn't decided what to do, but Andel's negativity made her determined to prove him wrong. "How do you know that? Have you ever even spoken with one?"

"No. They're Nox."

Evelyn folded her arms over her chest. "What if the Elders said I was Nox because I'm different?"

"You're not planning on attacking any mortals, are you?"

Evelyn shook her head.

"That's the difference. Fairies play with humans like they're dolls. It may be a game to them, but we have committed to protecting mortals."

"But Kalan wants to use the arrows to—"

"Protect themselves."

Evelyn huffed and walked over to the front door. They were walking today, and Evelyn looked forward to the distraction. Once the two Cupids bustled with every other tourist along Fifth Avenue, they turned to pass St. Patrick's Cathedral. After spotting Sydney and Roscoe, they walked a block behind the couple on their second official date.

Roscoe had mentioned some of the art he enjoyed on exhibit at The Met while on his date with Sydney the night before, and she asked him on a date for the next morning. Evelyn was thrilled. Not only had Roscoe dodged the sweaty palm and word vomit he anticipated having at the end of their date, but Evelyn was going to The Metropolitan Museum of Art. If only Andel had been as excited.

He made his argument again as they walked down the busy sidewalk. Out of all Andel's reasons for avoiding the fairies, there was one that resonated with her. "We don't know what other powers your arrows hold when they turn red." Andel's hands bounced in the air in front of him, almost poking the eye out of a passing pedestrian. "What if the fairies are attempting to trick you into providing them with a weapon to use against us?"

"Fine, you're right." Evelyn rolled her eyes. "I don't have a clue what my arrows are capable of, but I also have nothing tangible to go off of when it comes to my powers. The Elders haven't offered to help, but Kalan might exchange information for my arrows."

"Might? Evelyn, it's a dangerous game to barter with fairies," Andel warned. "They word things so you think you have the upper hand, but they're cunning. In the end, they always end up with what they want, no matter how it ends for their victim."

Neither of them said another word until they reached the corner of 5th and 59th. Evelyn replayed Kalan's words, trying to figure out if she'd been tricked somehow. The honking taxis, corner performers, and crowded sidewalks kept interrupting Evelyn's thoughts. The sun gleaming off high rises and cool air made up for the chaos, and once they stepped across 59ᵗʰ and into Central Park, the world transformed. Life didn't slow down, but the things that seemed necessary out there had become less important. The shift had reminded of her own change. Living to keep up with the world had never fully satisfied her. After she gave everything up for love, she gained a timeless existence.

"Have you ever been to The Met?" Evelyn asked.

Andel slipped his hands into his pockets as they walked past a sign for the Central Park Zoo. "I haven't."

"That's hard to believe." Evelyn skipped ahead a few steps. "Okay, but how many of the artists were you best friends with?"

"I promise, only one history lesson." Andel held up his hand like he was reciting a Boy Scout oath.

"You do realize I don't mind the art lectures, right?"

"History." Andel placed his hand over his heart and appeared to be wounded.

"Fine, history. I sincerely want to know everything you know about the city." Evelyn looked up through the trees and twirled. "It's amazing."

As they approached the front steps, Evelyn noticed Roscoe taking Sydney's hand. Evelyn's core buzzed with whatever Cupid-mojo she had, and she fought the urge to summon her bow and arrows. The new couple wasn't ready for her to intercede. Like, lust, and love could all be felt between them, and the first two blossomed. But love was still a seedling. If Evelyn pierced Roscoe and Sydney before love grew between them, it wouldn't be enough to carry them through a lifetime—even with her arrow's help. She would feel a symphony playing in her chest if they truly loved each other, and even though she didn't yet, she knew in her heart they were on the right path.

"Follow me." Andel reached for Evelyn's elbow and pulled her away from the direction Roscoe and Sydney walked.

"Where are we going?" Evelyn glanced back over her shoulder, trying to keep her assignment in sight.

"They'll be fine. I want to show you some of that *history*."

They meandered past portraits taller and older than Andel, and Evelyn squirmed as they passed by without pausing to let her take it all in. Working at MoMa had allowed her the time to really enjoy the art being exhibited. Evelyn had hoped to take her time visiting The Met today. She wanted to take a trek through time. In the first few minutes of walking through its halls, some pieces sang to Evelyn, and she knew they had to have been inspired by Muses. The art here was old. Evelyn could feel the age in each faint song, and the volume correlated with each piece's power to give life.

Stepping outside into a courtyard behind the museum, Evelyn gasped at the sight of a golden statue reflecting the setting sun. The woman stood on a column with her bow and arrow, impossibly graceful for an immoveable object. Evelyn didn't feel any melody coming from the art, but she noticed a change in Andel's demeanor.

He held his hands behind his back. "This is Diana."

"Did you know her?" Evelyn circled the sculpture.

Andel shifted his weight from one foot to the other. "No, but I have been doing a little digging on your behalf, and I think she was *like* you."

"She's a Cupid?"

"She was." Andel's face turned to the ground.

"How do you know?" Evelyn demanded. "Who's been talking to you?"

"I can't tell you."

"What? Why?" Evelyn held her hands out in front of her.

"Can I tell you what I learned?"

Evelyn nodded with a frown.

"Diana is believed to be the first Cupid. She loved nature so much she gave up her life to protect it, and that's not all."

Evelyn watched as Andel stared at the statue. Her beauty could have held the gaze of any man, but Andel wasn't admiring Diana. He looked more like her was working out a problem. She could take whatever he had to tell her, but she noticed his hesitation.

"Just say it!" Evelyn smacked one of Andel's arms. A few people turned to see what the commotion was about.

"The story, *history*, tells the tale of a young woman with many admirers." Andel rubbed his bicep. "Diana struggled to love any man with the same passion she had for hunting and being one with nature. She spent her life protecting the forest she loved, and one day, the huntress encountered an angry hunter. His unrequited love resulted in an arrow through her heart. The heavens welcomed and rewarded her devotion with immortality."

"Whoa. That's pretty awful, but what do Diana and I have in common that makes you think she had the same powers I do?" Evelyn tilted her head to the side, taking in Diana from arrowhead to toe.

Andel shook his head at her. "I'm not exactly sure yet, but I trust my source."

"Your source? Unless your informant knew her personally, I'm not sure how much I can trust them. And if you can't tell me who your informant is, maybe I can't trust you, either." Evelyn began to tear up. She had trusted him with the fairy confrontation, but he wouldn't tell her who knew about her powers.

Andel turned away, unwilling to meet her watery eyes.

Evelyn didn't know why she was on the verge of crying. Maybe it had to do with Andel keeping secrets, or maybe it was the overwhelming feeling she'd never get a solid answer. Andel had a tendency to hold back, especially if he thought he was protecting her.

"Tell me who your source is."

"I cannot do that." Andel placed his palm over his forehead. "I promised."

"Can you tell me if he or she knew Diana?"

"They did, but it was after she'd become a Cupid." Evelyn felt the air in her lungs evaporate. She didn't know if being immortal meant she could go without breathing, but she was about to find out.

"Why can't I talk to them? This is sherbet!" Evelyn sucked in some air and decided to walk away before she made more of a scene.

"Stop, Evelyn. Let me at least explain the rest of Diana's story. At least, the part I know."

"Fine." Evelyn didn't bother turning to face him.

"Diana made the same commitment we all do. She sealed her covenant, then pierced her heavenly quota of couples with love. But, then, she disappeared. Rumors spread that she'd fallen in love. The relationship resulted in her losing her purity and her powers. She blamed the man she'd loved and swore to never love again. Although, I'm questioning whether she really loved him at all. Some believe she moved on, while others think she's still wallowing in her hate and taking it out on mortals as a Nox."

"Oh."

"Exactly. There is more to what you're capable of, Evelyn. Having learned all of this, I'm almost positive there have been and maybe there are more like you in our ranks. All Cupids have died for love, but there must have been something special about Diana's love, about the measure or kind of love."

Running her hands through her hair, Evelyn looked for an exit. "I need to process all of this."

"I understand, but I think the Elders have remained tight-lipped to keep Cupids like you from taking the same path Diana took."

"Please, just give me a minute." Evelyn took a few steps, testing Andel. He didn't move to join her. The space would be good considering her head felt like it might explode. Her strides took her through the museum where she saw Roscoe and Sydney smiling at each other in front of a European sculpture. A tinge of jealousy rippled up her spine.

How could seeing a couple so happy make her feel that way? Suddenly, her guilt drove her to get as far away as she could.

Leaving the building, Evelyn made for Central Park. The line of trees reminded her of Diana's forest. The story she'd been told had to connect to her own somehow. Diana, the huntress, had loved the earth. Evelyn, the college student, had loved her boyfriend. They were both women, but maybe Evelyn was a descendant of Diana. Could Cupids even get pregnant?

Gah! I don't know anything! Evelyn mentally projected.

Well, instead of walking away, you could always ask me, Andel answered from a few yards behind her.

"You followed me." Evelyn stopped between two trees.

Andel caught up and leaned his shoulder against an elm. "Of course, I did."

"I need some space." Evelyn started to walk away again. "Physically and mentally, so if you're going to follow me, keep your distance."

Evelyn briskly made her way deeper into the foliage of the park. The winter grass became greener under the canopy of trees she ducked under. A peaceful stillness wrapped around her, and she stopped to sit at the center of the small meadow.

Grabbing a few blades of grass, she pulled them up and threw them in front of her. Her frustration made it impossible to focus on Diana and all she'd learned. In the corner of her eye, Evelyn noticed a rustling in the bushes and wanted to yell at Andel to leave her alone. What he considered help, she took as babying.

The sun had been blocked by a canopy of leaves, and in the shadows, Evelyn's enhanced sight refocused. She would never experience true darkness again—unless she chose the same path Diana took. Could Diana still be alive striking misery in others instead of love?

A bird's caw screeched above Evelyn, and she dismissed the sound, trying to target the link between her and Diana. It wasn't about gender or who or what they loved. The link could be a lineage of children and grandchildren who make the same sacrifice she made. But if it was something so simple, why wouldn't the Elders want to tell her about her distant relative?

"Your time is up, Cupid." Kalan stepped out from behind a gnarled, old tree.

Evelyn jumped up and tried to transcend, but thinking of her New York apartment didn't carry her to safety. Kalan had willed her to stay put.

"Kalan, I'm still trying to work out a few things. I need a few more days."

"The problem is we don't have a few days. One troll is attacking more frequently, and if you won't give me your arrows, I'll just have to take *you* back with me."

Help!

A red arrow, like her own, flew from the dense forest at her side. It streaked past her toward Kalan. The fairy easily dodged being shot, and Evelyn looked back over her shoulder to see who was there. It wasn't her brooding friend Andel, but a man with blond hair wearing dark jeans and a black shirt. He was the same guy who attacked the first day they transcended to New York. Before Evelyn could get a better look, Kalan had rushed to her side. Instead of fighting, she used Evelyn as a shield while yanking her away from the stranger.

Andel appeared a few yards away from the mystery immortal, and Jude ran with him into the small clearing. The arrival of the Cupid and

Gargoyle didn't seem to startle the stranger. They both looked over at him, and he disappeared into thin air. Evelyn could only guess he was able to transcend because he hadn't crossed into the circle of trees. Before she could warn Andel, he and Jude rushed to the middle of the lawn where she stood.

"Are you okay?" Jude asked while Andel made sure he positioned himself between her and Kalan.

"I'm fine," Evelyn answered. She rested a hand on Andel's shoulder, and the connection she felt a few nights ago was still there. It had frightened her before, but in that moment, their bond made her feel stronger.

"You won't be taking her," Andel said.

"I wouldn't be so sure about that," Kalan smirked. With a snap of her fingers, they were surrounded. Fairies, dozens of them, advanced into the open meadow.

Chapter 19

"Warn the others," Andel ordered under his breath to Jude.

He watched as Jude pulled his arms down to his side, the way he would call his bow and arrow to his side, but nothing happened. Andel knew who kept Jude from shifting, but Evelyn hadn't been around long enough to know much about fairy powers. One couldn't keep Gargoyles from transforming, but having so many surround them would dampen the power of a half dozen immortals. Usually, proximity had more to do with the strength of a fairy's power. It was probably how Kalan had kept Evelyn from escaping the stairwell the other day.

"Do we fight?" Jude's dark eyes narrowed, and his stance widened.

"No." Andel didn't think they could take all the fairies and ensure their safety. He'd rather surrender and insist they go with Evelyn wherever they planned to take her.

Andel felt a tickle in his thoughts, but only for a moment, and it felt dark. Andel didn't know of any other Cupids currently assigned to New

York City, so he assumed it was the immortal who shot a red arrow at Evelyn trying to communicate with him. He hadn't recognized the man, but his arrows looked all too familiar.

"Looks like you've won the affection of some prominent supernaturals, Evelyn." Kalan sneered at the sight of Jude. "Bring the Lux along." She pointed a finger at Jude and Andel, and with a wave, they were both bound with magic. Their wrists were magically glued together, and the essence of a blanket tightly wrapped around their body kept them compliant.

Once under their control, the fairies moved in and directed Andel to follow Evelyn. She hadn't been mystically tied up, but he trusted she wouldn't do anything that would put them in harm's way. Andel could feel Jude's presence behind him while Kalan led the way in front of him. The fairy's outstretched fingers danced in the air in front of them all and the plant life around them stretched and grew around the party. It allowed them to journey further into the forest.

Kalan approached a wall of foliage and whisked it to the side, revealing an ancient knotted tree. The trunk of the tree stood as wide as a house, and its lowest branches stretched higher than Andel or Jude could reach. He watched Evelyn fall into a trance as she glanced upward. The leaves waved at her in the breeze, showing off its golden fruit hanging from its limbs. Andel felt life trickle from behind the tree into him and guessed it called to Evelyn.

"Wait," Jude's voice called from behind Andel. "I want to strike a deal."

"Jude," Andel warned.

"I know what I'm doing. I've lived in the same park with these fairies for over a hundred years."

"I didn't think you'd noticed." Kalan pretended to have hurt feelings.

"I'll protect you from the trolls. Just let them go."

"Ha!" Kalan stepped closer to Jude. "What makes you think you have the power to help us? Your age? Not even your Lux Gargoyle commander has enough power to defeat the darkness of a troll," she seethed through gritted teeth.

"Fine, then what will it take to get you to promise me we'll all make it back here alive?" Jude asked.

"Jude," Evelyn spoke up. "Don't. This is my deal to make. It's between me and Kalan, or Queen Rhyan." She turned to address the queen's messenger. "They don't have anything to do with this. Let them go."

Evelyn met Andel's eyes. He knew she'd do or promise anything to see them get out of this unhurt. Being immortal meant you couldn't be killed, but it didn't mean you couldn't be tortured. They could be held by the fairies for an eternity if she didn't succumb to their demands.

"Oh, Evelyn. I need some assurance you'll cooperate. You understand, don't you?" Kalan's grin slipped into a sneer. "But I tell you what, I'll let you decide which one I let stay here."

Andel hadn't broken eye contact with Evelyn, and before she could speak his name Andel nodded in Jude's direction. Evelyn's brow wrinkled in confusion. He nodded toward Jude again, determined the Gargoyles had a better chance of fighting the Fairies. But he also struggled with the idea of letting Evelyn go.

"Jude," Evelyn whispered and swallowed down the emotion bubbling in her throat. "Let Jude go."

Immediately, Jude's invisible restraints released him. He hesitated, but only for a second. Kalan laughed as Jude bolted for the cover of bushes, but something solid stopped him. Andel had hoped Jude could report to Roscoe, who would then go straight to the Elders. But Andel recalled Kalan's promise.

"How long will he have to stay here?" Andel asked.

Kalan's lips twisted. "When you leave, he may leave."

"What?" Evelyn looked back and forth between Kalan and Jude. "Schnitzel!"

"Okay, now on to my realm." Kalan looked to the giant tree. The gnarled roots shifted and opened to reveal a glowing doorway. Evelyn's eyes glazed over as she stepped closer to the tree.

Kalan stepped in first, followed by two other Fairies. Evelyn made her way in next, and if Andel could have fit, he would have gone in at the same time but settled with entering close behind. Once inside the tree, Andel felt a shift in his power. His heightened senses felt flat. They weren't gone, but they felt like an old balloon struggling to stay in the air.

"Welcome!" Kalan swung her hands up in the air and Andel was released from his bonds. She had to know he was powerless here.

Stepping next to Evelyn, he took her hand and squeezed it. "I have no power here," he whispered.

Evelyn would have been shocked, but she'd been overwhelmed by their new surroundings. The grass was greener here, and it rolled on hills that stretched as far as their eyes could see. The flowers, vibrant with every color on the color chart, blanketed the hills. Taking a deep breath, thick, sweet air tickled Andel's nose. The sun didn't hang in the sky, but light still warmed their skin.

The hidden world lured its visitors with eternal Spring, and Andel had heard stories of immortals being lost in this place forever. He worried Evelyn had gotten them ensnared in a world they'd never be able to escape from.

Walking down a dirt road, beautiful fairy women passed them carrying goods. A few stopped to watch them. Fairy men didn't cross their path as often, but one band of misfits taunted the Cupids so loudly Kalan ordered them to be silent.

Kalan didn't take the time to explain that Evelyn was about to save their hides from the troll threatening their realm. Andel knew fairies could come along and twist his words, so even when he wanted to defend Evelyn, he kept silent. Evelyn continued to be mesmerized by their surroundings.

After a few miles of hills and valleys, a palace came into view. A waterfall served as background to the polished, stone structure. Turrets reached for the heavens at four corners of the building, and one rock wall hid under vines covered in purple flowers. The closer they came, the larger Queen Rhyan's home became.

Approaching the palace gates, Andel watched them shimmer as they opened. "We may never get out of here."

"We'll be fine." She squeezed his hand. "I have a good feeling about this."

"That feeling is fairy magic, and it's meant to entice you."

"I'm pretty sure I got this."

"You got what?" Andel asked. He doubted her strength since his had been smothered when they arrived.

Evelyn gasped as Kalan directed the group into a courtyard with an elaborate fountain standing at its center. A marble statue of five children holding hands came to life, dancing around the spray of water shooting up from its middle. Andel looked over at Kalan, and her hand stretched out toward the merriment. Her powers entertained them, but Andel knew it was more likely she used her strength to distract them.

The magic captivated Evelyn, but Andel searched for signs of a scheme. Above them, fairies ran along the tops of the walls surrounding their group. Each fairy armed themselves with bows and arrows. They were preparing for the queen's arrival.

Andel wondered why they wouldn't be taken down to the dungeons or secluded in an inescapable chamber. Everything he knew about the fairies came from Lux rumors. Fairies had been lumped in with the Nox because they never officially took a side. A paranormal Switzerland didn't exist, and the fairies hadn't done anything in centuries to prove they were one of the good guys.

"Please, move closer to the fountain," Kalan requested formally. "We must make room for the witnesses."

Two fairies perched on turrets above blew into horns that stretched over the edges of the castle into the air. Andel expected a burst of noise, but a lilting song played over the people as they crowded into the courtyard. Once the area had been filled, an enormous wooden door swung open, and a slender fairy with long white hair and a tangled crown of gold blossoms strode into their presence. She wore a white robe decorated with a golden pattern along its hem. The sleeves hung down past her hands, but Andel saw the tips of her white fingernails.

The colorful crowd came to a standstill in awe of their pristine queen.

She stepped up onto a platform that unfolded under her feet with magic. "Today we come together to witness the generosity of our new patron, our champion Cupid, Evelyn." Queen Rhyan's voice echoed over her people.

Andel felt Evelyn's fingers tighten between his as the crowd roared to life. This was a show for the people, to create hope and dissolve their fears. Andel's interest peaked at how the queen had referred to Evelyn, a *new* patron. Maybe the queen really could give Evelyn the information she wanted, so she could let go of this obsession. If she figured out why she was different, maybe she could accept herself. But, then, Evelyn would move on to working assignments without him.

"We will eat and drink to our heart's content in celebration!" Queen Rhyan turned and made her way back into the palace, and Kalan waved for them to join her. A line of fairies in uniform paraded out of the palace with trays held over their heads. Food covered each platter, but all Evelyn could see were red grapes cascading off the edges.

"Do not eat or drink anything," Andel warned Evelyn over the crowd's cheers.

"Even humans know that," Evelyn said.

Andel didn't understand how she was holding it together. Normally, she'd be on her third slice of chocolate cake. It took everything in him not to scoop her up and run. His logic teetered on being drowned by fear of the unknown. This realm was older than ancient Greece. As a boy, Andel remembered stories his father told him of the nymphs who held the power to lure men with their music. He'd always equated the myth with fairies.

"Maybe you should have kept Jude with you," Andel thought out loud.

"You nodded for me to choose him, right?" Evelyn tried to pull her hand away.

Andel tugged her back toward himself. "Yes, I'm sorry. I didn't mean to say you made the wrong choice. I had a momentary lapse of selfishness."

"I don't know how your brain computes letting another guy go in your place as selfish."

"I want to be here with you," he reassured. "I simply meant that Jude is older than the pyramids, and he was bound to know more about this realm than me. But, that makes him better suited to attempt a rescue. That is if he can figure out a way to get out of that meadow."

As they stepped inside the palace, the celebration outside faded. Stone walls that reached over thirty feet high canceled out the noise. Stained-glass windows were set high, and the light filtering through them created a mosaic of color on the marble floor. The collage circulated like a periscope, interchanging the red and turquoise tiles around each other to make new pictures with the shifting light.

"This way darling girl," Queen Rhyan called to Evelyn.

Andel moved with Evelyn across the entryway and into a receiving room. The open space drew their eyes to the end of the room where an ornate throne made from tangled white crystals sat. The queen glided down a gold carpet toward her seat but hesitated at the bottom of the steps leading to her chair.

Taking in Evelyn and Andel, the corners of the queen's mouth turned up.

"What?" Andel asked, holding back the urge to step forward and form a wall between her and Evelyn.

"Well, well, well. It seems we found you just in time." The queen ignored Andel.

"In time for what?" Evelyn asked.

"If you're not careful, you'll waste your power like most of the champions before you." Rhyan climbed the steps in front of her throne.

Andel couldn't help but wonder how many champions had come before Evelyn. "So, in bringing us here, are you forcing Evelyn to comply?"

The queen looked from Andel to Kalan. The queen's messenger looked to the floor, and it was the first time Andel had ever seen Kalan look worried.

"Forcing?" The queen asked. She ignored Andel and addressed Evelyn directly. "My dear, I will tell you what you what I know." She waved her hand, and a clear gem the size of a tootsie pop perched on her finger caught the light. "But first, the five arrows."

Andel fidgeted, unsure if he should interfere, but did anyway. "You cannot trust her."

"I think I've figured a way around that," Evelyn replied to Andel and stepped in front of him. "Queen Rhyan, do you promise the fairies will only use my arrows on trolls?"

The queen didn't hesitate. "I promise."

Andel knew fairies could be tricky, but he also knew they couldn't lie. "Nice one." He nudged Evelyn proudly with his elbow.

"I will have to summon my bow and arrows," Evelyn said.

"And you may." The queen sat and tapped her long, sharp nails on the sharp arm of her chair. "You're more powerful here than on the earth. The same as if you were in the heavens."

"Oh." Evelyn mentioned having a good feeling, but Andel hadn't thought it included her abilities. Knowing she had no restraints, Evelyn allowed the thought of her bow and arrows to be realized, and they appeared in her hands.

"In fact, you have an open invitation to join us here at any point during your existence as our champion."

Evelyn reached for an arrow from her quiver. "Thanks, but I'm enjoying New York."

"For now." Rhyan folded her arms over her chest.

Andel grew tired of the queen's insinuations and didn't want to be there any longer than they needed. "How about you give Evelyn a fact about the champions who came before her for every arrow?" Andel negotiated.

"Fair enough"—Rhyan turned from Andel to face Evelyn—"but first, I want to see you change it."

Evelyn glanced around the empty hall. "To do that, I need to point it at an immortal in love."

"You forget; I already knew that." Rhyan smiled and looked to Andel.

The queen's eye pierced his as if she could see into his soul. He worried she would mistake his protective feelings for Evelyn. Since she'd woken up in the heavens and he'd been assigned to be her mentor, he'd misunderstood his own feelings several times. Sometimes he felt frustration, other times it was annoyance, but most recently Evelyn had inspired hope in him.

Just then, a fairy couple walked into the room and stood behind them. Evelyn didn't have to look at first because she heard their love. But her curiosity got the better of her, and she wanted to see if the music, a string quartet, matched the couple.

The woman's black hair had been woven into a braid and she wore a lavender dress. As she walked closer, Evelyn noticed her eyes matched the light fabric. The man stood tall and slender like most of the fairy men, and his white-blond hair stuck out of the bottom of a beanie he had pulled down over his ears. His shirt was dark green and his pants brown. Evelyn could see the grass stains on his knees and gathered he worked as a farmer. The two clung to each other, and their song slowed as they approached the throne.

Queen Rhyan's hand rose in front of her to signal for the couple to stop. "That is close enough." They slowed, and the man wrapped his arm around the woman in an embrace. "Do you feel it?" Rhyan turned to ask Evelyn.

Evelyn nodded, but Andel didn't feel anything. How could Evelyn's power be amplified here, but his be weakened so much? He couldn't feel love in supernaturals, anyway, but the lack of his power altogether was frustrating.

"This is a great honor," Rhyan said to the couple. "The champion will take aim, but do not worry. She will only use your love to inspire the arrows we need for our peoples' protection."

Evelyn shouldered her quiver and retrieved an arrow. Taking aim, the arrow transformed before their eyes from gold to red. Evelyn's hand began to shake, and Andel knew she struggled to pull the arrow away from them. A Cupid was created to pierce love when it sang, not withhold it.

"Evelyn." Andel took a step behind her and placed his hand on her elbow. Her form couldn't be more perfect. Evelyn shuddered at his touch and slowly brought the glowing red weapon to her side.

The two Cupids turned to Queen Rhyan, and she dismissed the two fairies with a flick of her wrist. They scurried out of the room, and at the sound of a snap, Kalan moved to confiscate the arrow.

"Hold on, we had a deal." Andel moved between Kalan and Evelyn.

"We did." Rhyan stood and began pacing at the edge of her platform. "What to reveal first? Hmmm…"

One of her long, pointy white nails rested on her chin.

"Why don't you tell me why I'm different?" Evelyn asked.

"That is difficult to pinpoint. I know more about *how* you're different. You see, I've never been close enough to one of your kind to be friends. In the past, Cupids like you have always wanted something from the fairies, trading favors for arrows." Rhyan looked at Andel, "The others were always alone."

"How many are there like me?"

"Tsk, tsk." Rhyan motioned for Kalan to take the arrow, and Evelyn handed it over.

Andel clenched his jaw in frustration at the semantics. "You have it, now answer her."

"I've encountered three." Rhyan held up three sharpened fingernails. "Other than you, of course."

Evelyn's mouth formed a small *o*. It was more than Andel had dug up. He knew Diana had to be the first, but there were at least two more immortals out there like her. Andel had been told every Cupid was given the choice to move on at the end of their service, and he wondered if either of them would have chosen that way.

"So, *how* am I different then?" Evelyn asked.

Queen Rhyan summoned another couple into the room, and they went through the same spiel, assuring the fairies they wouldn't be pierced. Evelyn took aim, but this time it seemed easier for her to disarm herself. With each arrow, Evelyn became less wild. In the fairy realm, her power was stronger but also more controlled.

As the fairies left the room, Andel's curiosity got the better of him. "Why don't they want to be pierced? If they possess enough love to inspire Evelyn's arrow, wouldn't they want the security it affords?"

"Good question, Cupid." Rhyan sat down on the edge of her throne. "We have always believed our love is enough. Stories have been told of a fairy being pierced ages ago, but it ended in tragedy."

Evelyn handed over her red arrow and insisted, "How am I different?"

"You know you can assist mortals and immortals, but you can also telepathically communicate with both. Try it." Rhyan nodded at Evelyn to encourage her.

This explains a few things.

"I'm glad I could shed some light for you." Rhyan replied.

"Shed light on what?" Andel asked.

"Seems she's right. I can communicate with more than just Cupids." Evelyn turned to Rhyan and squinted her eyes. "Can you communicate telepathically?"

"Not the way you can." Rhyan smiled. "Fairies are more clairvoyant. We see and understand. It's less logical and more inspired."

"How else?" Evelyn wanted to know more.

"Well, the same way your arrows are more powerful, your abilities and senses are also intensified. But with heightened senses, you will encounter temptations that feel impossible to deny."

"Okay, cryptic much?"

Another fairy couple arrived, and Evelyn went through the process of changing her gold arrow into a red one. Andel and Evelyn learned that a link to Diana genetically was unlikely because Diana had never had children. Rhyan described Diana as a woman who'd love them and leave them.

The next couple looked so young Andel didn't think they'd inspire Evelyn. He knew fairies aged much slower than any supernatural race who still aged, but these fairies looked like teenagers. Evelyn pointed and looked surprised herself to see the gold shaft turn red. When handing the arrow over, Rhyan explained that Evelyn's red arrows only brought immortals with pure hearts together.

The information they'd learned so far led to more questions, and Rhyan became less forthcoming with each follow-up question.

There was only one arrow left to hand over, and Rhyan's eyes narrowed as she shared her last bit of knowledge about Evelyn's abilities. "Your red arrows can be lethal to Nox immortals. But you must remember even those whose light shines brightest can succumb to darkness. It's why we have to protect ourselves from trolls. They once walked in our realm as fairies but were overcome by their own darkness. Every race of supernaturals has to fight darkness, and the Lux will eventually have to see that truth. None of us are strictly light or dark."

Rhyan's observation had hit a nerve with Andel. He stepped closer to Evelyn.

"Killing Nox will only lead to all of our destruction," Rhyan spoke to Andel. "We must find a way to reach Nox and bring them out of the darkness and into the light. I believe Evelyn, and others like her, are the key."

Andel's arms folded over his chest. "Impossible."

"It's your kind's pride that makes it impossible," Rhyan snarled and slowly pointed a finger at Andel.

The queen's finger became blurry, and Andel's thoughts became hazy. He felt Evelyn's hand grasp his shoulder, steadying him.

"Adieu." She murmured.

Poof.

Chapter 20

Evelyn and Andel were safe in their living room before Queen Rhyan could stop them. Evelyn had grown more confident in her power with each arrow she transformed. Even though Andel couldn't use his power in the fairy's realm, she felt the strength of her own abilities surpass anything the queen could control.

"How did you two get away?" Leo asked from the kitchen of Evelyn and Andel's New York City apartment.

They were surrounded by Neomi, Zora, and Douglas. After Leo served Evelyn a plate of key lime pie, Neomi encouraged them to sit in the living room. Evelyn noticed the sun peeking over the city's horizon in the distance as she sat against the couch on the floor next to Leo's legs. The light filtered through the window where Andel still stood, covering everyone in an orange hue.

Andel took a step back from the window and looked to the Cupid Elder for answers. "How long have we been gone?"

"It's been close to thirty-six hours."

"What?" Evelyn exclaimed, with her mouth full of whipped cream.

Andel faced Evelyn and shoved his hands in his jean pockets. He made eye contact with Neomi then explained, "Time is different there. It's an element of the fairy's deceit that can cost a mortal their life."

"We'll have to go over fairy-lore another time." Neomi leaned forward in her seat to face Evelyn too. "Douglas, please go relay the good news to the others and make sure the message is delivered to Roscoe as well."

Douglas nodded and transcended. His demeanor had changed completely from when they'd last met in the heavens. Douglas had been light-hearted and a little goofy before, but as he disappeared, Evelyn noted that he seemed almost as militant as the Gargoyles.

Andel walked to a chair at the edge of the room and sat down. "Please tell me no one retaliated." He leaned forward and placed his head in his hands.

"No. We'd planned to move out this morning at sunrise," Zora spoke from the chair next to Neomi. Her words eased the tension that had built up in Andel's shoulders, and he relaxed back into his seat. Annoyance pricked at Evelyn's spine, and she couldn't sit still any longer.

After setting her empty dish on the coffee table, Evelyn started pacing in front of the window. She felt like a caged bird being teased with endless sky twenty stories high. "So, you all planned to launch an attack on Central Park while joggers and tourists lined the sidewalks? How were you going to get into the fairy's realm?"

"We don't have a lot of time to discuss it, but Roscoe found Jude a few hours after you went missing. The Gargoyles had worked out the details." Neomi's grandmotherly tone grew more clipped with each word. "I need to know what Queen Rhyan wanted with you."

"We had tea and crumpets." Evelyn fisted her hands at her side. "She's the queen. What else would we have done?"

Neomi closed her eyes and pinched the bridge of her nose. "Evelyn—"

"Don't," she interrupted. "Don't you think I know how *not* forthcoming you and the Elders have been with me?"

"Watch your—"

"She wanted Evelyn's arrows," Andel grumbled.

"Gah!" Evelyn's hands flew up into the air.

Neomi stood and moved toward Andel. "You're coming with me to address the Elders," she ordered.

Andel looked up, back and forth between Evelyn and Neomi, and nodded his consent.

"Douglas will return, and he and Zora will stay with Evelyn. Leo has also agreed to help."

Andel stood to join Neomi, and he glanced at Leo. The two exchanged a knowing look.

Really, Andel? Evelyn asked in thought. *They're not helping us, so why should we help them?*

Andel wiped his hand down his face at Evelyn's words. *I am doing this for you. Maybe they'll give something up, or maybe I can convince them to tell me about the others like you. Please, just stay here until I get back.*

Evelyn turned away from him to look out over the city. *I don't know if I can ever believe them.*

The truth hurt.

Andel frowned at Evelyn's last thought. *Then try and believe in me.*

He placed his hand on Neomi's shoulder.

Poof.

Chapter 21

Two cupcakes later, Evelyn felt like hashing out everything that had happened. She didn't trust Zora or Douglas, so even if she wanted to vent to Leo, they'd get suspicious and report back to the Elders. Plus, she had to get ready for work. Mondays. She felt just as much animosity for the day of the week when she was a student. Jane would need her at the museum, and even if the assignment belonged to Andel, she couldn't let Jane's love life suffer because she wanted to sit around and wait for Andel.

Evelyn didn't like that Andel was in the heavens talking to the Elders without her. It surprised her when she decided her issue had more to do with being apart than him finding out information without her. She knew he'd come back to tell her what he learned, but now she had both of their jobs to do, and she felt more compelled to worry about when Andel would be back at her side.

After putting on her favorite power suit and twisting her long brown locks into a messy bun, she stepped into the living room ready for the onslaught of arguments.

Douglas straightened, standing at the center of the room, when Evelyn made for the front door. "What can we do?"

"Um…" Evelyn's heels tripped up on the rug in the entryway. "Don't try and stop me?"

"No." Zora appeared from the kitchen with Leo behind her. "What he means is, what do you want us to help with?"

Douglas rolled his eyes at Zora. "I was getting to that, and what do you care anyway? You're busy entertaining the muscle."

"There's more to me than muscles, but I can see how it's difficult to look past that," Leo grinned as he walked toward Evelyn. "I'm in for helping, too, in any way you need. It's the least I can do."

"Seriously?" Evelyn couldn't believe they really wanted to help.

Do you trust them? Evelyn pushed her thoughts to Leo. Out of the three, she trusted him most, and if Queen Rhyan was right about Evelyn's abilities, this was the only way to have a private conversation with the Gargoyle.

Leo shifted his black-rimmed glasses up into his white hair and rubbed his eyes. "Huh?"

Zora and Douglas looked at Leo quizzically.

I'm trying to send you my thoughts, Leo, but you can't let Zora and Douglas know I'm communicating with you.

Leo coughed once. "Excuse me, guys. I think I need a drink of water."

Do you trust them? Cough once for yes and twice for no.

Leo coughed once, but before Evelyn could feel relieved he coughed again. He reached for a glass in the cabinet and filled it with water.

Well, that's not helpful. I wish there was a way for you to think back to me. We could be stuck here all day trying to figure this out. Let me try again. Do you at least trust them to help with Andel's assignment?

Leo coughed once and took another sip of water. When he didn't make another peep, Evelyn figured she could use them to get something done today. Anything would be better than being stuck in the apartment with a gender-swapped version of Lucille Ball and Desi Arnaz. Evelyn had a feeling Douglas would make as big a mess working in a chocolate factory as Lucy, while Zora would make men swoon with her accent and good looks like Desi did in the classic television show.

Evelyn tapped her chin with her pointer finger. "Okay, if y'all are really up for this, I need to orchestrate a girls' night."

"Ugh. Will I have to glamour myself as one of the girls?" Douglas whined.

Evelyn chuckled at the thought. "I'll actually need you to glamour yourself as Andel. I'm hoping you can convince Kendrick to crash our outing."

"And what am I supposed to do?" Leo looked offended at not being given a task.

"I'll need you to get Roscoe and Sydney to the event."

Leo winked. "But I'm supposed to be guarding you."

"How about you stay with me this morning and report my plans back to Roscoe. He may want to come just to add extra protection since we'll be out at night."

"You're pushing it, Evelyn," Zora spoke up, but one corner of her mouth lifted. "I'm in if I get to come."

Evelyn didn't know if she could trust Zora or Douglas with her own issues, but getting the two on board to help Jane and Kendrick couldn't hurt. She planned to orchestrate a girl's night with Jane, and if everything worked according to plan, it would turn into a date night. They would happen upon the guys, and once she got them talking, Evelyn knew Jane and Kendrick would hit it off more than they already had.

Andel had gotten them to meet on a professional level, but running into each other socially could shift their relationship from business in the front to party in the back. A mullet love story. Evelyn wanted to gently nudge the mission forward, so when Andel came back from his heavenly debriefing, he'd notice progress. She hoped to make him proud.

Chapter 22

Getting Jane Platt to agree to anything seemed impossible, so Evelyn used the oldest trick up her sleeve. She manipulated Jane into thinking girls' night was her idea. The only complication was Jane chose a club that carded, and technically, Evelyn hadn't turned twenty-one until after she'd died.

Evelyn snapped her compact shut and shoved it into her tiny purse. The taxi she sat in, with Jane and Zora packed snugly on either side, began to slow down. Jane pinched her cheeks, and Zora applied another layer of gloss while Evelyn picked at her nails. She had no clue how she'd get past the bouncer.

After the cab stopped, Jane placed a bill in the driver's hand and exited the vehicle. Zora placed a hand on Jane's shoulder to stop her from following. "Glamour a few wrinkles and they won't ask for your I.D."

"Got it."

Zora hadn't offered a truce verbally, but she'd been nice to Evelyn all day at the museum. The fact that Zora had noticed Evelyn's anxiety actually put her mind at ease. With relief, she pulled herself out of the car and joined Jane.

"Got what?" Jane asked. Then she rolled her eyes as Zora stepped out of the cab like a supermodel in a car commercial. Evelyn could tell Jane didn't like toting Zora along as their third wheel, but Evelyn had explained Zora was an extended family member visiting from out of town.

"I was just telling Zora she's still got it." Evelyn waggled her eyebrows. Zora placed a hand on her hip. "Of course, I do."

"Where is it you're from? I haven't ever heard an accent like yours." Jane folded her arms skeptically over her chest. Every exotic thing about Zora annoyed Jane. They were opposites in almost every way. Evelyn had a feeling that both women shared one trait in common, determination.

"Oh, I'm from a little bit of everywhere." Zora waved her off. "I travel a lot." Her immortal life had allowed Zora to travel across the globe, but her accent was even a mystery to Evelyn.

Jane looked the middle eastern beauty up and down. "How old are you?" Zora turned away, looking for the club's entrance. "That is if you don't mind me asking," Jane offered.

"I like to say I'm twenty-seven, but between us, I'm thirty-three." Zora spotted the line formed along the sidewalk and bypassed it for the bulky linebacker guarding the doorway. With a wink and her pointer finger, Zora had captivated the man, and he let the three of them through.

Evelyn thanked Zora with a nod.

Her timeless beauty had its advantages, and her little black dress didn't hurt, either. Relating her age to Evelyn's thirty-something boss helped solidify their girls' night comradery, and once inside, Evelyn hoped the atmosphere would do most of the work for them.

Zora, Douglas, and Leo had all worked to orchestrate the evening so Andel's assignment wouldn't be buried under Evelyn's personal drama. While the guys had invited Kendrick to the club, Zora had worked the hardest at the museum with Evelyn. She had almost been friendly.

"I'll get drinks," Zora announced. The room they entered was more like a hall, and the people packed inside moved to the beat of the booming music. Evelyn only heard Zora because of her immortal ability to hear a pin drop, but Jane wrinkled her nose up at Evelyn as Zora walked off toward the bar.

"I don't know about this!" Jane yelled over the bass. She tried to turn and walk back to the entrance, but Evelyn caught her elbow.

"We are here to have fun! Come on!"

Moving around a group of women closer to Evelyn's age, she deciphered a groan coming from Jane. The men didn't cluster together the same way women did, but they moved more freely through the club. Evelyn had planned to take Jane to the dance floor before making their way to Zora and the guys. Forcing back the buzzing mutual attraction, Evelyn passed couple after couple dancing in the middle of the room.

The flashing lights and lack of personal space didn't hinder Evelyn as she sought the perfect spot to keep an eye on Kendrick while dancing with Jane. Scanning the area around the bar, a man with blond hair had tucked himself in the shadows. Evelyn couldn't tell if it was the same guy from the park, but something about him bothered her. She recognized Douglas in her peripheral vision. He wasn't glamoured as Andel anymore, and he sat next to Kendrick at the bar. When she looked back to the dark corner, the man had disappeared.

Focusing on the task at hand, Evelyn noticed Kendrick had a full glass of clear liquid in one hand and two empty glasses in front of him. She knew better than to think it was water. Evelyn also knew too much alcohol could ruin this night for Jane, Kendrick, and Andel.

Zora? Evelyn thought.

Yes?

What's up with Kendrick?

Oh, Douglas received a message from the Elders that Andel is headed back, so he came as himself. But, Kendrick thinks he's been stood up by his buddy and now he's drowning his sorrows. Lame if you ask me.

Evelyn tried to sway her hips to the music and encourage Jane, but she got off beat while trying to stave off men attempting to dance with them. Andel needed to hurry up and get to the club, so they could get the night back on course. Evelyn couldn't concentrate on keeping Jane happy while watching the front door for Andel and the bar for Kendrick. She needed to put the night into second gear, so Kendrick wouldn't get fed up and leave.

Instead of accidentally running into the guys, Evelyn would have to risk Jane finding out that it was a setup. Evelyn considered sending Zora to distract Kendrick from his collection of shot glasses, but Kendrick falling for Zora would destroy Andel's assignment and all the work he'd done. The only way to make the meeting work would be to make Douglas's dreams come true, because for this to work, Zora couldn't be available.

Douglas? He straightened on his bar stool with Evelyn's mental prodding.

It only took a little more psychic effort and Evelyn was communicating with both Cupids at once. *I need you two to act interested in each other.*

Douglas' mouth spread into a wide smile. *Not a problem.*

Okay, I'll try. Zora didn't sound excited, but at least she didn't turn the idea down altogether. It was a good thing they couldn't hear each other's thoughts.

With the plan in motion, Evelyn bumped into Jane on the dance floor. "Let's go meet Zora for a drink!"

Taking Jane by the hand, Evelyn dragged her through the crowd as they jumped to the beat in unison. The elbows and shoulders jutting into their way were enough to keep Evelyn preoccupied from the lust echoing through the club. Couples made out along the outskirts of the dance floor, and it tempted her to summon her bow and arrows. The same way the music resonated in her chest, the mortal longing for more thrummed through her. Evelyn had felt the difference between the crescendo of love and the clanging between two people when they were being led by selfish desire. She hated that both circumstances called to her. Turning her thoughts to the potential Jane and Kendrick's relationship had, Evelyn's Cupid-instincts fell away.

Evelyn focused on Douglas and instructed him. *Come introduce yourself once we get to Zora.*

Introducing everyone would require smooth transitioning if she expected Jane to believe this was a chance meeting. Evelyn made every effort to stay in front of Jane, and it took some disjointed maneuvering to keep Jane from seeing Kendrick. Arriving at the bar, Zora turned around with two colorful concoctions. Evelyn glanced at Douglas a few seats over, and he took it as his queue to move in.

Once he made his way over, Douglas held a martini glass out to Zora. "I hope you'll join me for a drink."

"Well, I'm here with my friends," Zora began. She turned to face Evelyn and asked, "Would you mind?"

"Of course not. We can catch up later," Evelyn answered. She took the two drinks from Zora and handed one to Jane.

Zora's long black hair swished from side to side as she walked to a tabletop a few feet away with Douglas. Evelyn needed to act fast. She took a sip of her red, icy drink and it had no alcohol in it.

You are only twenty, Zora smirked at Evelyn from her table, pretending to respond to something Douglas said. Evelyn grinned back at her.

"I thought we agreed on no guys." Jane sniffed the pink liquid in her glass and took a sip.

Evelyn could explain away Zora flirting with a man at the club, but Andel would be showing up any minute. If Evelyn didn't get Kendrick's attention soon, Jane would think of herself as a fifth wheel. And Evelyn couldn't risk a guy other than Kendrick hitting on Jane. Evelyn didn't see how this could work if she didn't come clean.

Evelyn sucked air in through her teeth. "Well, Andel may be joining us in a little while, and I may have asked for him to invite Kendrick."

"Your boyfriend is coming?" At Jane's question, Evelyn twitched. "And you're pawning me off on a guy that didn't call the next day?"

Kendrick hadn't called her. Evelyn expected it to take a little more to get the two together. Neither one seemed to be looking for love, but there must have been some cosmic reason for the Elders to have assigned Andel to them. While she and Andel fought for love, it seemed like Jane and Kendrick were fighting against it.

"Hi there, ladies. Don't I know you?" Kendrick slurred from behind them.

Evelyn took her eyes off the bachelor for three minutes and he'd strolled up to them with a drink in hand. He threw an arm over Evelyn's shoulders. She squirmed out from under him, and noticed Douglas scoot closer to Zora and placed a hand on her arm. When Evelyn looked to Zora, her normally flawless face was twisted in concern.

Jane placed a hand on her hip. "Well, speak of the Devil."

"Actually, I'm Kendrick." He stuck a hand out in mock introduction. When Jane refused to shake it, he stuck his hand in his pocket. "What's the matter with her, sweetheart?" All of Kendrick's attention turned to Evelyn, and she noticed Jane gulp down a mouthful of her drink and frown.

Evelyn wondered how the heavens could think these two were a good match. The only explanation was if opposites attracted. And if that was the case, these two would be inseparable.

"It's Evelyn." Evelyn corrected Kendrick. "I'm Andel's friend."

"Where is that guy anyway? He was supposed to meet me here an hour ago." Kendrick lifted his drink and swallowed the remaining clear liquid. "How about we dance until he shows?"

He wrapped his hands around her waist and the smell of alcohol laced with Kendrick's proximity made Evelyn cringe. She attempted to wriggle out of Kendrick's arms, but he pulled her closer. His cologne rivaled his breath, and Evelyn felt an overwhelming desire to summon her bow and arrow for more protective reasons. Disgust bubbled up in her chest, and she fought using her immortal strength to shove him away.

"You know, I'm not much of a dancer. How about you take Jane?"

Jane's nose scrunched up like she could smell Kendrick too. "No, thanks. I think I'm going to call it a night."

"No, you don't have to do that." Evelyn stepped forward to try and catch Jane. Her heart ached for her friend and the hopelessness that emanated from her.

"Let her go, sweetheart. I'll show you a good time."

Spinning on her heels, Evelyn turned to face Kendrick and placed her pointer finger against his chest. "You let go."

Evelyn darted past Zora and Douglas, who looked as if they'd witnessed a car crash. Zigging and zagging between tables and people, Evelyn lost sight of Jane and figured she must have made her way to the exit. As she walked out the exit doors, Evelyn saw Andel enter the building. The noise from the music and buzzing crowd made it difficult to get his attention, so she resorted to getting his attention telepathically.

Andel?

Where are you? He'd stopped and swiveled to look around the club.

I'm sorry.

For what?

Douglas and Zora can explain, but I've got to go after Jane.

Evelyn broke the mental connection and jogged to the nearest intersection. Jane had already made it across the street and was stepping up to a taxi. Evelyn wouldn't be able to reach her in time to stop her.

When the intersection's lights changed, Evelyn recognized Roscoe walking straight toward her with a smile. He opened his arms wide as he approached, and Evelyn wondered what it would feel like to hug a Gargoyle.

She needed a hug after the nightmare she'd just put Jane through. The idea was to have both couples under the same roof, but all it took was an hour for Evelyn to epically mess things up.

"Evelyn, are you okay?" Roscoe asked as Evelyn let him embrace her on the corner. He was warm, and the joy and love that grew in him for Sydney helped balance Evelyn. "Where are you going? I thought we were supposed to meet in the club?"

"I was headed after Andel's assignment, Jane. I think I just ruined his mission."

"It can't be that bad," Roscoe reassured Evelyn, hugging her a little tighter. "Andel thinks very highly of you, and I don't think you're capable of getting into any amount of trouble he can't get you both out of."

"That's sweet, but you have no idea." Evelyn looked up at Roscoe with watery eyes. She should have let go of him sooner, but Evelyn knew he was unbreakable, and if she stayed in his arms maybe he'd keep her from falling apart.

"Uh...," Roscoe stuttered. His body tensed. "Sydney..."

Understanding what their situation might look like, Evelyn stepped out of Roscoe's arms and wiped her eyes. "I'm sorry. Gosh, this isn't..."

"It's okay. I just got off work, and Roscoe and I planned to meet here." Sydney waved Evelyn's words away. "Roscoe, should we do this another night?"

"No. Oh, no." Evelyn answered for Roscoe, wiping her tear soaked hands against her jeans. "I'll be fine. I'm just going to head back to my apartment. Y'all go have fun!"

The fake encouragement only made things worse and Evelyn let out a sob. Roscoe insisted on walking Evelyn back to her apartment, and Sydney agreed.

"I'll call you a little later, Sydney." Roscoe kissed Sydney on the cheek. "Can I get you a cab before we leave?"

"No, I'm fine. I'll talk to you soon." Sydney winked at Roscoe and waved goodbye to Evelyn. She turned the opposite direction Evelyn and Roscoe were headed in. Evelyn couldn't believe how well Sydney had handled that situation, but she still felt like sherbet.

"I'm on a roll." Evelyn slumped under Roscoe's arm as he guided them down the sidewalk.

"What's that supposed to mean?" he asked.

"It means I'm a joke of a Cupid. I make deals with fairies, ruin my friend—I mean, mentor's mission, and keep my own assignment from making headway with his true love."

"True love. I like the sound of that," Roscoe grinned.

Street lights lining the city streets kept the darkness at bay, and so did the joy overflowing from Roscoe. He had already fallen for Sydney, and Evelyn berated herself for not insisting he stay with Sydney a few minutes earlier. Most girls would have jumped to the worst conclusion when the guy they liked had another girl in their arms. Evelyn had a good feeling Sydney didn't simply like Roscoe. He had a way of making an impression. The kind that lasted.

"You know Andel's your friend," Roscoe took a chance and addressed the most sensitive topic first. "He's risked a lot to make sure you're safe."

"Risk?" Evelyn didn't consider Andel a risk taker, but he'd taken a few chances with her. "You know, I didn't ask him to go with me into the fairy realm."

"No, he went willingly. He also refused to take on any new Cupids until your hunt for the truth was satisfied. He even insisted that the Elders work with the Gargoyles because he knew they'd offer the best defense if anything threatened you. Andel may be a Cupid, but I'd accept him into our ranks in any fight."

"Oh." Evelyn felt a little hope knowing that Andel hadn't been ordered to babysit her. Although, she still hated to be the reason his mission was falling apart.

"You still have a lot to learn about Andel, as well as the other immortal races. The Elders like to make it look two dimensional, good vs evil, Lux and Nox, but you know as well as I do that we live in a three-dimensional world. We exist in the light and the darkness. It kind of makes us *all* gray"—Roscoe smiled—"not just us Gargoyles. What matters is what we choose to fight for."

Chapter 23

Andel stayed at the club long enough to hear Zora's account of the train wreck. Before leaving, he knew he needed to have a brief conversation with Kendrick. Andel's knuckles still throbbed from their contact with Kendrick's jaw. The guy hadn't actually hit on Evelyn, but he'd crossed a line. Andel realized that he'd blurred that line when it came to Evelyn way before he met Kendrick.

Douglas and Zora walked with Andel back to the apartment. The cold air, and the extra time for Evelyn to cool off, allowed Andel to go over everything that had happened between them. In an attempt to explain to the others why Evelyn had run off and why he'd hit one of his charges, Andel started from the beginning. He told Douglas and Zora that he and Evelyn had posed as a couple to convince Jane and Kendrick to go out on a date. It had all been a show, and he needed to play the jealous boyfriend so their cover wouldn't be blown.

The problem was Andel had felt like a jealous boyfriend when he'd popped Kendrick in the eye. Andel knew Evelyn still struggled with letting go of humanity, and that included her ex-boyfriend. She'd made huge strides to focus on her duty as a Cupid. It was Andel who'd most recently succumbed to his emotions. He needed to clear things up between them. If only drawing a line between him and Evelyn was as easy as drawing a line in the sand.

As Andel approached St. Patrick's Cathedral, Andel turned to Douglas and Zora and asked, "Would you two mind giving me a few minutes with Evelyn before you come up?"

With a nod from Douglas, Andel stepped into a shadowed doorway and transcended.

Appearing in the middle of the living room, Andel couldn't *feel* Evelyn. He'd become very attuned to her emotions, and the lack of frustration and energy spilling out of her room sent him into a panic.

"Evelyn?" he called.

Without a response, Andel went to the front door and opened it. She might have decided to walk the whole way back. One thing they had in common was their need for a physical outlet. Evelyn diverted her stress through eating or walking or training. He would have guessed she did the same as a mortal.

Still standing in the frame of the doorway, Andel watched the lights above the elevator light up. Once the double digits lit up, he started pacing, wondering why they didn't have an apartment on the second floor.

With a ding, Evelyn and Roscoe finally stepped out of the lift and came face to face with Andel. He'd stopped pacing and rubbed at his sore knuckles. It only took a frown from Andel, and Roscoe shuffled back into the metal box. The door slid shut, and Andel stood alone with Evelyn.

Her eyelids were puffy and pink. She twisted her lips together like she was trying to keep something from spilling out.

"It'll all work out." Andel opened his arms to her, and she sank into his chest. After a moment, her shoulders started shaking, and she let out a sob. "We can fix this."

Evelyn pulled back. "Are you sure about that?"

Andel squeezed her tighter and answered, "Yes."

"Your assignment just flirted with me in front of your other assignment." Evelyn's words were muffled in Andel's shirt. "Not to mention we were kidnapped by fairies, I've been babysat by fellow Cupids, and some creeper keeps following us. Don't get me wrong, I don't mind the creeper because he seems to be on our side."

"You saw him again tonight?"

"Yep."

"Well, we can deal with him later." Andel placed his hands on Evelyn's shoulders. "You need to understand that what happened tonight might set us back, but it doesn't make anything impossible."

Evelyn smiled up at him. "Thank you."

Maneuvering up to her tiptoes, Evelyn stretched her neck to the side of Andel's face and kissed him on the cheek.

"What's that for?"

"Knowing what to say and not taking thirty minutes to say it in a lecture," Evelyn chuckled, and the sound resonated in Andel's chest. Her laugh sang to him.

Before he could stop himself, Andel reached a hand behind Evelyn's neck and brought her lips to his. He froze for a moment, waiting for his better judgment to take over, but it didn't, and Evelyn kissed him back. Pressing his lips to hers, he focused on her full bottom lip, pulling it between his.

She sighed.

Evelyn's hands glided up Andel's chest and around his neck. Tangling into his curls, she pulled him closer. He lost himself in the moment, and he lost his balance. The two fumbled, and Andel pressed a hand against the wall behind Evelyn. The harmony they produced flooded Andel's senses. He was consumed with the sight of Evelyn's neck lengthening for him to kiss her there, the sound of her heartbeat, the hint of rose in her perfume, the taste of berry on her lips, and the soft curve of her hips.

Nothing else mattered as he brushed his lips along Evelyn's ear.

The rules and assignments had faded away—until the elevator doors slid open with a ding.

Jude stepped into the narrow hallway, eyes narrowed. He folded his arms over his chest. "Andel, a word please," he requested.

Andel steadied Evelyn and straightened his shirt. As he loosened his grip on her, Andel realized he'd just lost control of everything. He'd finally given into his feelings. His promise to pierce mortals with love had been enough until he'd met Evelyn. She'd changed his perspective on a lot of things about their world, but he still had a duty to the mortals he'd been charged with.

"Give me a minute, Jude." Andel needed to explain to Evelyn that they couldn't let anything like that kiss happen again. He was so close to completing his service as a Cupid, and she had him second guessing the plans he'd been making for centuries.

Jude grabbed Andel's arm before he could step into the apartment behind Evelyn. "Actually, this can't wait."

Andel's brows furrowed. "What is it?" he asked.

"We got him."

Evelyn looked back and forth between the two men. "Got who?"

"Evelyn, before I left to meet with the Elders I asked Jude to keep an eye out for the man, or creeper as you like to call him, that's been following you."

"You mean following *us*."

"No, he's definitely been stalking you," Jude pointed out. "He's being held at the cathedral. You can meet Leo and me there, or if you two need to talk about…" A dimpled smirk spread across Jude's face.

Jude's cynicism was aged like a fine wine, and his determination to avoid love rivaled Andel's. They'd spent several conversations justifying each of their choices to remain alone, but Andel had allowed someone in.

"We should poof there together. We can *talk* later." Evelyn winked at Andel as she jumped into the elevator after Jude. Andel wouldn't argue because he wanted to know what this stranger wanted with her. The mystery guy had known about Evelyn's abilities but had also exhibited similar ones.

"Poof?" Jude asked.

"Transcend," Andel corrected. He moved to stand with them and placed a hand on Evelyn and Jude's shoulders. The thought of a shadowy doorway at the cathedral crossed Andel's mind. It would be the perfect place to appear without drawing attention.

"Adieu."

Chapter 24

Evelyn, Andel, and Jude appeared in a dark, secluded archway. The oversized wooden door before them was covered in ironwork with a knob at its center. Evelyn didn't feel the bustling city behind her, so she looked over her shoulder to confirm they were still in New York. They had accessed one of the small gardens on the St. Patrick's Cathedral property. Evelyn wished she had a map of the church with a "You Are Here" star to mark where they stood.

"I'm never going to get used to that." Jude stepped out into the courtyard behind them and took a deep breath.

"Not a fan of poofing, huh?" Evelyn walked into the moonlight.

"Poofing, transcending, whatever you call it. My mojo doesn't mix well with it. Actually, let's not talk about mixing anything."

The door opened at Andel's hand and creaked loudly. "We need a plan."

He was right. They needed to figure out a way to interrogate the immortal and get him to talk. "I want to talk to him." Evelyn pushed past Andel.

"I had a feeling." Andel looked to Jude for support, but the Gargoyle shrugged his shoulders. "If you want information, I think it would be best to send one of the Gargoyles in," Andel countered.

"I agree." Jude lengthened his gait to enter first and lead Evelyn and Andel to the room they had bound the prisoner in.

"Have you learned anything yet?" Evelyn asked.

"He claims his name is Benjamin Callahan, and the church seems to have the same effect on him as the rest of us immortals."

"Are you sure?" Evelyn followed Jude into the church, and she wondered if the sacred ground kept this Benjamin character from using his power like the others. If he could create red arrows, he probably had more in common with her. And she didn't feel the same restrictions Andel had described.

"So far, the guy hasn't tried anything. He said he wants to talk—it was almost like he turned himself in."

Andel's pace picked up. "Good, maybe he'll cooperate."

The three turned into a narrow hallway, and suddenly, the two feet Andel walked behind Evelyn felt more like two inches. Heat rose to her cheeks as she thought about how close they'd been a few minutes ago. How had she gone from feeling ready to take on the world to defeated to passionate in the span of an hour? Could the buzz of the desire she felt in the club have affected her judgment?

Kissing Andel had heightened her emotions, and thinking about their kiss made Evelyn restless. If they'd sat in a cafe instead of walking through this holy place, Andel's Cupid abilities would have allowed him to feel all her pent up emotions. Evelyn thought she picked up on some of Andel's anxiety, but she already knew he was concerned because he couldn't slow down. Evelyn didn't know if his anxiety was a result of what happened with her or the stalking stranger they were about to confront.

"You got quiet. What are you thinking?" Andel asked.

Evelyn wanted to be honest, and trying to communicate with him mentally might be a good way to test her power in the church. If Evelyn's abilities worked in the fairy realm, where Andel's was dulled, maybe her powers would work in the cathedral, too. *Can you hear me?*

"Evelyn?" Andel footsteps stuttered.

Well, I'm still picking up some of your emotions, and since I could do stuff in the fairy realm, I thought I'd try. I know it should be impossible in the cathedral, and last time we were here, I didn't even know to try.

"You're abilities are amazing." Andel was stunned.

He did put out a vibe of amazement, but when Evelyn tried to dig deeper, his emotions felt hard. It was like he'd successfully constructed a brick wall around his heart.

Andel? What's the matter?

"I can't," Andel answered.

Jude stopped ahead of them and faced the Cupids. "Are you two ready for this?"

"Yes," Evelyn answered. "Why?"

"I think what's going on between you two could really mess this up."

"And what do you think is happening?" Andel asked.

Jude answered, "Nothing good."

"You know, you should mind your own danish business!" Evelyn argued. "This other Cupid might give something away that you can't pick up on. If I'm close enough, I can read him."

"Good to know." Jude's eyebrow quirked up. "So, when were you going to tell us you could use your powers in here?"

"Oh, for heaven's sake! I just tried for the first time. I attempted to have a telepathic conversation with Andel—" Evelyn bit her lip to stop from getting into it with either supernatural. "Let's just get to Leo and the creeper-Cupid."

After a few more turns through cold, gray stone passageways, they entered the main sanctuary. Jude led them behind the altars and ornate chairs to a set of stairs hidden behind a curtain. They led down. Evelyn didn't want to know why a church needed a dungeon level or what they might have kept in a place like it.

Once underground, they only had to walk a few feet before encountering Leo. He stood outside a wooden door with ornate carvings lining its edges. "Took you long enough." He rolled his eyes at Jude.

"You don't want to know." Jude passed Leo and patted his shoulder. Banging on the door three times, Jude asked, "Has he been out long?"

"He's not unconscious. He's been cooperating."

Andel stepped between the Gargoyles. "It'll be a trick to get to Evelyn."

"What could he want from me? If he's like me, he won't need my arrows. Maybe he's just curious like I am."

"I don't like it, but we have to find out." Andel opened the door and walked in.

Evelyn followed, and the blond man sat strapped in an ornate chair with red velvet cushions. The stranger didn't struggle or look irritated but grinned at Evelyn when she met his eyes. "Finally."

In one word, this Cupid exuded more feelings than Evelyn had read from every mortal she'd come in contact with since becoming a Cupid. The flood of relief took Evelyn off guard, and she stumbled to the wall for stability. All three men immediately darted toward their prisoner.

"What are you doing to her?" Andel had Benjamin in a headlock before he finished his question.

"How do you expect him to answer? You've blocked his airway with your bicep." Evelyn held up a hand to prove she was okay.

"Summon your bow and arrows, and I'll feel better about releasing him." Andel relaxed his grip, but only after Evelyn held her bow and aimed an arrow at their target.

"I've got him covered." Jude pulled a short blade from behind his back. "You can put your bow down."

Andel slowly pulled away from the Cupid. He felt better knowing two weapons were aimed at the stranger and began his questioning. "What's your name?"

"Benjamin. Ben Callahan." He spoke to Evelyn, not taking his eyes off her, "I heard about you, Evelyn, and had to know if it was true."

"If what was true?" Evelyn asked, but the scowl on Andel's face made her second guess her question.

If you're like me. The stranger's brows lifted in communications with Evelyn.

Stunned, she dropped her bow and arrow to her side.

"Stop," Andel growled. "Or I will make you."

Evelyn couldn't breathe without tasting the tang of Andel's anxiety. "Our ability to use telepathy in this place is one thing we have in common, but if you want this conversation to continue, you'd better start using your vocal chords."

"I became a Cupid in the early 1800s," Ben began, "and went rogue a few years later."

"A rogue Cupid," Andel contemplated with a frown.

"There are a number of us, but I wouldn't call us Cupids. I mean, we are, but we're non-practicing. We want to stay off the Elders' radar."

"Why?" Evelyn asked. Andel might have skipped over the Elders being mentioned out of respect, but Evelyn felt something off at her last meeting with the ancient Cupids.

"I can't speak for everyone I've met, but I can personally attest to their disregard for other immortal races...and me."

"Do you enjoy being vague?" Jude interjected.

"Look, if you'd untie me, I might feel more forthcoming."

Leo looked at Jude, who raised an eyebrow in Andel's direction. Determined to get answers, but not give in to Ben, Evelyn lifted her bow again and aimed an arrow at his face. "Go ahead. Untie him."

She smirked at Ben, daring him to make a move.

Leo and Jude removed the ropes with ease while Andel stayed close to ensure their safety. Evelyn couldn't believe she had an arrow pointed at the only other Cupid like her, but it was the only way to make sure everyone in the small, dank room got what they wanted.

"What do you plan to do next, now that you know about Evelyn?" Andel stepped around Ben to stand at her side.

"I'm not sure. It was a long shot, and I guess I didn't think that far ahead. I've been on the run for a long while."

"Have you ever met another Cupid like you?" Andel asked.

"Once." Ben crossed his legs. "It's why I went into hiding to begin with."

"And…" Leo encouraged.

"And she warned me that the Elders only wanted to use me up like a battery. It had happened to a Cupid before me."

"And you just believed her?" Jude blurted. "What was her name?"

"I can't tell you. I promised." Ben looked down at the tile floor, and remorse filled him. Evelyn could sense a hint of joy being covered by his remorse as well. In response, she tightened her grip on her arrow.

Andel, reacting to Evelyn's strained bow, looked over to Jude and nodded. The two moved to switch places, and as they exchanged responsibilities, Andel took the knife from Jude and stood ready for an attack. Jude placed his hand on his chin, thinking of their next line of questioning. Leo remained still, like a lion waiting to attack. Evelyn wanted a chance to ask her questions but observing Jude and Andel work so seamlessly led her to believe they'd done this before. Hopefully, they'd been successful.

Jude knelt down on one knee in front of Ben, surveying everything from the type of boots he wore to the style of his messy hair. "Maybe you won't tell us the name of your informant, but would you be so kind as to tell us the warning she gave you?"

"Of course. If it means keeping Evelyn out of harm's way, I'll tell you every word."

Jude managed to roll his eyes, giving Evelyn the distinct impression he didn't believe Ben. Having Andel, Jude, and Leo to read gave her more perspective, because while Ben appeared to be worried about her well-being, that didn't rule out any selfish motivations. Evelyn wanted to give Ben some room to explain.

"How about you start from the beginning?" Evelyn interjected.

Ben sat up to face her and threaded his fingers together in his lap. "I died, like you, for someone I loved. She was the only love I'd ever known, but I sacrificed myself for her before we were married. Sound familiar?"

"Somewhat," Evelyn prompted, but couldn't look anyone else in the face. She hated that this stranger knew so much about her without actually knowing her.

"I was deemed worthy to be a Cupid, and I went through training. On my first mission, I was walking through the streets of London when I encountered a couple walking hand-in-hand. They were clearly in love and the energy surrounding them sang to me. It wasn't until after I pierced them with a glowing red arrow that I found out they were a Warlock and Witch. Needless to say, the Elders quickly found out about my ability. They treated me like I was extraordinary. I went fifty years before I knew there were other Cupids like me."

While Ben told his tale, Evelyn let her arms relax and brought her bow to her side. Spending a half-century on assignments...working alone was bad enough. Evelyn didn't look forward to parting ways with Andel. Living out an immortality without companionship and thinking you're the only one of your kind would be horrible. "Why'd it take so long to get answers?"

"Because I didn't ask questions. I blindly followed the Elders, and they kept me secluded. Until you, they'd operated the same way with several Cupids before us."

"So why was Evelyn different?" Andel interrupted, gripping the knife tighter.

"It had something to do with the first assignment they sent her on with you. I'm just guessing, but seeing your markings, the Elders probably thought you'd be preoccupied with meeting your quota and moving on. They knew Evelyn would need assistance, but they didn't plan on you wanting to help her after that initial mission."

Evelyn had been thrown into being a Cupid in an unorthodox way. The Elders needed her help in New Orleans with a warning from another supernatural race. She thought she was chosen because she was the newest Cupid, but it turned out, she was special.

"I don't want to talk about me," Evelyn spoke more to Andel than Ben. "I want to know what you know."

"Diana found me when I was on a mission in Australia," Ben continued. "The encounter lasted all of ten minutes, but it motivated me."

"So, it *was* her," Jude muttered.

"We want to know what she told you, not how it inspired you to become a stalker." Evelyn was tired and emotionally all over the place. Jude's realization cleared up who Andel's source was, but it stung that Jude hadn't just told her himself.

"She advised me to drop my bow and arrows and walk away. Forever." Ben ran his fingers through his hair, making it even messier but not in a bad way. "You should do the same."

Ben let the weight of his suggestion grow heavy in the following silence. The idea of never reacting to the call of love seemed impossible to Evelyn. The euphoric emotion inspired Cupids. They were created and lived, forever, to share the feeling with the world.

"But you didn't," Evelyn remembered. "You shot an arrow in the park when the fairies kidnapped me."

"I did, but that was the first time in over a hundred years I've summoned my bow and arrows." Ben stood, oblivious to the restraint Andel struggled to maintain. "A mistake, but one I'd willingly make again to ensure your safety."

Ben took a step toward Evelyn.

"Move another muscle, and I'll take my lion form." Leo threatened. "Cupid tends to taste too sweet, but I am a little peckish."

"Why me?" Evelyn asked.

"Diana warned me against sharing my arrows with any immortals, especially the Elders. They use our red weapons to protect themselves against Nox, but also as an intimidation tactic against other Lux races, like the Gargoyles. You're a grenade, Evelyn, and the Elders won't hesitate to set you off if they feel it'll protect them."

"I kinda get why I shouldn't hand out my arrows, but I still feel like it should be my decision. I want to know—why did Diana warn you to stop piercing immortals with love altogether?" Evelyn asked.

"The Elders track us. Ask him." Ben looked over at Andel, who continued to grip Jude's knife menacingly. "When we shoot an arrow, they can track the love it dispenses and who it's tied to. Diana's different, now, and not in a Lux way. That's how she's been able to elude them for so long. But the rest of us, even Cupids with the ability to pierce supernaturals, we still have the ability to blend in with humanity. We just have to avoid our calling."

Evelyn's face scrunched up together toward her nose. "I didn't know why I was chosen to do this Cupid-thing for an eternity. And at first, I would have rather wallowed in my own misery, but being able to give this gift is freeing. Even if I currently suck at it." She looked to Andel.

Evelyn used to feel numb after her parents died. And living without love was possible, but it was also lonely, painful. "How do you live without it?" she asked Ben.

"You'd be surprised how easy it is once you find out you only have so much love to share."

Evelyn watched as Ben's hands tightened into fists. He didn't need to survey the room because he'd been waiting. He'd wanted each of them in specific places before he made his move. And Evelyn stood paralyzed for a moment too long.

Chapter 25

It had all happened at a supernatural speed, and Andel came to in a panic. "Evelyn?"

She was lying under him. Inhaling. Exhaling. "I'm okay." Her hands pressed against his chest.

Andel shoved the chair Ben had been sitting in to the side, revealing Jude kneeling over Leo. Jude mumbled, "No, no, no, no, no." His head shook from side to side.

He was dead. Ben had killed Leo. It shouldn't have been possible.

Leo hadn't flinched when Ben pierced him in the chest. Shards of Andel's memory slashed through his mind.

Ben reached for Jude.

Evelyn drew her arrow into its bow.

The shot.

It had been lightning fast, but Ben caught the golden arrow. He'd anticipated it.

Ben darkened physically and emotionally. His black pupils spread out over the blue and whites of his eyes, and loathing crept up from whatever he had left of a heart.

Leo stepped between Ben and his friends as the weapon turned inky black in Ben's hand. With an immortal throw, the arrow stabbed Leo. Ben attempted to grab Evelyn, but when she fought back, he knocked her unconscious to distract Jude and Andel. Andel wasn't going to let Ben take Evelyn anywhere.

"Andel, are you okay?" Evelyn wriggled beneath him.

He shifted to the tile floor beside her, blocking her view. "Evelyn, let me take you back to the apartment."

"No. I want to check on everyone." Evelyn pushed up to see past Andel's broad shoulders.

Andel placed a hand on Evelyn's arm. "Please."

"Leo? Jude?" Evelyn's eyes stung with tears. She shoved Andel's hand away and scooted around him to crawl to Leo's side. Crouched next to Jude, she whispered, "Oh, God."

Evelyn pressed her palms to her eyes and wiped away her tears. Leo's body lay placid without a mark or any indication of how he'd died. The arrow had disappeared the same way it did when Cupids pierced mortals with love.

Jude looked from Andel to Evelyn and growled, "Get out."

"Evelyn," Andel walked up to her from behind.

"No!" Evelyn argued.

Jude turned his back to Evelyn but didn't dare leave Leo's side.

"Please, let me help," Evelyn pleaded.

Andel didn't need telepathy to know exactly what Jude was thinking. The weight of his guilt pulled his mouth into a frown. "This is all my fault."

"Let me take you back." Andel reached to pull her up with him and get her out of the way of Jude's anger. "I'll get you to the apartment and come back here to help Jude."

"Don't," Jude spat at Andel. "If you want to do anything, get Roscoe. That's all I need from you. Either of you."

Neither Andel or Evelyn could bring themselves to respond, and as they walked out of the cathedral in silence, Andel felt a flood of remorse. Once in the courtyard, Andel didn't bother with their code word and transcended himself and Evelyn to their apartment. Evelyn wrapped her arms around Andel, seeking more security than the safety of their living room could provide, but Andel had a job to do. He began to peel Evelyn's arms off him, and she let out a sob. "Please."

"I have to find Roscoe," Andel took a stoic tone.

Evelyn tried to suck in all her emotion and focus on Andel. "Take me with you."

"No."

"I can help."

"No."

"I should be the one to tell Roscoe." Andel didn't want to break the news to Roscoe, but Evelyn was too distraught. Andel had been friends with the Gargoyle long enough to know he'd take Leo's death as a personal attack.

"Ben could try and come back." Evelyn was playing the victim card, but Andel knew better. Keeping Evelyn safe was still a priority, only there wasn't a place safe enough as long as Ben was out there. She would have to come along.

Andel folded his arms over his chest. "Since the sun hasn't risen, he'll be patrolling."

"As in flying over the city?"

"Maybe." Andel searched her for any reservations, but Evelyn didn't balk. "Lucky for us, I know his patterns and we can probably catch him at the Empire State Building."

"Okay, let's go."

Andel took Evelyn's hand, and his pinky grazed her wrist. Recognizing her pulse, Andel couldn't help but feel relieved she still had one. His feelings for her were beginning to cloud his judgment, and the affection he felt for her might have even been a factor leading to Leo's death. Andel wouldn't let his guilt take over. Instead, he'd direct it into a new mission: hunting Ben down.

In a blink, Andel and Evelyn stood in each other's arms on the observation deck at the Empire State Building. Rod iron obstructed some of their view of the city, but it didn't keep a gust of wind from sweeping Evelyn's hair up off her neck. She tightened her grip on Andel instinctively, and he savored the feeling of her arms draped over his shoulders. The longer Andel held on to Evelyn, the more it would hurt when he'd have to let go. Loosening his grip, Evelyn slipped away from Andel and they searched the night sky for Roscoe.

"Do you think you could try and call on him mentally?" Andel asked.

Of course. Evelyn answered, opening her mind to Andel and Roscoe. *Roscoe, it's an emergency. We need to talk. You can find me and Andel on top of the Empire—*

Roscoe's stone dragon-form circled overhead before she could finish. It was incredible how his solid, long body rolled through the air with grace and speed. Approaching the deck, he shifted into a sweater-vest wearing human and touched down on the tower.

"What is it? Is Sydney alright?" Roscoe's eyes widened.

"Yes," Andel answered.

"Then, what's the emergency?" He relaxed and slipped his hands into his pockets. "It's not the fairies again, is it?"

Evelyn shifted from one foot to the other. "Ben escaped," she began. "He got hold of one of my arrows and used it against us. Leo, well, he was trying to protect us, and we didn't know what Ben was capable of."

Roscoe lifted one hand to his forehead. "Capable of what?" he asked as he rubbed along his hairline like he could understand if he rubbed hard enough.

"Leo is dead." Andel walked up to stand beside Roscoe and placed a hand on his shoulder. "I'm not sure how to explain because it should be impossible. But the prisoner got a hold of one of Evelyn's arrows and changed it. He turned it black. I vow to search with you until we find Ben. You will have justice."

"What are you talking about?" Roscoe's looked back and forth from Andel to Evelyn. "He's probably just recuperating in his lion form."

"No, Roscoe, something happened. Something I've never seen before," Andel tried to explain, placing a hand on Roscoe's shoulder.

"No." Roscoe stepped out of Andel's reach.

"I'm sorry," Evelyn said.

Roscoe's knees buckled, and Evelyn moved to his side. She bent over him and wrapped her arms around him. Andel watched as Roscoe's shoulders shook in heart-wrenching pain. One of his closest friends was gone. Andel watched as Evelyn pulled Roscoe up to his feet.

Roscoe straightened his vest. "A black arrow? How?"

The two Cupids didn't know. Evelyn had only begun her search for answers, and during his two hundred years, Andel had never heard of an arrow turning black. They'd only heard of an arrow turning red a few months ago.

Andel just knew he needed to get Roscoe to Jude. Jude had existed as a Gargoyle, an immortal, longer than anyone Andel had ever met. If anyone had heard of an arrow being deadly to immortals, it would be Jude.

"We need to get you to the church."

"No, not the cathedral, the library. That's where Jude would have taken Leo."

With one hand on Roscoe's shoulder and the other stretched out to hold Evelyn's hand, Andel transcended them to the front steps of the New York Public Library. Jude stood with a fist held to his chest in front of the lion statue lying to the right of the entrance. His solemn demeanor made Andel and Evelyn feel like they were intruding. So, they waited as Roscoe marched to Jude's side and saluted to his lost friend with the same fist clutched to his chest.

"He moved on with honor." Jude's chin fell to his chest.

Andel could only guess what happened to Leo's human form. He must have supernaturally transformed into his lion when Jude brought him to the statue. To think he'd never shift back into human his human form made Andel wonder where he existed. If he'd been hit by the arrow, where would he be?

Roscoe looked to Jude and proclaimed, "He will be avenged."

"I wish to be given the mission," Andel spoke from Evelyn's side and walked over to join the other men. "I will devote myself to you. You are like brothers to me. There's no reason for this attack to tear our supernatural races apart."

"There isn't?" Jude scowled at Andel.

Roscoe placed himself between the two. "Calm down, Jude. Andel's heart is in the right place, he has proven himself to be one of us."

"I wouldn't be so sure." Jude glanced between Andel and Evelyn.

Evelyn swallowed back her tears for Leo and crossed her arms over her chest. "This is because of me," she spoke to Jude. "And if you want to take it out on anyone, it should be me."

Andel worried that Evelyn's words could be twisted to prove Jude's point, but he waited to see if Roscoe had an opinion.

"Ugh, why do guys have to be so stubborn?" Evelyn called them out. "You, too, Leo!" she yelled up into the sky.

Andel's eyebrow rose, and Jude smirked.

Looking back to the men lined up, ready for battle, Evelyn admitted, "I know, I'm just as bad. But we should be remembering Leo right now."

"She's right," Roscoe agreed.

"Agreed," Andel announced.

After a few seconds of silence, Jude relented, "Agreed."

"So, what's next?" Evelyn asked.

"That will be up to each of you." Roscoe positioned himself next to Leo's lion statue. "Whether you choose to fight with us or not, this could lead to a war. It won't simply be Lux against Nox. Fear will determine the side most immortals take."

"Does that mean you'll be giving up Sydney?"

With a wide smile, Roscoe thought carefully before answering. "I don't think Leo would've wanted that."

"Me neither, but what if I hurt one of you?" Evelyn's doubt in herself felt like a gut punch.

Andel shifted uncomfortably. Love sang to him, and Evelyn's lack of hope sounded like a harmony being sung in the wrong key. Because her arrow had been turned and used to kill, she would struggle to trust herself and other Cupids from this day forward, and so would he.

Andel wondered if he could trust the Elders or their assignments. He hoped Douglas and Zora had witnessed enough to know the truth had become convoluted. Evelyn would need their help.

Andel would avenge Leo, for himself and the Gargoyles. Finding Ben would give Andel purpose without the messy emotions Evelyn stirred in him, but ultimately it would benefit her. He'd taught Evelyn everything he knew, and if he chose to follow her, he didn't know if he could keep their friendship platonic.

Andel took Evelyn's hands in his. "While you figure out how to pierce Roscoe and Sydney, I'll begin the hunt for Ben." He took a step back, releasing her. "Good luck." He transcended so quickly, he didn't see Evelyn wince.

Chapter 26

Evelyn walked back to the apartment from the library. She marched through the city, needing her heavy footsteps on the pavement to ground her. When she stepped through the front door, all traces of Andel had been removed. She peeked into the bedroom where he'd never slept because Cupids didn't typically take naps. The perfectly-made bed hadn't given his departure away. It was the closet—door hanging open and empty. Andel had removed all his clothes and gear: bows, arrows, and ancient leather archery stuff.

Evelyn parked on the couch in the living room and watched as the sun rose over the city's skyline. For the first time in a long time, the idea of soothing herself with sugar turned her stomach. Why would Andel just up and leave like that? Maybe he was upset about what happened to Leo, but they all were. Could he blame her? Did he think Jane and Kendrick's relationship didn't deserve saving?

Evelyn couldn't leave things the way they'd ended the night before.

A quick shower and glance in the mirror brought her back to reality. She may have been immortal, but she didn't look any different. The tragedy of Leo's death had taken its toll, and the circles under her eyes didn't lie. Evelyn's humanity is what made her different from the other Cupids she'd encountered. She wouldn't let her supernatural abilities define her. She wanted her actions to reflect who she was, and living in resentment and wallowing in her loss had been numbing.

Evelyn wanted to deal a crisp deck of cards, and if anyone needed a fresh start more than Evelyn, it was Jane. Evelyn determined to take Jane on. Not as an assignment, but as a friend.

Evelyn dressed in a pair of wide-legged navy dress pants and a white blouse with navy polka dots. Since Jane's ego had been bruised, Evelyn was betting she'd be kept busy, so as not to bring up the previous night's unfortunate events. So, she wore a pair of red flats just in case Jane sent her on back-to-back errands.

She poofed in an alleyway near the museum and walked through the employee's entrance. Evelyn hoped to get a read from the receptionist before heading up in the elevator. "Good morning, Gloria."

"Morning, Evelyn. Have you heard from Ms. Platt?" she asked.

"No." Evelyn twisted her lips. "She's not already here? I thought I was running a little late."

"You are, and you better be glad Ms. Platt isn't here to witness it, or you'd be on basement duty the rest of today."

"True. I guess I'll just go up to her office and wait for her."

"Sounds good."

Evelyn walked over to the elevator and pressed the little arrow pointing up. "If you hear from her, will you let me know?"

Ding.

"Sure will. I'll page the phone in Ms. Platt's office to let you know when she arrives."

Evelyn rode the elevator to the administrative floor and made her way to Jane's office. The lights were out, not that they were really needed. The wall of a window let in enough light for Evelyn to confirm that Jane hadn't yet arrived. The late morning start didn't sit right with Evelyn. Jane had been angry the night before, and maybe she needed time to get a handle on her feelings.

Evelyn sat in Jane's office for thirty minutes, and she'd only ever sat still that long for Netflix and dessert. To feel somewhat useful, she decided to head to the delivery dock. Kendrick wouldn't have Andel down there to guide him, so Evelyn would have to step in and get him back on track, too. But she drew the line at glamouring herself as Andel. It made her feel all kinds of icky to imagine herself as him, even though she knew she could pull off a perfect impersonation.

It hadn't occurred to Evelyn that the Elders could be wrong about matching Jane and Kendrick. That is until Ben exposed the Cupid leaders as misleading. She'd felt the connection between Jane and Kendrick at their first dinner. Their harmony had lulled Evelyn into thinking the unlikely was still attainable.

Passing through the gallery, Evelyn stopped to admire the swirling Van Gogh paintings and soft, winsome Monet's. She let herself sit on the bench facing Starry Night, and magic from the painting poured over her. The power used by Muses to elicit the art hanging before her was strong.

Evelyn didn't fully understand how a Muse inspired magic into art, but she knew her own power to wield her bow and arrow gave her a similar peace. Working toward accomplishing her mission and piercing pure hearts with love soothed and strengthened her.

Should I help the Cupids or the Gargoyles? Evelyn thought. The canvas didn't answer, and honestly, Evelyn hadn't expected it to. She did wonder if the magic could help guide her.

How about working with the fairies? Kalan's thought pushed into Evelyn's mind. Evelyn twisted in her seat to see the fairy step into the room. *Evelyn, you need to start thinking like an immortal. If you did, there would be no end to what you could accomplish when partnered with us.*

"That's what scares me."

"Fear will hold you captive and keep you from greatness." Kalan sat down beside her. The glamour Kalan wore didn't alter her fairy features too much. In the fairy realm, Kalan's ears were pointed. Kalan had always let her dark, velvety skin and braided hair add depth and mystery to her beauty. Evelyn could see past the glamour, though. She appreciated Kalan for not trying to hide too much of herself.

"If you're referring to the same *greatness* that consumed and turned Ben and Diana into whatever they are, I'm fine with staying normal."

"I'm not a fool. I just saw you in here, connecting with the creative magic inside you. You can have whatever you want, even that Cupid, Andel." Kalan's observation made Evelyn fidget in her seat. "That is, if you wanted him badly enough. You have the ability to do more than piddle with matchmaking."

"I don't know what you're talking about, and I'm not sure I want to know anymore from you."

"Whether I tell you or not, you'll figure it out eventually. Your power can't be contained or restricted. It will find a way to reveal itself."

Evelyn stood and walked away, not looking back. She left Kalan, not sure what to make of the fairy's very intrusive observations. Having been warned about the fairies, Evelyn knew they were capable of twisting their words to get what they wanted, but at no point had they lied to her. Evelyn couldn't let herself trust them, but she wouldn't discount the fairies, either.

Once at the delivery docks, Evelyn was even more determined she would convince Kendrick to apologize to Jane. And she'd do it without her Cupid powers. She'd use good old-fashioned, mortal manipulation.

After asking a few of the employees if they'd seen Kendrick, one of the drivers informed Evelyn that Kendrick hadn't shown up for work. His absence made more sense than Jane's because he had probably lain on his bathroom floor and passed out.

Evelyn grinned all the way back to Jane's office thinking about the hangover he must be suffering from, and it served him right after the mess he'd made of things. But hadn't the whole thing been her fault? She was the one who interfered in Andel's assignment.

Evelyn decided against using her supernatural abilities with the mortal couple. In fact, she wasn't even sure Roscoe and Sydney needed her help. She wouldn't sway emotions. There would be no poofing from place to place. No glamouring herself. No aiming her bow and arrow until she knew without a doubt that the couple was ready. She wanted to know if love would be enough, at least for Jane and Kendrick. But Roscoe and Sydney would be different.

There was more at stake.

By sealing the Gargoyle's agreement with an arrow, Evelyn would be siding with the Elders in a way. She couldn't ignore the feeling she had when she was with Roscoe and Sydney, and she wanted to do everything she could for them. If she shot her arrow, it could be misunderstood as choosing a side. She just wasn't sure where she belonged. The battle lines between light and darkness were blurred, and she wasn't sure where everyone stood.

Chapter 27

Three weeks later, the air had turned from cold to crisp.

Three weeks and no word from Andel.

Three weeks with Zora and Douglas.

Spring tried to push through the wintery gloom with its sunlight each day, but gusts of icy wind bombarded the city every night. Work at MoMa was as bearable for Evelyn as the weather, and Douglas and Zora staying with her at the apartment had become less like an episode of "I Love Lucy" and more like "Three's Company." The two Cupids tasked with protecting Evelyn had made themselves at home. Evelyn wasn't sure where Douglas went every night, but like a gentleman, he excused himself at ten o'clock and didn't return until six in the morning.

Once, Zora had mentioned him going on patrol, and Evelyn wondered if Douglas worked with the Gargoyles until he returned each morning at eight. She also suspected he could be reporting back to the Elders. Zora made sure Evelyn didn't go hungry, and they'd entered a level of friendship when they shared a chocolate chip pecan pie one night while watching reality television.

The bodies in the apartment kept Evelyn from going crazy the first week. She didn't really interact with Zora or Douglas, but they'd grounded her just by being in the next room. After not using her abilities for several days, Evelyn had become more irritable than normal. No amount of chocolate cake could bring her mojo back. Each day, she wanted less comfort food and conversation, and more solitude. Zora took on a nurturing role, and Evelyn acknowledged her efforts with tight smiles and nods of thanks.

At work, the art surrounding her became the highlight of her existence. As the second week dragged by, Evelyn felt like a cold, mute zombie. She could barely hear the paintings and sculptures singing to her. Evelyn hadn't used her powers, and she avoided going anywhere she'd feel the tune of love calling. Her emotional tank was empty.

Jane and Kendrick had hardly needed her. They both came into the office after lunch the day after the club-catastrophe. Jane explained that Kendrick had gone after her after Andel punched some sense into him. The reason they hadn't come to work the next day was because they had fallen asleep after talking all night in Jane's living room.

At first, Jane hadn't confided in Evelyn why Kendrick had acted so irrationally the night everything turned upside down for them all. But, a few days later, Kendrick showed up to the museum in a black suit to pick up Jane. His uncle had passed away. It had explained so much since his uncle had been the one to encourage him to pursue more than the family business. Kendrick wore his black and blue eye proudly at the delivery docks. And Jane talked incessantly about their nightly dinners, walks, and late night conversations.

Each day Evelyn grew more reclusive, making excuses to leave work early or stay in when the others went out to patrol. Roscoe quit pressuring her to pierce him and Sydney with one of her red arrows, but he still visited to bring her updates about the Gargoyle's search for Ben.

It only took fifteen powerless days to drive Evelyn to barricade herself in her room permanently. Evelyn felt useless. No one had needed her Cupid abilities. She felt like no one needed her. The problem was she hadn't counted on needing to use her power for herself.

"Evelyn, are you awake?" Zora poked her head into Evelyn's room, letting in enough light to jar Evelyn out of a sleepy stupor.

"Ugh."

"I'll take that as a yes." Zora pushed the door completely open, revealing Jude close behind.

"Go away," Evelyn grumbled.

"We aren't going anywhere, you are." Jude stepped around Zora and into the room. "I think I can handle her from here."

"If you say so." Zora turned and left. "I'll be in my room if you need any help," she offered over her shoulder.

"When was the last time you had sugar?" Jude stepped up to Evelyn's bed and lifted the comforter off her body. "You need a shower or a really good glamour, and chocolate."

"I don't give a strawberry danish what you think I need." Evelyn yanked her blanket away from Jude and over her head.

Jude sat down on the bed at Evelyn's side and sighed. Evelyn peeked out from the top of her blanket and watched Jude give her room a once over. He mulled over something, rubbing at his jawline.

"Why are you still here?" Evelyn asked.

"At least hear me out." He nudged her. "I have a message for you, but before I give it to you—"

"Did you find Ben?" Evelyn didn't really care about Ben but hoped finding him would lead to Andel's return.

"No, and the only reason we're back is because Douglas couldn't stand seeing you this way. Neither can I. I need to tell you the truth about Diana. Seeing you like this has me wondering if I should have just told you everything the day I met you."

"Andel told me." Evelyn wiggled over to sit up and make a little more room for Jude.

He shifted, kicking his legs up onto the bed beside her. "He didn't tell you everything. He doesn't even know everything."

Evelyn tilted her head but didn't interrupt.

"A long time ago, when I—or the Obelisk—still stood with its twin in Egypt, I met Diana for the first time. She was magnificent." Jude shook his head. "If only I knew then… The only immortals I've ever met who rivaled her beauty were the Muses, and I've only seen two in my existence."

"Was she like me, then? I mean, not in beauty, but did she have the same powers I do?"

"Yes, a lot like you, even in beauty." Jude reached over and placed a hand over Evelyn's. "I fell in love with Diana. I'd spend half my time as a stone tower and the other half in her arms. I believed she truly loved me, but I found out later she was only capable of loving one thing. Herself."

"Did you know her when she changed? You know, from good to bad? Or Lux to Nox, or whatever?"

"I'm the reason she changed, Evelyn. It's my fault."

"How?"

"Diana explained once that she'd dedicated her mortal life to loving her forest and all the creatures who lived in it. When she died, her Cupid powers overwhelmed her. In her loneliness, she created the fairies to be her companions, but eventually, she became bored with them. That should have been a red flag, but she had me enamored. As I was the oldest Gargoyle, and a creation of the Muses, Diana hoped to develop a relationship that would get her an introduction."

"So she used you to get to the Muses. How's that your fault?"

"Stay with me," Jude encouraged. "I arranged a meeting with the Muse who inspired my artist, and I stood at Diana's side while Clio listened to her proposal. It was the first time I'd ever heard Diana discuss working together with the Muse to create a supernatural army—all to take over the mortal realm."

"Are you kidding me? She had plans to take over the world? That's a little cliché, don't you think?"

"It's still her plan. Before I was in the picture, Diana had a brother, Apollo, who adored her. Together, they had used their power to create half of the supernatural world. The same way Diana had created the fairies, Apollo had created the Muses. And the same way Diana grew bored, Apollo searched for something more. He found love with a mortal and asked Diana to pierce them. But she wouldn't because she was angry with the mortal for stealing her brother's attention and affection. Immortality means there's no time limit. And Diana has held a grudge against her brother and mortals ever since. She'd used me to get to the Muses and wanted to use them against their creator."

"I guess it makes sense, but it's hard to believe someone can stay that angry for so long." Evelyn waved her hand in a circular motion.

"Clio tried to explain to Diana their purpose as Muses and hers as a Cupid. Supernaturals are meant to help bring balance to the mortal world, but Diana was done helping mortals. Diana lost her temper and stormed out of Clio's presence, and before I could follow Diana out, Clio cautioned me against a relationship with the Cupid. Red flag *numero dos*.

"Evelyn, immortals aren't meant for love, at least not the way you think. Diana tried to love an immortal before me. She told me she used one of her own red arrows to pierce them, but something went wrong." Jude wiggled three fingers in front of her. "Third red flag."

Evelyn whipped the covers off and got to her feet. Pacing in front of the bed, she fidgeted with the bottom hem of her T-shirt. "I'm still not getting how Diana turning Nox is your fault."

"If I tell you the rest of the story, I need you to promise it won't ever come up again. It's not something I'm proud of, and at the time, I had no idea it would wreak so much havoc."

Evelyn nodded her agreement.

"After that meeting with Clio, Diana convinced me that she'd given up on her scheme and wanted to live out her eternity with me. I knew she still harbored feelings for the man she'd loved before me, but I thought if we were together those feelings would eventually go away. So, we took our relationship to the next level, regardless of the warning from Clio and numerous red flags. That night, Diana's heart was divided. I'd given myself completely to her, but during the months that followed, Diana withdrew more and more. She changed. The darkness in her didn't reveal itself overnight, but it grew. She broke my heart, Evelyn. And if you're not careful, you'll break Andel's heart."

"But I'm not the same as Diana."

"Aren't you?"

Evelyn's head fell and her hands hung at her side in defeat. "I'm going to take a shower."

"Evelyn."

"You can give me your message when I'm done."

"Alright, but I was actually going to tell you that I do see differences in you. It's just that your story parallels so closely to Diana's that I can't risk my friends getting hurt. Andel and you. I do count you a friend, Evelyn."

"Thanks, Jude."

Evelyn stepped into a scalding hot shower, hoping to burn some of the crusty weight of guilt and sadness she'd been clinging to for weeks. She did have a similar story to Diana, but there were distinct discrepancies. Evelyn hoped it wasn't in her to be as power hungry or selfish as Diana. And Andel didn't love her, not the way Jude had loved Diana. Knowing Diana's story, Evelyn could avoid taking the same path.

After getting dressed, Evelyn stepped back into her bedroom where Jude waited. He looked rough. Evelyn hadn't noticed before, but he had dark circles etched beneath his eyes, and his normally, styled dark hair was grown out and frizzy. They might be immortal, but worry and revenge still took their toll.

"So what's your message?"

Jude looked up at her, his drawn-in eyebrows giving away his anxiety. "Andel wants to meet with you at the cathedral."

"Okay." Evelyn folded her arms over her chest. "I wasn't expecting that. I thought you meant you had a message from Roscoe. I've been avoiding him lately. It's just that—"

"Stop yammering and let me explain. Andel and I have been friends for a long time. He knows everything I just told you, and he's been putting the puzzle pieces together for a while."

"I get it, but I still see major gaps in your theory. Andel isn't like you. He was a mortal and loved someone before; he had a family."

"Have you ever asked him why he was deemed worthy to be a Cupid?"

"We've talked about it. He saved his family from a fire."

"Exactly. His family. Andel loved his wife, but the Cupid who pierced him with an arrow hadn't had the guidance of the Elders. They weren't ready for the kind of love they'd been imbued with. There are so many kinds of love, and from what I've experienced, we only get one chance at the kind of love Cupids bless."

Evelyn had known that kind of love. She'd had to remove her half of the arrow that pierced her and Tate. Andel had helped her through the painful experience of moving on, and she'd thought she was doing a good job of focusing on this new immortal life. In fact, she hadn't thought of Tate in weeks.

"So I'm supposed to go meet Andel and unfriend him? Is that why you're telling me all of this? Because this isn't Facebook…" Evelyn said through gritted teeth.

Jude stood and lifted his hands in surrender. "Don't be angry, I'm trying to help you both and keep our realms from going into a civil war. If you change and can no longer create red arrows but create black ones, you will be considered a threat. And some will jump to the conclusion that all Cupids are a threat."

Shaking her hands out at her side and rolling her shoulders, Evelyn relaxed. "And because the Gargoyles are aligned with the Cupids, you'll be considered a threat. I can't promise anything, but I'll go and hear Andel out."

"That's all I ask."

Evelyn didn't wait for Jude to excuse her or take him with her. She poofed to the small courtyard outside the cathedral, hoping to get a few minutes with Andel alone. When he wasn't waiting in the garden, Evelyn worried he would be waiting inside the church where Leo had died. It was difficult enough to stand in the small garden knowing Andel would be saying goodbye. Taking a deep breath, Evelyn looked up at the stars and saw movement out of the corner of her eye.

Chapter 28

"Thank you for coming," Andel welcomed Evelyn after he transcended to the middle of the courtyard. She looked tired, and that's how he felt. He'd been searching for Ben for the last three weeks, and none of the leads they'd been given resulted in capturing the rogue Cupid. He wondered if Ben was a Cupid anymore.

Evelyn took a few steps toward him and stopped an arm's length away. "What did you want to tell me?"

She folded her arms over her chest, like she was trying to block the overflow of Andel's dread. The emotion was like foamy suds spilling from an unattended bubble bath, but underneath warm affection was brimming.

"Douglas wrote, and he might have alluded to some problems." Andel knew Evelyn hadn't come out of her room for three days, and he also knew seclusions were more dangerous than being on a battlefield for someone like her. She thrived on interaction.

"Problems, huh?" Evelyn asked.

"Well, he might have mentioned that you weren't eating or helping Roscoe or getting out of bed."

"How are those *your* problems? I'm actually wondering how they're problems at all. Aren't you the one who told me Cupids don't have to eat? Maybe I'm simply accepting my role as a Cupid. And, if I'm in bed, I can't cause any more problems or mess up any more relationships."

"Evelyn. You need to flex your supernatural muscles, even if it's just training."

"No one needs my help, not even you. And if you feel the same way Jude does, maybe I should poof to some deserted island and live out a miserable eternity alone."

"You could still help Roscoe if you wanted. He's your friend. And I never said I feel the same way Jude does. I don't think you'd have this power if you weren't supposed to help immortals."

"But Sydney's not an immortal," Evelyn argued. "If I were to take Jude's advice, I'd hang up my heart and Cupid abilities—But wait, that's what Diana's doing!"

Andel closed the distance between them and placed a hand on each of Evelyn's shoulders. "Stop this."

"Stop what? Ever since becoming a Cupid, I've been strung along." Evelyn attempted to brush Andel's hands off her. "I'm not supposed to turn out like Diana, but you all want me to do exactly what she's doing."

"We have a duty, Evelyn. I'm not asking you to ignore yours."

She stepped away from him and began pacing. "I've heard this one. Isn't it the lecture titled *Cupidity, Part 2*?" Evelyn shook two fingers in the air. "If I remember correctly, it comes after learning why I was chosen to be a Cupid and before the lesson explaining how I have to give up everything to become a Cupid."

"Your sarcasm isn't helping."

"Your flaking out on me isn't helping, either."

"I didn't flake out on you. I'm trying to keep us all from breaking apart." Andel noticed a tear in the corner of Evelyn's eye.

"By letting me go?"

Andel shook his head and rubbed at the tension building along the back of his neck. "I think you need to reconsider helping Roscoe and Sydney."

"I don't *need* to do anything."

"Evelyn, you're struggling to get out of bed. You ignored the cakes and pies I had Zora stock the kitchen with, and if you're not careful, the Elders will remove you from this realm. I never thought you'd take it this far."

"The Elders can't take me back to the heavens if they can't find me" she threatened.

"You seriously cannot be planning to go on the run. You just said you don't want to do what Diana's done."

"It seems to be working for you."

Andel squeezed his fists at his side. "I'm not running, Evelyn!"

"You are. You're running away from your mission and me—"

"That's not why I left. Did you ever stop to think who Ben might go after next? What if his plan had been to pierce you with his black arrow?" Andel looked up at the cathedral spire towering over them. "I can leave here tonight on good terms with you. When you think about it, our relationship would have been over before it began anyway. I have four more couples to strike, and I'll be moving on."

"So why don't you pierce Jane and Kendrick? Then, you'll be that much closer to moving on and never having to see me again."

"Finding Ben isn't merely about protecting you. I have to make sure the Gargoyles remain our allies. It's the best way to end…this." Andel's hands dropped open in front of him. Andel was a company man, but something other than serving as a Cupid drove him now. He'd given up on what Cupids were supposed to be fighting for or at least the chance of it. Love. Instead, he'd given into fear.

"You don't *have* to do anything, Andel," Evelyn argued. "When did being a Cupid stop being about following your heart?"

"You tell me." Andel's verbal gut punch hurt, but it also sparked emotions in her that Andel hadn't felt until just then.

Evelyn had turned her heart off the same way she had when she'd lost Tate. By not helping Roscoe, she'd been doing what Ben wanted. Even Jude had influenced her decisions with his past choices. She'd been as wrong as Andel. He'd realized he didn't want to be a deciding factor in any decision she made. Evelyn had to choose her own path.

Evelyn needed to dig deep and follow her heart.

She took a step closer to Andel and struggled to find the right words. She'd always blurted out her thoughts. So he waited silently. She took another step closer, and Andel held his ground. He broke eye contact and looked down to the ground. Maybe she'd be able to say what was on her mind if she didn't have to face him. One more step and he could feel her breath brush across his neck.

Andel's eyes closed, and his jaw tightened. "Don't, Evelyn."

If she tried to kiss him, Andel knew he wouldn't be able to stop himself from kissing her back. She reached up and placed a hand on his chest. His muscles tensed under her fingers.

"Why?" She gathered up some of the fabric from his shirt in frustration.

"Just try to see it from my perspective," he begged. "The Gargoyles needs me right now."

"The Gargoyles or Jude?" Evelyn let go of Andel and created some space between them.

"Jude sees love as a weapon that Diana wielded against him," Andel explained. "He just lost Leo, and his closest friend, Roscoe, has a chance at love. If you pierce Sydney and Roscoe, it'll solidify their relationship and cement the Gargoyle-Cupid ties. I need to keep Jude on the sidelines, focused on finding Ben. This is the best way I know to help you, help all of us. It won't be long before I'm in the heavens for good—"

"What if I shoot Roscoe and things get worse? You have to admit, I'm good at screwing things up."

"Can it get much worse?" Andel smiled, bringing a much-needed lightness to the conversation. "Even though you're hesitant, you should spend some time with them and then decide. Hiding out in your room isn't going to solve anything."

"And you think you're solving the world's problems?"

"I'll be doing my part. Love isn't all passion and desire, Evelyn. Love is humble and hopeful."

Evelyn felt a hot tear roll down her cheek. "Okay, fine. I'll give Roscoe and Sydney a chance."

"You promise?"

He'd expected the call of Evelyn's heart to lead her to pierce Roscoe and Sydney, but without hesitation, she wrapped her arms around Andel's shoulders and pulled him close. The move surprised Andel. She pushed up on her toes and lifted her chin, pressing her lips to his. He was right, he'd never be able to put a stop to this. He welcomed her kiss with his own and ran his hands across her lower back. His fingers grazed the skin exposed between her shirt and jeans.

In an exhale, Evelyn said, "I like it when you follow your heart."

Andel stepped back from Evelyn. "You may not always feel that way." His eyes looked to the sky and his chest rose and fell with a deep breath.

"Are you going to deny what's happening between us?"

"Nothing is happening from here on out, and you know why it can't. If I choose you, the way Jude chose Diana, it could lead to you being ruined. It will be better if I finish my covenant and move on." Andel couldn't look Evelyn in the eye. "You need to be careful."

Evelyn walked away from him, unwilling to concede.

"I'll request for Douglas and Zora to remain at your side if you want."

"Please, don't go out of your way to do me any favors." Evelyn waved him off. He had to push his feelings aside for what he thought was the greater good.

Evelyn didn't wait for Andel say goodbye. She poofed out of his sight, but he'd expected that. He had asked Roscoe and Jude to patrol the sky. Evelyn may not be happy, but Andel could rest easy knowing she was safe.

Chapter 29

Evelyn appeared in front of the lion statue she knew as Leo. She wasn't sure if the person she knew as Leo was caged in the stone or if his soul had moved on. Alone, standing outside the New York Public Library, the night was cold. If a mortal had seen her there wearing a T-shirt and jeans, they'd wonder why she hadn't frozen solid.

"I wish you were still here," Evelyn talked to Leo. "I could really use some comedic relief right now. You know, like inappropriate flirting or teasing about how awful I look." She shoved her hands into her pockets and kicked at a small piece of paper wadded up on the ground in front of her.

"You don't look that awful." Roscoe touched down, transforming from his dragon into his bowtie-wearing human self.

Evelyn waved away the weak attempt to make her feel better. "Aw, you're just saying that."

"You know everything's going to work out, right?"

Evelyn frowned at Roscoe, not really sure it would all work out at all. "You know as well as I do that I'm screwing everything up."

Roscoe laughed and held out an arm for Evelyn to take. "You're not screwing *everything* up, but you might think I have a screw loose"—he tapped his forehead—"after you hear what I have to ask."

"If you still want me to shoot you with one of my arrows, it's going to take some serious convincing," Evelyn said as politely as possible. She and Roscoe strolled down Fifth Avenue. They passed a homeless person who was buried under layers of clothing, pushing a grocery cart with all their belongings.

"Please, hear me out," Roscoe pleaded.

If his manners weren't reason enough, the fact that he could transform into a stone dragon would have had Evelyn listening. Roscoe guided Evelyn in the direction of her apartment. His hipster appearance would have had them blending in if it were daytime. In fact, his good looks had probably gotten plenty of attention over the years, but in all that time, he'd never fallen in love with anyone else. He only had eyes for Sydney.

"Fine, but my tank is close to empty."

"Thank you, Evelyn." As they walked around a fence, Bryant Park revealed itself. "If Andel didn't tell you, I've been assisting in the hunt for Leo's killer. I don't blame you at all for what happened that night, but like Jude and Andel, I feel the need to seek justice. I've returned every few days to meet with Sydney and our relationship is progressing faster than I'd imagined."

"You came back to check on Sydney?" Evelyn's pace slowed. If Roscoe cared for Sydney enough to return to her so often, what did that say about Andel's feelings for her?

"I did." He patted her hand as it tensed over his forearm. "I have a feeling I know where your thoughts are at, or should I say who your thoughts are on? Andel is a complicated immortal. Of course, not as formidable as our friend Jude, but close."

A lit fountain proudly stood at the end of their path, and trees concealed her and Roscoe from anything or anyone flying overhead. Shadows danced in the moonlight as Evelyn and Roscoe walked closer to the open green field at the park's center.

"What do Andel or Jude have to do with your favor?"

"Nothing, actually. As you know, Jude is against solidifying my love for Sydney, but he has his reasons."

"I know. I mean, he gave me the abbreviated version."

"Did he tell you about Diana or Cleopatra?"

"Cleopatra?" Evelyn yanked on Roscoe's arm. "You mean *the* Cleopatra?"

"Yes. Of course, Jude was created a thousand years before her reign, but he loved Cleopatra before Diana. Where do you think his statue got the nickname, Cleopatra's Needle?" Roscoe tried to clarify his friend's love life. "Jude sought to be pierced with Cleopatra by a Cupid's arrow, but before Diana arrived, Jude's twin tricked Cleopatra, promising her immortality and winning her affection."

Evelyn's chin dropped. "There are two of him?"

"I guess their sister doesn't count—"

"Sister! Wow. I'm guessing after the Cleopatra love triangle, they don't get together for family reunions."

"You guessed right. And poor Jessie, she's always caught in the middle. But anyway, if you know history, Cleopatra eventually chose the mortal Caesar to align herself with. She never did achieve immortality even though she claimed to be a goddess. Who knows what would have happened if Diana had shown up earlier. Instead, she arrived after all the drama and ended up taking advantage of Jude while he was still weak from his first heartbreak."

"So Jude has two really good reasons to persuade you to give up Sydney."

"And two reasons to convince Andel to break things off with you."

Evelyn and Roscoe had walked to the edge of the fountain. "What did you want to ask me?"

He cleared his throat. After a long pause, he turned to face her. "Please, don't decide to leave before you're able to come hang out with me and Sydney. I considered bringing her tonight, but I didn't want you to feel harassed. The Elders may have assigned you to pierce us, and I may have orchestrated that to begin with, but I don't want you doing anything against your better judgment."

"So, if I don't want to after—"

"I just hope you'll at least give us a chance and see if you feel compelled to help us," Roscoe urged.

"What happens if I still refuse to mark the two of you?"

"Then, I won't argue with you."

"Will you break ties with the Cupids?"

"No." Roscoe shook his head. "I can't believe I'm saying it, but I will still uphold the agreement. If Andel used that as an excuse to try and get you to help me, I apologize. I worry Andel will become as hardened as Jude if they spend much more time together hunting Ben."

Evelyn thought if anyone could convince Andel to do something that went against his very existence, it would be Jude. She'd seen a glimpse of what Andel's heart looked like when he'd opened it up to her, but now it was closed off from everyone in the same way Jude had buried his heart. Thousands of years of bitterness and resentment made a convincing argument.

Evelyn squeezed Roscoe's arm playfully. "Let's set a date."

"Do you mean it?"

"Of course, I do. We can hang out. Well, maybe I can hang around inconspicuously while you and Sydney hang out. I don't want to put her in danger, and I can sense love from a football field away. If I'm called to pierce you two, I'll consider it. I'm just worried about what I saw happen with Leo," she admitted. "Everyone keeps telling me it's not my fault, but if I hadn't shot at Ben, we wouldn't be in this mess and Leo would still be here."

The two turned to walk out of the park, and Evelyn focused on the rhythm of her footsteps.

"I'm not sure that's true. Leo would have died to keep Ben from taking you hostage." Roscoe took Evelyn's hand in his. "I understand your concern, and maybe we can come up with a way to safeguard the shot you take. We could set a perimeter and clear it before I bring Sydney in, and there could be a patrol on land and in the air. Douglas and Zora would even be welcome."

"It sounds a little militant, but I guess that's kinda who you are." Evelyn shrugged. "Speaking of that, are you going to tell Sydney who you are beforehand?"

Roscoe let go of Evelyn's arm and wrung his hands together as they walked. "I want to tell her, but I don't want to scare her away."

"And you don't think it'll be worse if you shock her with your dragon form after the honeymoon?"

"I don't know?"

Evelyn stopped Roscoe and placed her hands on his shoulders. "I can make the decision easy for you, ya know."

Roscoe's brows rose in bewilderment.

"I won't agree to summon my bow and arrow until you tell her everything."

"Everything?" he asked.

"Every. Thing."

Chapter 30

Evelyn expected Roscoe to come over to the apartment before his and Sydney's date. He was going to go over some more details about the evening with the Cupids, and they'd be on their way. Convincing Douglas to pose as a couple with Zora again had been easy. But Zora continued to argue that they could protect Evelyn better if they split up. After Evelyn felt the joy her first idea had brought Douglas, she couldn't bring herself to yank his hope away.

Knock, knock.

Evelyn rushed out of her bedroom to answer the door. Checking the peephole, Evelyn was surprised to see Jude. "What are you doing here?" She asked as she opened the door. After the last time they spoke, she figured he wouldn't want to have anything to do with her potentially piercing Roscoe.

"Roscoe's nervous"—Jude rolled his eyes—"and he wanted me to work with you on the plans for tonight to prove I'm willing and able to play nice."

Evelyn didn't know what Jude meant by play nice, and that made her curious. Jude could be referring to welcoming Sydney into the fold or it could be about him accepting Evelyn's abilities. Of course, Roscoe could have been trying to get Jude involved to provide more protection.

Evelyn let Jude into the apartment and offered him a seat on the couch. While Jude spouted off the places Roscoe would be taking Sydney on their date, Evelyn made her way to the kitchen and opened the refrigerator. It was loaded with desserts, and a yellow bowl caught her eye.

Banana pudding.

"What's your definition of playing nice?" Evelyn figured if he didn't want to talk about it, he'd shut the topic down. She pulled a spoon out of the drawer and sat down in the oversized black chair diagonally opposite of Jude.

"I promised Roscoe I wouldn't interfere if you think it's best to take a shot."

"Ok, can you also promise not to bring up Andel?"

"That won't be possible because I'm supposed to give you a message from him."

"Then give it to me, and then you can make the promise."

"Deal." Jude leaned back and spread his arms over the back of the couch. "He wanted you to know that he's on an assignment."

Evelyn shoved a spoonful of pudding into her mouth waiting for Jude to explain. But he didn't say another word. Savoring the bite of softened vanilla wafers, she wondered if this would be how they communicated from now on.

"That's it?"

"Yep. I promise not to mention *you know who* again."

Evelyn took a turn rolling her eyes.

Jude enjoyed her annoyance too much. "Looks like you've got your appetite back." He pointed in the direction of the bowl in her hands.

Evelyn responded by savoring another spoonful of gooey-banana-goodness. Jumping back into her Cupid powers had not only revived her cravings but the time she had spent visiting Sydney's coffee shop the last two days had also filled her emotional tank back up. Love saturated the air. Roscoe had stopped by during Sydney's breaks, and the small cafe brimmed with their affection for each other. There were other couples who crowded over tiny round-tops with their lattes who also exuded love, and Evelyn soaked up every ounce.

"Where are *we* headed tonight?" Evelyn had never been very good at small talk. So far, the list of places Roscoe planned to take Sydney wouldn't cater to an arrow-shooting Cupid. And Evelyn wanted to have the option of piercing them if their love sang "Clair de Lune."

"Central Park. Roscoe will expect us to start tracking them on Bow Bridge then follow them to the Great Lawn."

"Great!" Evelyn scraped some whipped cream off the top of the pudding and shoved it in her mouth. "No pun intended. You know I never thought, being a Cupid, I would get to be so stealthy."

A corner of Jude's mouth turned up. "Maybe you should wear all black."

Evelyn looked down at her comfy jeans.

"I'm kidding." Jude shook his head. "Do you want to poof or fly?"

"I assume they'll be having dinner before heading that way?"

"You assume correctly."

"Then, I'll finish my pudding and poof over."

"Fine. I'll meet you. Do you plan to have your bodyguards there?" Jude looked over his shoulder to the bedroom on the opposite side of the apartment.

"Douglas and Zora will be discreet." She nodded in the direction of the closed door. "You know, I'm kinda glad I have back up. Central Park and I don't have a good track record. Is Roscoe sure about this going down in such a public place?"

Jude stood and stretched his arms up over his head. "You sound like you've made up your mind. Are you sure about this?"

"I'm sure they love each other, but Roscoe knows I won't pierce them until he tells Sydney the truth about who he is."

"Really?"

"Really."

"That's a twist I didn't see coming." He shoved his hands in his pockets. "I like it."

"You mean we agree on something?"

"Don't get ahead of yourself. I still think using your arrow will complicate things. Right now, he loves Sydney, but once you introduce heavenly love, the stakes get too high for my liking. Roscoe has been my closest friend for over a century, and I'll support him however he needs, but to be honest, I'm not sure he'll be able to tell her."

Evelyn jumped to her feet with a half-empty bowl. "Oh, ye of little faith. I've felt what he feels." She poked herself in the chest with her spoon. Once in the kitchen, she returned the bowl to the refrigerator.

"I have, too. And after she freaks about him being a Gargoyle, I'll have to be there while his world comes crumbling down around him."

"Just because you've suffered heartbreak doesn't mean everyone else will." Evelyn dropped her spoon into the sink with a clang and scampered back into the living room.

"But what about your arrow?" Jude's eyes narrowed, gauging how far to take the debate. "We don't have a clue what it'll do to Roscoe or Sydney, and after what happened with Leo—"

"Don't you dare." Evelyn pointed a finger in Jude's face. "Roscoe will react to the red arrow the same way any supernatural would, it's Sydney I'm not sure about. With her being mortal, I wish I could create an arrow half gold and half red. And I've finally come to terms with what happened to Leo, and I won't let you throw it in my face. If anything, you should work on coming to terms with your own love life. You should be questioning your taste in women, not my instincts."

"Feel better?"

"A little." Evelyn's head fell. "Look, I'm sorry for the way that came out."

Jude moved to the window and looked over the city he'd been charged with protecting, but maybe it had been protecting him.

"No, I needed to hear it." Jude crossed his arms over his chest. "I'm just not sure I was ready to hear it."

"Would you have ever been ready?"

"No. And I'm—" Jude hesitated. "I'm not sure I'm ready to lose Roscoe to Sydney."

"Is that really bothering you?" Evelyn stepped next to him.

"Maybe a little."

"You're not losing him," she assured. "And if you'd taken any time to get to know Sydney, you'd have realized you're gaining a coffee-wizard who loves your best friend better than anyone else on the planet could."

"Lattes for life, huh? Well, when you put it like that…" Jude joked. "It's going to be extra hard with Leo gone. But, for Roscoe, I'd do anything."

Evelyn knew what it felt like to lose someone you loved the same way Jude had. She hoped it was the only thing they had in common because she didn't want to end up like him—thousands of years of crusty resentment and hollow loneliness. Evelyn would fight for love.

"We should get moving," Jude interrupted her thoughts. "Do you need to let Curly and Moe in on the arrangement?"

"Nah, they probably heard every word through the door over there." A fumbling thwack sounded from the extra bedroom Zora had been getting ready in. "Let's get going."

Evelyn grinned at Jude and poofed to Bow Bridge.

Chapter 31

Just as Evelyn appeared at the edge of Bow Bridge, Zora and Douglas came into view. They'd transcended more discretely and approached hand in hand. Douglas nodded his head when they walked past, letting Evelyn know they were prepared for whatever she needed them to do.

Thank you for coming, Evelyn thought in their direction.

You bet, I wouldn't miss it, Douglas answered.

What do you need from us? Zora asked.

Right now, I like that you two can be out in the open without giving us away. The fairies won't recognize either of you. I'm thinking you should stay ahead of Roscoe and Sydney. When they arrive at the bridge, you can head over to the Great Lawn and be on the lookout for any possible interference.

Sounds good. Zora being on board meant more to Evelyn than she'd wanted to admit. They hadn't exactly become close over the last few weeks, but she'd been a constant for Evelyn. Looking at her, Zora wouldn't come across as motherly, but she'd constantly been bringing Evelyn food and checking in with her the past few weeks.

A bird shrieked overhead, and Evelyn knew Jude was announcing his presence. Anyone in Central Park would have heard his call, but maybe he'd planned it that way. Jude's job was to patrol the sky and watch for any unwanted company. His falcon form cast a shadow over the water beneath Bow Bridge, and Evelyn watched as he flew, interrupting the moonlight's mirror reflection on the water. The city sounds didn't reach this far into the park's center, but Evelyn's core stirred at the magic Bow Bridge held. Its intricate banisters should have given Evelyn a hint as to the power they might hold.

Standing out in the open, a gust of wind stung her cheeks. The shocking cold reminded her to find cover. She needed to find a place where she could keep an eye on Roscoe and Sydney and follow them without being detected. Tucking herself at the foot of the bridge, Evelyn watched for the couple. It had grown late, and the park lay sleeping in the midst of a thriving metropolis. Evelyn could feel the quiet as much as she could hear it. Bow Bridge made her feel a peaceful hope, that is, until Roscoe and Sydney approached.

Before they stepped onto the wooden walkway, their emotions raced to Evelyn. The mixture of love with friendship and passion immediately called to Evelyn. She yearned to pierce them with love, but she needed Roscoe to tell Sydney the truth about himself first. Fighting the reflex to summon her bow and arrow, she focused her hearing toward them. In her gut, Evelyn knew Sydney could handle Roscoe's existence as a Gargoyle.

"Have you ever walked across this bridge?" Roscoe asked.

Sydney surveyed the area around them as they walked to the middle of the bridge. "I've walked past it several times, but nope, I don't think I've ever crossed it. Does it lead anywhere?"

"There's an unmarked path back there, but it's not one many people would take, especially this late."

"What are we doing out here, anyway?" Sydney leaned with her back against the railing to face Roscoe.

Roscoe stepped closer to Sydney, giving her nowhere to go, no reason to want to go anywhere. "I know it's fast, but you need to know that I'm falling in love with you."

"I know. I mean, yes it's fast, but I know what you mean, Roscoe. I feel the same way." She wrapped her arms around his waist and pulled him even closer.

Roscoe looked down and Sydney looked up. Their lips met over and over in soft kisses, and the magic from the bridge blended with the power of the couple. Without a second thought, Evelyn's bow and arrows rested at her feet. When she looked down to see them, she noticed a breeze had blown over the water, creating ripples that distorted the reflected image of the stars above.

Roscoe lifted Sydney up to sit on the railing and she tangled her hands in Roscoe's hair. Her legs wrapped around his waist, and they were in the perfect position to be pierced. Both pure hearts had to be aligned for the shot to count. She could shoot through Sydney and strike Roscoe, but something at the edge of her conscience seemed off. As another breeze brushed Evelyn's skin, her nose wrinkled at an acrid odor it carried.

Looking over her shoulder, Evelyn knew the smell couldn't have come from behind her, but Roscoe hadn't reacted to the scent. The sour aroma had to have come from somewhere between them. Evelyn looked up to the sky for Jude, but he'd disappeared. Scanning the park around them, Evelyn wanted to ensure no one was advancing on them. When she determined the area was clear, she moved toward the bank of the lake to check under the bridge. The scent of rot got stronger with each step.

An earth-shaking rumble had Evelyn stumbling toward the bank of the lake. She grabbed hold of the bridge's ledge to keep from falling in the water.

A murky darkness slithered over the water, and Evelyn sensed something or someone very wrong lurking nearby.

Glancing up, Roscoe and Sydney continued to embrace while whispering to each other. She couldn't believe Roscoe hadn't heard the disturbance below them. Evelyn would rather be safe than sorry, so she thought, *Roscoe, run!*

Roscoe picked Sydney up without hesitation, and he darted off the bridge using his supernatural speed. In her line of sight, Roscoe set Sydney down next to Douglas and Zora on the lawn. With everyone out of harm's way, Evelyn peeked back under the Victorian bridge and met two glowing yellow eyes.

Evelyn scooped up her bow and looped the strap of her quiver of arrows over her shoulder and rushed up to higher ground. Running over the bridge in her friends' direction would only take the danger to them, so she looked over her shoulder to the dense woods.

Water from the lake sloshed violently over the shoreline in front of her. Giant hands with ragged, dirt-crusted nails gripped the underside of the bridge and a head the size of an exercise ball revealed itself next. The creature had long brown scraggly hair falling over his face. Beneath the hair, a bulbous nose and sagging skin accompanied its yellow eyes. Stepping out into the open, he was the size of one of the trees behind her. As it waded out of the water, she didn't have time to wonder how the monster fit under the bridge.

Evelyn froze in terror.

Evelyn? Zora thought to her. *You need to get out of there. Now!*

Zora's warning surprised Evelyn out of her disbelieving trance, and Evelyn gradually scooted one foot back. The creature let out a growl.

Getting away would be next to impossible on foot. Evelyn didn't know how fast this thing could attack, but if size equaled strength, she was in for a world of hurt. Her arrows might be able to slow the thing down, but the weapons would have resembled pins in a pincushion if she shot the giant.

She needed to poof to her friends and then poof them all far, far away. Thinking of the grassy spot next to Roscoe, Evelyn squinted her eyes. Nothing happened. Why couldn't she transcend?

I don't think it's going to let me just go. I'll need a distraction, so I can have enough time to reach for an arrow, aim, and shoot. If it's injured I might have a chance, and it might go back where it came from,

Evelyn thought to anyone who had the ability to hear her. She'd be grateful to whoever stepped up to the challenge, but she couldn't bring herself to ask any one of them to step into the line of fire.

A loud screech sounded overhead, and Evelyn slowly exhaled waiting for Jude to show himself. In his falcon form, the ancient Gargoyle swooped over the monster and clawed at its face. The beast swatted at Jude like he was a fly. Hitting him, the stone bird, the size of a small car, careened into the turf at Roscoe and Sydney's feet.

Roscoe instinctively burst into a marble dragon to protect his girlfriend and best friend. Behind him, Sydney fainted and Jude lay unconscious. With a ferocious roar, Roscoe warned the beast. Both supernaturals were bigger than tow trucks, but Roscoe had the advantage of a tail.

The putrid creature had brute strength, and the distance Jude had been flung indicated to Evelyn she probably didn't have the ability to overpower him. But Jude's attack had given Evelyn a split second to clutch an arrow, nock it, and aim. Naturally, she marked his barrel of a chest.

Roscoe flung himself in front of the monster, blocking Evelyn's shot. The dragon's talons tore the beast's flesh, and then he ascended protectively over the others, giving Evelyn an opening. Her arrow turned from gold to red, glowing in the night. Releasing it, the arrow hit its target, vanishing into the giant's heart.

A flash of light blinded the group from the lake's edge, and as Evelyn blinked away the spots in her vision, she spotted a young man lying unconscious in the creature's place. Douglas stood guard in front of Sydney while Roscoe flew to Evelyn's side and transformed back into his mortal form.

"Who, or what, is *that*?" Evelyn asked as she stepped closer to him. A scrap of tattered, brown fabric kept his privates concealed, and mud coated the rest of his skin.

Roscoe squinted his eyes and tilted his head. "I believe it's a fairy."

Evelyn, are you alright? Zora asked in a thought.

Yes, I think so. Evelyn answered. *Roscoe thinks it's a fairy, but how is that possible?*

We can figure that out later, you need to send Roscoe over here, Sydney is coming to.

"Sydney's waking up, Roscoe," Evelyn warned. "You should go explain things."

Roscoe looked over to the field across the bridge. "This was not the way I'd planned to reveal myself." He looked back and forth between Evelyn and the body.

"I'll be fine. You go."

It was all the encouragement Roscoe needed, and he sped across the bridge to Sydney's side. The care he took in helping her up and the gentle tones he spoke as he began to explain what had just happened made Evelyn's heart swell up. She knew the call she felt to pierce them with her arrow would never go away.

A few yards away, the figure on the grassy bank twitched. Evelyn armed herself. A low groan escaped his lips from behind a curtain of dark hair. She didn't know if she should shoot the fairy again, check on him, or run across the bridge to get away.

"Where am I?" he asked more to himself in a European accent. He hadn't acknowledged Evelyn's presence.

Feeling less intimidated after his transformation, Evelyn slid her arrow out of her bow and let them dangle at her side. She didn't anticipate shooting the slender, worn-out figure, but she'd be ready if he tried anything. "Bow Bridge, Central Park."

He flinched and looked over at Evelyn. His eyes were golden instead of the violent yellow they'd been earlier. "Who are you?"

"Evelyn Bowden."

"Mortal?"

"Immortal. I'm a Cupid. Who are you?"

"Avery," he began. "I'm a fairy, but I can't remember how I got here. Did you help me or"—he looked at her weapons—"hunt me?"

"There's definitely no hunting going on, but I'm not sure help is the word that best describes what just went down."

"Then how would you describe it?"

"Before I tell you anything, I need to check on my friends."

"Fair enough." He nodded.

Evelyn hesitantly asked, "Are you well enough to walk over with me?"

"I would much rather gather my strength here for a few more minutes. That is if you don't mind."

"Will you wait for me to come back?"

If Avery was a fairy, he couldn't lie to her. "I'd like to clean up a bit in private, but you can rest assured, I won't leave the area until I understand what happened to me."

Evelyn would have to be okay with his answer. Her brain couldn't work out any loopholes he'd worked into his wording because she worried more about how Jude and Sydney were. Evelyn didn't turn her back on the fairy until she absolutely had to halfway across the bridge.

Her bow and arrows disappeared into thin air, but she knew they'd return if she needed them. Evelyn had worried she wouldn't ever get the courage to shoot her arrows again after Leo's death, but when the others' lives were in danger, she didn't hesitate. The relief she felt when her arrow hadn't kill the man-beast mixed with her fear of who he could be. What if the fairy hidden underneath proved to be worse than the ogre-like monster?

"Everyone okay?" Evelyn asked as she approached Douglas. He paced around the group, on the lookout, while Zora tended to Jude and Roscoe spoke softly to Sydney.

"Seems like it," Douglas answered. "Is it dead?"

"No. But it's not the same *thing* anymore. It's a fairy."

"Really? I can't believe it." Douglas' forehead wrinkled.

"You can't believe what?" Zora asked.

"The rumors were true." Douglas' eyes brightened. "Cupids have never had much to do with the fairies, and the Elders have always referred to them as Nox. But gossip has always had them hovering between Nox and Lux. Some fairies are good, and others are bad. The juicy rumors always surround the really bad fairies because it's said they change—or morph—into trolls. I've never seen one before."

"Me neither." Evelyn looked back toward the bridge. "I thought trolls were supposed to be short, and don't they roll up into rocks to camouflage themselves? But I also thought fairies were only three inches tall and flew around spreading sparkly dust."

"You've seen way too many movies." Jude sat up on the ground behind Douglas. "Trolls are the darkest of the fairies. As their power is used against mortals or for self-indulgence, they transform into the ugly nature of their conduct. Then they begin to hide from the light under bridges and in caves, truly becoming Nox. But they prefer to remain as close as they can to their realm."

Jude began to stand up but then buckled at the waist. His midsection had been slashed by the troll when he was hit. The gashes were crusty with scabs, and Jude's clothes were ruined. "I need to shift into the Obelisk if I want to heal faster."

Looking over at Roscoe, Jude hoped for his approval, but Roscoe tended to Sydney's tears. Jude gritted his teeth as he stepped a few yards away from the group. He transformed into a falcon and flew off into the night sky. Cleopatra's Needle stood at the end of Central Park, and Jude would be able to rest easy and heal in the light of the new day.

"I can't. I can't," Sydney whispered while shaking her head over and over again.

Evelyn tried not to hear Roscoe and Sydney's very private conversation. He had pleaded with Sydney to hear him out, but she insisted she needed to go home. Scrambling to her feet, Sydney looked around at Evelyn, Douglas, and Zora. Luckily, Jude had left out of her line of sight.

"I just need some time." Sydney walked away, alone.

"Do you want me to go after her?" Evelyn asked.

Roscoe stood, his shoulders rounded, and his hands slipped into his pockets. "No, I'll watch over her." Instead of transforming, Roscoe followed on foot. The sadness trailing behind him left Evelyn aching.

"Should we, maybe, check on the fairy you left at the lake?" Zora asked.

"Yes. Absolutely, but I think if we all go, we'll spook him." Evelyn started back toward Bow Bridge. *We can communicate this way until I convince him y'all are friends.*

Fine, but I want to go on record that I think this idea is a bad one, Douglas interjected his thoughts. *We'll split up and be ready on both sides of the lake if you need help.*

As Evelyn reached the bridge, she looked to the bank where she'd left Avery, and there was no trace of him. Douglas had planted himself among some bushes to her left, and Zora found a bench to sit on to her right. Evelyn slowed her pace and decided she may need her bow and arrows with Avery again and summoned them. Once at the lake's edge, Evelyn peered under the bridge looking for any sign of movement.

Avery isn't here. Evelyn informed the others.

Douglas started pacing, glancing back and forth. *Did you say he would wait for you?*

Yes. Evelyn answered.

What exactly did he say?

Evelyn thought back on the fairy's words. *Something like, he'd wait in the area until he figured out what happened. Maybe he's walking it off?* Evelyn shrugged. *Zora, do you see Avery over there?*

Zora transcended to Evelyn's side. "Did you say his name was Avery?"

"Yep, but I don't understand how he could disappear like that. He looked like he'd been hurt, and he barely had the strength to sit up." Evelyn walked further back to the edge of the forest behind them. She hoped he was merely seeking shelter or looking for food.

Douglas transcended inches away from Evelyn, and she jumped. "If he said he'd stay in the area, that would include the fairy realm."

Evelyn pressed her palm to her forehead. "Well, if he got there on his own, it's one less thing for us to worry about." She turned to Zora. "And, yes. His name is Avery."

Zora's olive skin tone turned green, and the corners of her mouth turned down.

"What is up with you two?" Evelyn threw her hands up in question.

Douglas and Zora looked at each other, and Zora answered, "Avery is the ruler of the Fairies, well, he *was*."

"He's been gone since before our time. He's closer to Jude's age than any of ours," Douglas added.

"Then, who the hot-fudge is Queen Rhyan?"

Chapter 32

After a thorough search of the area surrounding Bow Bridge, Evelyn poofed back to the apartment. Douglas and Zora felt the need to check on Roscoe and Jude, but Evelyn had a feeling the two Cupids were up to something else. No matter how much she trusted them, she would always worry they'd be reporting back to someone. It only took a slice of apple pie and a long scalding shower to calm her nerves enough to settle down. As she curled up on the couch, she noticed someone else had returned to the apartment for a shower in the other bedroom.

Her eyelids grew heavy, but instead of going to her bed, she let herself fall asleep in the living room. She didn't feel as alone out in the open. A warm, soft blanket slid over her shoulders, and she squinted out one eye to identify who she needed to thank: Zora or Douglas. But Andel stood over her. He wore a white T-shirt and plaid pajama pants. His smile widened when he realized Evelyn saw him.

"What are you smiling about?"

"Just glad to see you," Andel admitted. "You good?"

"I'm doing great." Evelyn sat up, and as the blanket fell to her waist, she realized the tank top she'd chosen to sleep in left little to the imagination. Pulling the blanket back up, she narrowed her eyes at Andel. "What are you doing back?"

"I finished my mission, and instead of waiting in the heavens for my next assignment, I thought I'd wait here. Are you okay with that?"

"So this little visit has nothing to do with Douglas or Zora tattling about the troll incident?"

"Troll?" Andel crossed his arms over his chest and sat on the arm of the couch. "To be honest, I heard you might need some extra protection today because Queen Rhyan's husband appeared in the fairy realm after centuries of being presumed dead."

"She has a husband? She never struck me as the commitment type."

"Me neither." Andel shrugged. "I can only guess that's why her husband was a troll. Did you have something to do with his return?"

"I might have shot him with one of my red arrows." Evelyn stood up, straightening her white cotton shorts. She suddenly had a craving for something sweet and headed for the kitchen. "Why wouldn't Zora or Douglas have told me Avery was Rhyan's ex?"

She shivered at the thought of the Queen possibly becoming an enemy. Evelyn had experienced some relationship drama in college with one of her roommates. Everyone felt the need to pick sides during her break up, and even when the couple got back together, no one forgot the choices each other made. It had felt like everyone had a secret alliance.

Evelyn pulled a box of brownie mix out of the pantry along with some oil. She also grabbed a measuring cup and spoon from the drawer and eggs from the refrigerator. With the push of a button, she started to preheat the oven.

Andel joined Evelyn in the kitchen, propping himself up on the countertop.

"I made Douglas and Zora promise me they wouldn't talk about you or talk to you about me. They're good friends like that."

He watched her pull out a bowl from the cabinet and mix everything together. "So do you plan to face a new day with a nap and brownies?"

"Actually, I'm ending a pretty rough day with them." After getting the batter to the perfect consistency, Evelyn looked from the gooey spoon to Andel. "What, exactly, is so bad about baking?"

"You and I both know this isn't just baking. Right now, you're debating whether to lick that spoon and the bowl clean. Turning to dessert will not fix anything."

"But it'll make me feel better."

"Okay, I understand there is an emotional attachment to the sweets, but if you're busy eating brownies when Rhyan is looking for answers, it could look a lot different to her."

"She could be mad, but she could also be overjoyed. It's not like she's going to come after the Cupids for this. And if she comes after me, I'll handle it." Evelyn waved her hands out, forgetting the spoonful of batter. Chocolate splattered across Andel's shirt. "I'm immortal, and she wants something from me."

Grabbing a dish towel, Andel started to wipe away the globs of brown. "I thought the same thing before Leo died. But we aren't sure who the fairies have aligned themselves with. What if that Ben-guy lends one of his black arrows to the Queen?"

The truth of his words hit Evelyn hard. It may not have been her fault, but Ben's black arrow put an end to any security an immortal felt. She'd been deemed worthy to be a Cupid just in time to see them fall at the hands of a deadly, dark Nox.

Evelyn shoved the fudge-battered spoon in her mouth.

"Why don't you tell me what happened tonight." Andel scooted off the counter and reached under the stove for a pan.

She handed the bowl over. "I gave Roscoe a chance to prove he and Sydney should be pierced by my arrow. Then, Avery attacked, in troll form, of course. He must have heard or smelled us, and when he started to attack me, Jude intervened. Roscoe got Sydney out of the way, but after the troll threw Jude like a football, Roscoe transformed in front of everyone and joined the fight. Jude had been knocked unconscious, Sydney fainted, and I had time to aim a red arrow and fire. In a flash of light, the troll turned into Avery."

"What did he say? Andel poured the batter into the pan and placed it in the oven.

"Not much. Once I got his name and saw he wasn't a threat, I went to check on the others. He looked to be in pretty bad shape, and it led me to believe he wouldn't be going anywhere. He said he wouldn't leave the area, but I hadn't considered that the Fairy realm was in the area."

"Interesting."

"Am I in danger?" Evelyn set her spoon in the sink and headed back to the couch. "Rhyan seemed to like me. I mean, as much as a fairy can like a Cupid. She got the arrows she wanted and I saved Avery from trolldom. Neither of them could be that mad at me, right?"

"You haven't known the fairies long enough to understand their way of thinking." Andel followed Evelyn.

"So catch me up."

"First off, you've learned firsthand they won't take no for an answer. They also don't like airing their dirty laundry. We may never know what happened between Rhyan and Avery. Fairies will do anything to get their way, and that could mean Rhyan did something to make Avery a troll or Avery did something horrible to land himself under the bridge.

You know the saying *keep your enemies closer*? We should definitely consider putting it into practice with Rhyan."

"You're right."

Andel couldn't believe she'd admitted it. "I am." He yawned. "So, what will you do about Sydney and Roscoe?"

"Follow my heart like I promised."

"And, what is your heart telling you?"

"I'm not sure I want to share that information with you." Evelyn flopped down on the couch. It hurt her to say it, but letting him in on what her heart was leading her to do would be the same as letting him in. He'd left to do the Elders' bidding, and she had begun to understand that she wouldn't be able to follow their missions anymore unless they lined up with her own.

Andel slumped into the chair next to the couch and watched as Evelyn pulled the blanket over her legs. "I can only assume you'll go through with piercing Roscoe and Sydney, but I wonder why after what you've seen can happen."

"What I saw tonight was hope. The love in my arrow saved a fairy from darkness."

"Did it, Evelyn? We don't know where Avery's coming from, and we don't know what he'll do now."

Evelyn sighed and sank into the pillows. She'd been in danger from one thing or another since the moment she laid eyes on Andel in the heavens. "I'm willing to risk danger, and a lot more, when I'm following my heart."

"Then you should do it."

"I will, and I plan to follow it from here on out." Evelyn closed her eyes. She knew it would be easier to say what was on her mind if she didn't have to look at Andel. "I'm not going to let the Elders use me as a bargaining chip anymore. I won't be manipulated, fooled, or toyed with if I can help it."

"It's not their intention—"

"Stop. Don't defend them. I get it, you're one of them, or you could be someday. But I don't want to hear it. I have an idea, and if I'm right, you won't have to worry about Roscoe or Sydney...or me."

Silence pulled Evelyn and Andel further apart. He sat in the chair, and she lay on the couch, both unsure if the next thing they said would rip their friendship apart. Evelyn felt unsure of Andel and the feelings he stirred in her. The divide threatened to grow so wide they wouldn't be able to hear each other anymore.

"Do you mind if I stay?" Andel's question reached across more than the room—he wanted to stay with her, even if it was just for the night, and that warmed the center of Evelyn's chest.

"Of course not," she answered.

Chapter 33

Warm sun spilled into the living room and prodded Andel's eyes open. He hadn't slept that long in years. Looking over at the clock on the wall, he cringed as pain shot down his neck from sleeping in a chair. He'd dreamed for over five hours. The whirlwind of scenes all had one thing in common: Evelyn.

A dream of he and Evelyn on the cliff near his home in Greece lingered more like a memory. He also had a vision of them at St. Patrick's Cathedral surrounded by their friends. Andel had woken up in more emotional turmoil than he'd fallen asleep with, and the crick in his neck didn't compare to the hurt he'd felt when Evelyn kept him at arm's length the night before.

"Are you awake?" he whispered.

Evelyn yawned and rolled over to her side. "What?"

"Never mind."

"What is it?" Evelyn peeked out one eye. Andel still sat in the chair across from her, minus his brownie-splattered T-shirt.

"Do you dream?" Andel leaned forward, and his biceps flexed as he placed his elbows on his knees.

"Sometimes." She stretched her arms up over her head. "Why do you ask?"

"No reason." Andel got up and hobbled to the kitchen. "Want something to eat?"

"Nice move trying to change the subject, but that's my trick. What's really going on?" Evelyn knew him too well, and even though he hadn't used a bare-chest tactic in the past, she wouldn't put it past him. "I'll take a bowl of ice cream while you're in there, though. It's like having a glass of milk, right?"

Andel ignored her reasoning. "It must be because I don't normally sleep that my subconscious was overactive last night."

"Do you think it was trying to tell you something?"

Andel opened the freezer door, and the cool air brushed goosebumps across his skin. He reached in and pulled out a carton of vanilla ice cream. "Probably, but that doesn't mean I have to listen to it."

"Why wouldn't you listen to *you*?"

"Point taken." Andel used a spoon to scoop some of the sugary milk into a bowl.

Evelyn held out her hands for her breakfast, and Andel's warm fingers brushed against hers. "I'm not a dream interpreter, but I'd be happy to give it a try."

"I'm pretty sure one was just a memory."

"A good one?"

"I like to think so. I think it was when you and I went for target practice in Greece that last time."

"Did you dream of my face at the center of the targets?"

"No." Andel pressed his lips down into a frown. "It was just a dream of us sitting on the cliff's edge together."

"That *is* a good memory." Evelyn shoved a spoonful of ice cream in her mouth.

"That's enough about my dreaming. What do you plan to do—"

Knock, knock.

"I'll get it." Andel, relieved at the interruption, opened the front door to find Roscoe. Andel didn't want to tell Evelyn about his dream of them in the church, so Roscoe's timing couldn't have been better. The two Cupids had been at the church together before, but never standing at the altar hand-in-hand. It definitely wasn't a memory, and Evelyn would think he was crazy if he told her. Andel thought he was crazy for having it.

"Shouldn't you be resting up?" Evelyn asked, scooting over to make room for Roscoe on the couch.

He fell into the cushions beside her. "I never went to sleep."

"Is everything okay?" Andel asked.

A smile spread across Roscoe's face as he closed his eyes and leaned over to lay his head on Evelyn's shoulder. "It's more than okay. Sydney noticed me following her home last night and invited me inside. She had a million questions, and I got to explain everything. She must have just felt overwhelmed in the park with everyone there watching. I think this is going to work out."

Evelyn patted Roscoe's leg. "I'm so happy for you."

"I just wanted you to know the good news before I headed back to the cathedral, but I'm glad I caught you both at the same time." He looked to Andel.

"Me too," Andel nodded. "Now, you better get back to your post before you fall asleep and transform into a boulder. You'll bust that couch and crush Evelyn."

"He wouldn't crush me," Evelyn argued.

Roscoe smiled and stood to leave. "Technically, I don't think I'd crush you, but it wouldn't feel too good."

As curious as Evelyn was, Andel didn't want her finding out firsthand how much Roscoe weighed as a Gargoyle. Andel held out a hand to Roscoe and helped him to his feet. Evelyn followed, setting her bowl down, and scooted him toward the front door with a wave of her hands. "Then go, get some sleep. And I'll work on a plan to complete my mission and our agreement."

Evelyn shut the door behind Roscoe with a wink and turned to face Andel.

"What do you need from me?" he asked.

"I'm thinking I need to get Sydney and Roscoe to St. Patrick's Cathedral this afternoon. We know my abilities work there, and I figure, if we do this during daylight hours, we don't have to worry about any Nox getting in our way."

"Clever." Andel wiped a hand over the stubble along his chin. It was a great idea. One that, in theory, would ensure everyone's safety and hopefully their success.

"Thanks, but what else?"

"What do you mean?"

"You have never given me a one-word answer to anything regarding strategy."

"True."

"So—" Evelyn scooped up her bowl and took another bite of ice cream.

"Well, I'm curious. If you believe that Ben's power is dark, do you also think he'll only be able to come out at night?"

"I'm not sure what Ben is," she conceded. "But there's not much more I can do to keep everyone safe."

"Am I invited?"

"I hope so. I'm depending on you to get the Gargoyles to the church on time."

"If Jude is hurt as badly as you say, you should give him until at least three to heal before I wake him."

"Perfect. I plan to whisk Sydney away before she has her shift at the coffee shop."

"How do you plan to convince her to go with you?"

Evelyn scraped the last spoonful of ice cream out of the bowl. "Leave her to me." She stood and headed for the kitchen.

Tossing her bowl in the sink, she leaned forward, and Andel caught himself eyeing her white pajama shorts. When Evelyn looked up, she grinned, having noticed him noticing her. He blinked and turned his attention to his bare feet.

"Do you trust me?" she asked.

"I trust you." Andel did trust her, but he didn't think he could trust himself with her.

"So we'll meet at the church at four o'clock this afternoon?" Evelyn walked to her bedroom then peeked back into the living room, waiting for his answer.

"I'll be there."

Chapter 34

Evelyn waved across the street to get Sydney's attention, but the taxis lining up at the red light like a Tetris game kept her from seeing the brown-haired girl who blended into the crowd. In the mass of people navigating around each other, Evelyn felt like, even as a heavenly immortal, she didn't stand out.

When the light changed, a flood of bodies washed over to Evelyn's side of the street, including Sydney. She didn't want to take Sydney by surprise, but she also didn't want to have to explain her plans via text message. "Syd!" Evelyn popped up on her toes and waved a hand in the air.

"Hey, Evelyn. What are you doing here? Is Roscoe okay?"

"He's fine. He's actually planning to meet us at the St. Patrick's."

Sydney glanced at her watch and tilted her head. "I have a shift in thirty minutes."

"I know, Roscoe told me." Evelyn raised her eyebrows. "He also told me you're still up for being with him. Even if he's a you-know-what."

Sydney straightened, looking Evelyn in the eye. "I am."

"Then, I have an idea that could help the two of you in the long run…if you're up for it." Evelyn nudged Sydney to walk alongside her down the busy New York City street. "I'm not sure if Roscoe explained, but I'm a Cupid."

"He said something about you being an immortal, too, and explained that you have a special ability that could be helpful to us. Normally, I'd have you both committed, but after what I saw last night, I'd believe anything you told me."

"Good, because I'm going to need you to trust me and have a whole lot of faith. What I'm about to propose might sound a little more than crazy."

"Okay, shoot."

"No pun intended, I'm sure." Evelyn smiled at the irony. "But seriously, we're headed to the church where we'll meet up with Roscoe and the others. The Nox are having a little too much fun at night, and I don't want any more distractions."

"Are you really referring to that troll as a mere distraction? It wasn't a hangnail but an overgrown monster who attacked us."

"I'm not trying to come across as flippant, but I'm immortal, even if it's only been a year and a half. Now, Roscoe's friend Jude might equate a tsunami to a waterpark, but he's ancient. I don't plan to ever get that cocky, and hopefully, you won't either."

Sydney grabbed Evelyn's arm and stopped in the middle of the sidewalk. "What do you mean *hopefully I won't either?*"

"Hmmm, maybe I should have arrived at that point more delicately, but we don't have time. Let's keep moving." Evelyn stepped a few paces ahead of Sydney before she followed.

"We're going to the cathedral because my powers work there, but other immortals can't interfere, at least with their supernatural abilities.

The thing is, Gargoyles don't have a problem using their power in churches, either. Gargoyles are all over the oldest cathedrals, so I'm pretty sure some of Roscoe's power will transfer to you when I shoot through his heart first."

"Are you kidding? Will I turn into—"

"No, no." Evelyn shook her head. "I mean his immortality. His stone form is actually his original condition. The magic or power in him allows him to be human some of the time."

"I'm not sure about taking his power. What if it hurts him?"

Evelyn turned the next corner, and St. Patrick's rose into her line of sight. "I thought of that, and if you'd rather I can shoot through your heart first. But then you'll only have each other as long as your mortal life allows. Before that troll attacked last night, I felt compelled to shoot through Roscoe first. I've learned to trust my Cupid instincts."

"Will it hurt?"

Evelyn took Sydney's hand in hers. "Not at all. The arrow is heavenly, and the last couple I pierced didn't even know it happened."

"Well, I guess if Roscoe's fine with it, then I will be, too."

Reaching the steps of the church, Evelyn took them two at a time. She squeezed Sydney's hand and released it. Sydney and Roscoe weren't even in the same room yet, but Evelyn felt their love resonate in her. The feeling hinted at something familiar, something she'd felt before.

Out of respect, and to avoid unwanted attention, the two women moved with the tourists through the cathedral. Once they arrived at the center of the building, Evelyn could sense other immortals. They felt close, so Evelyn scanned their surroundings, trying to come across as a visitor admiring the architecture and ambiance. No Andel.

"What's wrong?" Sydney asked.

"They're here, but"—Evelyn held out her arms wide—"they're not right here."

"I have no idea what you mean." Sydney turned in a circle. "How do you know they're here?"

"I can feel them."

"Well, this place has a bunch of secret rooms and a couple of bell towers, right?"

"Yeah, but Andel wouldn't expect me to…" Evelyn winced at the realization that her friends were waiting for her in one of the rooms below them…in the same area where Leo had died.

Andel, really? she thought.

Sydney placed a hand on Evelyn's shoulder. "Now I know something's wrong. Does your head hurt?"

"I don't know if I can do this." Evelyn leaned into Sydney as a wave of guilt and remorse crashed over her. Sydney pulled Evelyn to a nearby pew and sat her down. "I'm so sorry."

"Don't be sorry," Sydney reassured. "I'm going to love Roscoe whether you shoot me with some hocus-pocus arrow or not. Maybe it's for the better?"

"No." Evelyn gripped the back of the pew in front of her. She tried to absorb some of the love in the room but thought of Leo. She'd mourned for the loss of the Gargoyle over the last few weeks. Leo had been loved, and he'd loved his friends. Evelyn welcomed the relief of her realization and was surprised to find that love had come from her grief.

"Are you sure we should do this?" Sydney's question opened a floodgate of memories for Evelyn.

"As a human, I was pierced with a Cupid's arrow."

"Really?"

"His name was Tate, and I'm not sure when in our relationship it happened, but the arrow anchored us. After I became a Cupid, I had to remove it, and that hurt like honey."

Sydney squinted in confusion, but Evelyn waved it off. She leaned forward and put her forehead in her hands. She could do this, right?

"Ummm, Evelyn," Sydney whispered, "There's a really big guy walking this way."

Evelyn's head popped up, and Andel only had a few more steps to take before reaching them. Worry lined his forehead. Andel nodded to Sydney and moved into the pew in front of them. "Roscoe is waiting for you around the right side of the stage." He told her.

"Are you okay if I go?" Sydney patted Evelyn's hand.

Evelyn nodded, and as Sydney walked away, Andel turned in his seat to face Evelyn. "What just happened?"

"What do you mean?" Evelyn tried to play ignorant. Maybe she could explain away the mental plea she'd made in a panic.

"You reached out to me, but in addition to hearing your thoughts, I felt every drop of the emotion that overpowered you."

"You did?" Evelyn laid a hand on Andel's arm. "I'm sorry. That couldn't have been fun."

"Not for you, either. What brought it on?"

"The idea of going back down there and reliving what happened to Leo," Evelyn admitted. She looked at the front of the church where they both knew a hidden door led to a floor beneath them.

"If you didn't want to meet there, where had you planned to pierce Roscoe and Sydney?"

"Here." Evelyn looked at Andel. "I imagined them embracing at the altar, each of us making a promise. Them to each other, and me to them. I know I'm not a Gargoyle and I can't physically take on a troll or whatever else is out there waiting for us in the darkness. But I know I want to fight for love. At least, their love."

Andel placed his hand over hers. "I understand." He wove their fingers together, and she thought she'd like to have his steady hand in hers forever.

"Would you like me to go get the others or would you like to mentally nudge them?"

Evelyn twisted her lips in thought to Roscoe and Jude, *Do you guys mind coming up here?*

"You have to admit, it's an ability you wish you had," Evelyn teased Andel. "If they aren't up here in a few minutes, then we'll know even my power can't get through their thick skulls."

Andel laughed, patting Evelyn's hand. He turned to face the altar, sliding out of Evelyn's grasp. "They know by now they can't ignore you."

"Do you?" Evelyn asked.

Andel rubbed the back of his neck along his hairline. "Not now, Evelyn. Please."

Evelyn had given Andel one more chance to lay everything out between them, but instead of a magician pulling the tablecloth and everything staying in place, it tumbled to the floor. She felt like she'd been shut down, again. Standing, Evelyn moved out of the pew to walk to the restroom. She could poof from the stall up to the restricted balcony and shoot her arrow. Mentally relaying her plan to Roscoe, she asked him to tell everyone else. It wasn't until she poofed to the balcony that she saw Douglas and Zora posted on either side of the altar. Roscoe and Sydney stood at the center of the room talking, and Jude stood near them like a best man.

Andel? Evelyn remembered that he couldn't answer her back in the cathedral just as she finished calling him. *Sorry, mental fart.*

"Mental fart?" Andel's voice shocked Evelyn.

"What are you doing up here?" She spotted him in a doorway twenty feet away. "How did you even get up here? You can't poof."

One of Andel's eyebrows shot up. "I never *poof*, Evelyn."

"Fine, transcend."

"I've lived a long time and have some experience picking locks."

"Good to know."

Andel took a few steps toward Evelyn, shrinking the distance by half. "Can we talk?"

"Not a good time." Evelyn summoned her bow and arrows, taking on a more professional demeanor with Andel. "I'm glad Zora and Douglas made it. It's a good idea to have witnesses in case something goes wrong."

"Stop, Evelyn. They're part of what I need to talk to you about." Andel closed the distance and reached for her. Evelyn took a step back and bumped an organ pipe with her backside. Gripping both of her arms, Andel anchored Evelyn to the floor. "The Elders might bring them in for questioning when this is all said and done. They won't be able to lie."

"Why would they need to lie?" Evelyn asked accusingly.

Andel made eye contact and didn't blink, "I heard you explain to Sydney what might happen. How you think your arrow could transfer power, immortality?"

"It's just a gut feeling."

"How are you going to explain all of this to the Elders?"

"Why can't you just let me pierce Roscoe and Sydney? Then you can all go about your business. Jude may have to share Roscoe, but he'll get over it. You can report back to the Elders and finish your last few missions, and Douglas can go on pining for Zora."

"What are you going to do?" Andel frowned and his voice grew soft. Evelyn shrugged.

"What if I told you I didn't want to lose my best friend?"

Evelyn's breath left her lungs in a slow exhale. "Best friends don't kiss like that."

"In today's culture—" The corner of Andel's mouth turned up.

"Don't give me that. I don't have time for a lecture. Plus, this generation doesn't define me, and neither do you."

"I want to be with you, but *we* can define things later." Andel nodded down to the others in front of the altar. "You have an assignment to complete."

"You make it sound so romantic."

Evelyn looked over her shoulder; Roscoe had taken Sydney in his arms. Evelyn's instincts took over, and she slid out of Andel's grasp and pulled an arrow from her quiver as she lifted her bow. Once the couple was in her sight, the arrow changed from gold to red. She only waited a second, and as Sydney looked over Roscoe's shoulder up to the balcony, Evelyn released her arrow. The red instrument harmonized with their love as it sang to Evelyn. The arrow plunged into Roscoe's heart through his back and disappeared as it drove into Sydney's heart.

Sydney's eyes glowed red for a moment and closed. Roscoe caught her as she lost consciousness. Evelyn panicked at first but then used her powers to reach out to Sydney.

Sydney?

She didn't respond, but Evelyn could detect the magic from Roscoe's veins slowly beating through Sydney's heart. Douglas had rushed to them and peered up into the balcony, looking past Evelyn. She glanced at Andel, and the corners of his mouth sagged with the weight of worry. None of them could feel the change in Sydney because of the protection the church offered.

She'll be fine, Evelyn thought to each of the immortals, including Sydney now. *Everyone meet me in the garden.* At the surprise of having Evelyn in her head, the newest immortal's eyes fluttered open.

Dismissing her bow and arrows, Evelyn moved closer to Andel. She took his hand, but before she could poof them to meet the others, Andel squeezed her hand to stop. "Before we go out there, I need to know if you still want me to stay. The Elders will expect me to report to them, but I will refuse if you give me a reason."

"Stay."

Poof.

Chapter 35

Andel and Evelyn appeared in the courtyard first. Dusk reflected off the New York City skyline and hues of purple and pink softened the blow of last few minutes of daylight. Neither Cupid knew where their hearts would lead them next, but standing together hand-in-hand felt right.

Evelyn stood close, and Andel didn't plan to let her go. "I think you should let me try to convince them not to say anything about Sydney's new immortal status to the Elders."

"Why? They'll find out eventually," Evelyn pointed out.

"All the Elders need to know is that you completed your mission. That way, Roscoe and Sydney can enjoy being together. If other supernaturals find out you can transfer power from a supernatural to a mortal, I have a feeling the demand for your services will be even more coveted."

"Okay, but how are you going to convince Jude, Zora, and Douglas?"

"Well, Jude's a loner, and I know a little about that. His reason for trying to stop me was more protective than hurtful. The so-called damage is done, and he still has his best friend. There's also the potential for a new friend in Sydney. If you and I feel compelled to follow our hearts, then Douglas and Zora must have felt a similar way at some point or they wouldn't have shown up."

Evelyn shrugged. "They've stayed to help me all this time and never tried to stop me. I'm not sure it'll work, but I won't stop you from trying."

Andel turned to face Evelyn and ran his fingers up her arm to her shoulder. The door creaked open, and Evelyn jumped. Andel's hand fell to his side.

The group filed out of the cathedral, and as Sydney stepped outside, Evelyn and Andel searched for any differences. When Zora and Douglas stepped out behind her, they announced they'd already performed their own inspections.

"How do you feel?" Evelyn rushed to Sydney.

"I'll tell you what I told Roscoe. I feel better than I've ever felt in my life. It's a little scary but exhilarating all at the same time."

"What's better? Your hearing? Sight?"

"Yes, both. Everything. I can see more clearly, and there's a fullness to your voices that wasn't there before. Sounds almost hurt after you struck us, but I just had to tune them like I would a radio station. Roscoe's embrace covered me and went from suffocating to captivating, and his voice slid into harmony. Everything is crystal clear. Our connection and immortality aren't just parallel but entwined. The scary part is I have a strong feeling if something happened to me, it would happen to Roscoe, too."

Everyone stood to take in Sydney's observation. Andel didn't know how Evelyn's arrow transferred the power, but if Roscoe's magic resided in Sydney, it would make sense that they would be tied to each other in more than an emotional way.

Douglas first broke the silence with another inquiry. "What about your strength and speed?"

"How about we let her figure that out in time?" Roscoe wrapped his arm around Sydney's lower back. "I know your Elders will want a report, but can't we let Sydney breathe a little first?"

"Technically, she may not need to breathe anymore," Douglas retorted and folded his arms over his chest. "And we have a job to do." He looked to Zora and Andel.

Zora pulled her lips into a tight smile. "I think we can agree to hold off for a few hours. The Elders will want a more thorough statement, and we can provide that if we allow Sydney some time."

"I'm standing right here." Sydney placed a hand on her hip.

"Wait." Evelyn moved to stand next to Sydney. "We'd like to throw an idea onto the table." She looked over at Andel to explain.

"Would any of you consider keeping this development a secret for more than a few hours?"

Douglas shifted his weight from one foot to the other and looked down at the ground. "You can't expect us to lie to the Elders," he answered.

"You're right, but what if we omitted the part about Sydney being immortal? You can still tell the Elders about the successful mission," Andel reasoned.

Douglas ran his fingers through his hair, still unable to make eye contact with anyone. "I don't know."

"I can do it," Zora spoke up. "Neither of you signed up to be poked a prodded. You should spend this time together, not in the heavens being interrogated. Especially you, Sydney."

Andel noticed Douglas' mouth fall open, but before he could argue, Andel wanted to move the discussion on to something else. "Thank you, Zora. Evelyn has done exactly what the Elders requested, and our partnership with the Gargoyles is solidified. Right?"

Andel looked from Evelyn to Roscoe to Jude.

"Yes," Roscoe confirmed and patted his friend Jude on the back. "I will continue to protect mortals and Lux with the help of the North American Legion of Gargoyles, but thanks to Evelyn, I will do it with Sydney by my side."

Zora looked at the couple with a smile and caught Sydney's eye. "I wish you all the best and hope to see you again."

"Thank you." Sydney smiled back.

Zora took a more formal tone with Roscoe, "I'll take the agreed upon news to the Elders."

"I'll go with you." Douglas nodded to Sydney and Roscoe.

Evelyn wanted to express her own appreciation and walked over to hug Zora goodbye. The gesture left Zora speechless and glassy-eyed. As Evelyn released her new friend, she caught Douglas' arm. "I know this isn't how you'd prefer to handle this, but thank you."

He nodded, and both Cupids transcended, giving the others some room to move around in the small courtyard. And that's exactly what Jude did. He paced like a caged animal. Andel walked over to him and placed his hands on Jude's shoulders. "Brother, this battle is won. But there is a war ahead. I'm grateful you are with us."

"You can both count on me," Jude saluted, placing his fist over his heart. He also made eye contact with Roscoe, Sydney, and Evelyn. Taking a step back, he transformed into his falcon without another word and pushed off the ground into the night sky. His pain at losing a part of his best friend would grow duller each day, but things would never be the same between them.

"I'll walk you to the coffee shop if you'd like." Roscoe turned to Sydney and took her hand in his.

"Do I really have to go to work?" she asked with a grin.

"It's up to you." Roscoe turned to the cathedral door and opened it for Sydney. "We have an eternity together."

"True." Sydney looked down at her wrist. "Crap! I'm so late, so how about I just call in sick?"

Roscoe laughed and tugged her inside. Sydney didn't budge. She untangled herself from Roscoe's hand and bounced over to embrace Evelyn.

"Thank you for everything."

The gratitude took Evelyn by surprise. Her hands stuttered before returning the hug. "You're welcome."

Sydney bounced to Roscoe's side with the same enthusiasm. Her immortality hadn't changed her; rather, it had amplified her zeal for life.

"We'll see you two around." Roscoe waved over his shoulder, as they disappeared into the dark hallway.

"Yeah, we'll see you around. Right?" Sydney peeked back through the doorway.

"I'm sure you will," Evelyn tried to sound convincing.

"You will," Andel nodded, and the two closed the door behind them. He turned to face Evelyn. "What next?"

The garden went from being overcrowded with immortals to brimming with emotion. Andel wanted to be closer to Evelyn, but a cloud of uncertainty kept them at a distance. He didn't know if the hesitation he felt was his own or Evelyn's. He exhaled as he waded through the emotions between them, hoping to blow them away.

Once he stood in front of her, Evelyn pushed past her own reluctance and placed a hand on Andel's chest. "You have another couple to pierce."

"I don't want to use one of my arrows." Andel looked away. "It's selfish, I know, but if I pierce them, I'll be that much closer to the end of my service." He managed to move his eyes to meet hers and grazed his hand across her cheek. "Moving on isn't an option for me anymore. Not while you're here."

"Andel—"

Andel covered his mouth over hers in a breathtaking kiss. He lingered long enough for Evelyn to kiss him back. She took his bottom lip between her lips and gently tugged him closer. Her hands wrapped around his neck, and he hooked his fingers into the belt loops of her jeans.

Andel would stay for Evelyn. He'd stay an eternity. Tightening his grip on her hips, Andel kissed her with an urgency he'd never felt before. He heard Evelyn's heart race, exhilarated. She broke every mold and challenged everything Andel had taught her. Neither of them had felt so much courage and fear in one moment.

"Evelyn, we need to slow down." Andel rested his cheek against hers.

They held each other in the quiet provided by the trees around them. "What's the matter?"

"Nothing, it was—" Andel pulled his head back to make eye contact. "I want to be with you, but I lose control when we're together. I feel tormented, in a good way, when I'm with you."

"I'm not sure I follow."

"Me either," Andel admitted. "I do know I want as much time as possible with you, and if I pierce Jane and Kendrick, it would inevitably cut that time short."

"But they deserve to be given the same love we just gave Roscoe and Sydney," Evelyn argued.

"I know. That's why I was wondering if you would like to complete the assignment on my behalf?"

Evelyn's arrows worked on mortals as well as immortals, so the request didn't sound unreasonable coming from Andel. Evelyn loosened her hold on him and checked for any pause. "I'll go to them and listen to my heart."

Andel nodded. "Fair enough."

"The sooner the better, though. I don't want to take a chance on Queen Rhyan looking for me or the Elders finding out more than we intended."

"Then we'll go tonight." Andel pulled Evelyn close again.

"Kendrick and Jane had planned to attend an event at the museum tonight. I have a feeling they'll still be there."

Poof.

Andel had transcended them to Jane's office on the administrative floor. She glamoured herself in an emerald cocktail dress while Andel used his power to give off the illusion he wore a three-piece suit. They made their way down the elevator, and Andel expected they'd have to travel to one of the new exhibits to find Jane and Kendrick. The couple should have been entertaining museum board members, but love's melody led Evelyn to her favorite gallery, and Andel followed.

Jane had made herself comfortable on the bench in front of one of the swirling Van Goghs. She wore a black dress, and her red hair had been swept up into a gold clip. He heard the solo her heart sang, but Evelyn turned to him with a frown.

What is it? he mentally asked.

I don't recognize her song.

You mean, you don't feel it? Andel couldn't imagine not experiencing the joy in Jane's heart.

No, it's there, but it's changed. I'm sad I didn't get to feel it grow in her. It hurt too much to check in with her emotionally after you left.

Jane and Kendrick had found love their own way, and that fact tipped the scales for Andel. He knew when he saw them last that Cupids weren't necessary for their love to find its way.

The sound of footsteps approaching pulled Andel out of his thoughts. Kendrick, in a black suit and tie, joined Jane on the bench. Their love reached a crescendo as he took her hand in his.

Andel felt Evelyn's hand slip into his.

I think I'll get a better angle from the stairwell door. Evelyn squeezed his hand gently and let go. *You stay here and keep an eye out. If anyone comes, you can warn me.*

Okay.

Evelyn disappeared, and Andel looked over at the stairwell door. It slowly crept open, and he knew she watched the couple for an opportunity to pierce them. *I'm going to need them to stand up to pull this off.* She thought from across the room.

Give them a few minutes. I have a feeling. Andel listened in on Jane and Kendrick's conversation. The couple spoke in whispers, but it sounded like they were inches instead of yards away.

"You know, I never would have guessed we'd be here holding hands," Jane observed.

"But I wouldn't want it any other way." Kendrick leaned in to kiss Jane.

Is there a clear angle now? Andel asked.

No, I'd have to come out in the open. It wouldn't be a problem with glamour, but they might get suspicious when a phantom opens and closes the door.

Andel sighed impatience. On the outer edges of the love that filled the room, a tinge of worry irritated him. Something felt off. He thought the annoyance probably emanated from a couple downstairs.

Jane stood and pulled Kendrick along with her. "We should get downstairs. The dinner will be starting soon."

Kendrick looked down at his watch. "We have a few minutes." He pulled Jane to his chest and kissed her deeply.

Now! Andel's anticipation met silence as the stairwell door slipped shut across the room.

Evelyn?

Chapter 36

"Evelyn, dear. So good to see you, and in such a familiar setting," Kalan teased as she climbed the stairs in designer heels.

"What are you doing here?" Evelyn let the door slide shut behind her, and her bow and arrow vanished from her hands. She hoped to hide the couple and Andel from the fairy's view.

"Don't worry, I don't want anything to do with your little project out there. I'd actually hate to intrude, but felt it would be unkind if I didn't warn you."

Evelyn shoved her hands into her pockets. "Warn me about what?"

"Benjamin. He was spotted in Central Park, and Queen Rhyan is worried he might be looking for King Avery."

"How do you know about Ben? Or Avery?" Evelyn wondered out loud.

"The Gargoyle, Jude, asked us to keep an eye out for Ben. And Avery was hard to miss. You unleashed the king on our turf. Remember how we needed your arrows to help with a troll situation?" Kalan's eyebrows rose. "The problem is as abruptly as Avery appeared, he was gone. The queen wants to know if you've been in contact with him."

"I haven't seen Avery since that night in the park, but if I see him, I'll tell him you said hi." Evelyn offered Kalan a tight smile.

"Fine, be that way." Kalan started down the stairs. "But I was going to give you another bit of information about Diana if you weren't being such—"

"Sorry, sorry. I apologize." She waved Kalan back. "I'll let the Gargoyles in on the news about Ben, and I'll ask them to keep an eye out for Avery."

"That's better." Kalan straightened the sleeves of her jacket. "Rhyan remembered that it was Diana's love for another immortal that lead her to darkness."

"How could loving someone turn them into a Nox?"

"It wasn't the actual love, but he left her. She replaced love with revenge. Everyone she's ever claimed to love and everything she's ever done after losing love has been part of a vendetta. It's created a monster the same way Avery became a troll."

Evelyn swallowed down the fear that threatened to choke her. She could become the same monster if she let herself. It could happen to any of them. "Thank you. I think."

"Good luck, Evelyn. If anyone asks, the fairies call you friend."

Evelyn blinked, and Kalan vanished. So much had been implied in her news, but Evelyn had to push her curiosity to the side and focus on Jane and Kendrick.

Evelyn, where are you? Andel's voice echoed in her mind.

I'm here. She pushed the door to the gallery slightly open.

What happened?

I'll have to explain later. Evelyn canvassed the room filled with priceless paintings, but the couple had left.

"Actually, you can explain now." Andel stepped into the room from the opposite hallway.

"No, we have to go after Jane and Kendrick."

"No, we don't." Andel's hand rubbed the back of his neck. "I pierced them."

"What? I thought we agreed I would do it."

"When you didn't answer their call, it grew so loud I couldn't ignore it. My bow and arrows appeared out of habit, and I took the shot when I had it." Andel wore a grimace that pulled the features of his face downward.

"It's okay." Evelyn moved closer, placing a hand on his shoulder. "You still have three more targets to hit until you're off to the pearly gates." Evelyn joked.

"Evelyn, I don't plan to go anywhere that isn't with you anytime soon." He looked her in the eye and tightened his jaw.

Her chest vibrated with power from the gallery. The magic held in each canvas around the room resonated so loudly Andel could feel it through Evelyn. "What was that?"

After the feeling faded, Evelyn hesitantly pulled away. "I'm not sure, but we need to leave." She moved toward the stairwell. "Follow me."

Once the door shut behind them, separating the Cupids from the overactive art, Andel looked around them. "What happened in here earlier?"

"Kalan."

"Did she try to take you?" Andel gave Evelyn a once over, checking for who knows what. "Are you hurt?"

"She wanted to warn me, and now we've got to warn the others."

Chapter 37

Evelyn stood at Cleopatra's Needle, waiting. She had poofed there to find Jude. Explaining the situation to Andel, he exploded at her transcending them to Central Park after Kalan's warning.

"We have to find Jude," she argued.

"We have to stay alive, Evelyn," Andel begged. "If you'll transcend with me back to the apartment, I'll go out and look for Jude."

Standing close to the inscribed tower, Evelyn leaned against the base of the structure. "We should wait for him since we're already here." She figured Jude wouldn't mind, especially after the day they'd had. Evelyn's weight slid down to the ground in a stubborn effort to make it hard for Andel to remove her. Sitting, Evelyn curled up her knees and patted the ground next to her.

"No, Evelyn, this is—" Andel's body slumped forward, falling on top of Evelyn.

She screamed, gliding her hands over Andel to check for a wound. She heaved his body to the side when she didn't find blood. Pressing two fingers to his neck, she checked for a pulse. Andel's heart beat steadily.

"Did you really come here to hunt me down?" Ben's voice sounded from the darkness surrounding them. She'd been an idiot to bring Andel here. Instinctively, she summoned her bow and arrows. There wasn't time to dwell on her mistake because Ben slowly strode into view.

Evelyn's eyes widened at his boldness. "Honestly, I didn't think you'd be crazy enough to come here. Staying in the park when so many supernaturals are looking for you is a dumb move. But showing up where Jude calls home—after murdering his best friend—proves you have no sense of self-preservation."

Ben stepped out from behind a row of bushes. "Who's to say it wasn't my intention to be found?"

Evelyn stood and aimed her arrow in the blink of an eye. "Stay where you are, or I'll shoot."

Ben armed himself just as fast. "I don't plan to end you, Evelyn. Tonight, I merely play the messenger again."

"Have you ever thought that doing Diana's bidding is the same as completing the Elders' missions? They're both giving orders and expecting you to turn off your heart. The one thing we can always rely on as Cupids *is* our heart."

"My heart? Who says I have one?" Ben took a step forward but froze when Evelyn pulled her arrow tighter against the bow's string. "I won't be threatened into explaining myself or Diana to you. Soon, you'll understand for yourself. You'll beg Diana to let you fight with her."

Ben smirked, leaving Evelyn speechless. He slid back into the shadows of the bushes and trees and disappeared. She immediately regretted not taking a shot at him. Ben had killed Leo, and she would have been justified, but she hadn't had the guts to release her arrow. The unknown of what might happen had kept her arrow from piercing Ben. After hearing about Diana's vendetta, Evelyn didn't want to take revenge. She wanted justice.

Diana had a plan, and her endgame was to get Evelyn on her side. She'd already placed herself in the middle of the chaos by choosing to follow her own heart. She wouldn't be taking assignments from the Elders, and her independence would affect any supernatural who wanted her help. Sliding back down to the ground with her bow propped up at her side and her arrow gripped in her fist, she'd be ready if Ben came back. Evelyn had no qualms with shooting first and asking questions later to protect Andel.

In the corner of her eye, Evelyn noticed a figure appear out of thin air. Jude had arrived, and she really didn't want to have to explain what just went down with Ben to him. She would give Kalan's message to Jude but save Ben's communication for later when she and Andel were alone.

"What's going on?" Jude asked as he approached Evelyn. "Is Andel alright?"

At the sound of Jude's voice, Andel began to stir. Evelyn stood and dismissed her weapons into the thin air. "Kalan visited me."

"And what does that have to do with me or the Gargoyles?"

"Quit acting like you didn't ask for their help. She told me about your request to keep an eye out for Ben, and one of the fairies spotted him in the park. They're also looking for Avery, and I'm starting to wonder if Ben may be working with him."

Evelyn bent over to help Andel up. He groaned and rubbed his hands over his head.

Jude rubbed along his chin. "Did she say where?"

"No, but I figured you knew how to get in contact with her." Evelyn couldn't help but wonder if this strategic alliance might grow into a friendship between the two supernatural races.

"That can't be all she went to you with, or she would have just come here to inform me."

"What happened?" Andel asked as he looked around them. "What are we doing here, Evelyn?"

Evelyn realized he must not remember transcending to Cleopatra's Needle, and it must have been a result of whatever Ben had done to knock him out. It was a pretty powerful trick, and she wondered if she had the same card up her sleeve.

"It's okay, Jude's here." Evelyn grabbed Andel by the arm and turned him around. "Kalan gave me some more intel on Diana. She told me your involvement with her wasn't what changed her." Evelyn didn't want to go into more detail with Andel silently observing. It was Jude's business.

"How about you and I go for a walk?"

Evelyn looked to Andel and he nodded. "We'll be right back, I promise. But you should be on alert, maybe arm yourself, in case Ben shows up."

Andel's jaw tightened, and before he could argue that they should just leave, Evelyn had an idea. "How about you transcend to your favorite training ground? I'll meet you there after Jude and I talk. We can work out some frustrations on the targets you set up."

Andel's mouth relaxed and he released the fists he'd made at his sides. "Evelyn, I don't—"

She closed the distance between them and kissed Andel. She whispered, "I'll be fine. I'm with Jude. I'll tell you everything when I get to Greece."

Reluctant to let go of her, Andel held Evelyn with one arm while reaching the other out to Jude. "Friend, until we cross paths again."

"I have a feeling it will be sooner than later." Jude gripped Andel's forearm and they shook.

Andel wrapped his arms around Evelyn one more time. "I'll be sitting on the cliff waiting for you to come and fulfill my dream. Adieu." Letting her go, Andel transcended.

"You're treading in dangerous territory," Jude warned. "I've tried to talk some sense into Andel, but the more time he spends with you, the less he's willing to heed my warning."

"About that, it seems that all the guilt you feel about turning Diana into some monster is unwarranted. Her first love must have come before you because Kalan explained that he left her. Since then, everything she's done has been for revenge. I'm sorry."

"Sorry? Don't be. I'm almost relieved." Jude's eyes brightened, and he stood taller. He breathed easier with the realization that he wasn't completely to blame for the love of his life turning to darkness.

Jude and Evelyn had wandered further into the park. Trees lined each side of the path and shadows lurked behind them, but Evelyn didn't fear what lay ahead because she had friends who called the park home.

"So you've been secretly working with Kalan?" Evelyn's eyebrows bounced up and down.

"Keep your arrows in their quiver, Cupid." He warned.

"She told me I can consider the fairies my friends now."

Jude grasped Evelyn's arm and stopped her in her tracks. "Don't get too comfortable. Those creatures are tricky, and not all fairies are in Queen Rhyan's court."

"Point taken." She shook off his grip and kept walking. "Now to figure out what Diana's planning."

"You didn't tell Kalan you were looking for Diana, did you?"

"No! I'm not that dense. Plus, I'm not sure I want to find her. But I may need to help stop her. I'm only bringing it up to you because someone needs to know what Andel and I are up to in case there's trouble."

Jude stepped off the path onto a grassy, open field. "I have a feeling you and Andel will get into trouble without Diana's help if you're not careful." Now, his eyebrows danced.

"Shut it, Jude. I'm sick and tired of hearing you bash what Andel and I have." Evelyn pointed a finger at him. "Which, I'm not saying we have anything. I mean, we have something, but we're still figuring it out."

"We're immortal. There's more to loving someone than you can fathom."

Evelyn walked onto the field after him. "I'm not her, Jude. I'm not Diana."

"I know that. And Andel is definitely not me, but I'm right about your purity, aren't I?"

"So big-freakin'-what! I've never been with a guy. I'm pure. At least I'm not some floozy." She slapped her hands on her thighs. "Gah! It's none of your business."

"I'm only pointing it out because you and Diana are starting on a similar path."

"That's why I have to find her before she finds me. I need to understand why we're different, so I can stop whatever plan she's set in motion and keep myself from turning into a modern-day version of her. I won't be a pawn."

"You might not be a pawn, but a key. Have you thought about that? Finding her could be what she wants."

"If I think like that, I'll end up being the Elders' pawn, or key, or whatever symbol you want to use." Evelyn walked a circle around Jude. "Can I really count on you? I know Roscoe will help me, but I'd like to let him enjoy this honeymoon phase."

"There you go thinking like a mortal again."

"It's not all bad, you know, thinking like one of them." Evelyn put a hand on her hip.

Jude stared up at the stars. "I don't think I'll ever get used to your voice in my head, but you can call me if you need me."

"Thanks—"

"Just be careful." Jude reached out and took Evelyn's hand. "You've seen what Ben, and anyone like him, can do. Don't go throwing yourself in front of one of those black arrows."

"You can count on that." Evelyn squeezed his hand.

"Good, now, get out of here." He released her and jumped into the air, transforming into a fierce, granite falcon. With wings spread wide, he screeched his goodbye and flew toward the stars.

Poof.

Chapter 38

The salty air brushed Evelyn's skin at the cliff's edge. Gray clouds rolled overhead, blocking the warm sunlight, and a chill rushed through Evelyn. Goosebumps spread over her skin. The small rocky opening appeared normal, but Andel was nowhere in sight. Evelyn walked to a large boulder and sat down on a rocky extension shaped like a boot.

Andel could have decided to run the course once without her. Or maybe he was setting targets up in new places to challenge her. He would always want to strive to be better. He would always want to protect her. Andel gave his life for his family, he constantly trained to be the best Cupid, and Evelyn knew he wanted to make sure their relationship was right. He wanted them both to be better for it.

"Andel?" Evelyn called out over the sound of crashing waves below. She wanted to see him, to take him into her arms and thank him for supporting her. She knew it would be next to impossible to go after Diana on her own. Andel's experience paired with her determination could add up to stopping Diana before she became strong enough to see her plan imposed on the supernatural world.

They didn't have a clue what Diana was plotting, but seeing her lackey Ben in action had left Evelyn worried for more than just the Cupids. Ben didn't care that he'd ended an immortal's life, let alone that Leo existed as a Gargoyle to protect mortals. From what Evelyn understood, the supernatural races didn't mix unless in an official capacity.

Evelyn knew she'd always side with light, but she struggled with being different than most Lux.

Sliding down off the rock and walking over to the line of trees serving as a gateway to the forest, Evelyn searched for Andel. The green canopy shifted from side to side with the breeze. She used her enhanced vision to inspect the blooming branches and fallen trunks. She noted a few targets hanging in the same places they'd been the last time she trained here.

Something felt wrong.

"Andel!" She cupped her hands around her mouth and shouted. "Where are you?"

The sound of rustling leaves and the tide swelling didn't calm her.

When Andel didn't respond, she walked back toward the cliff. Could he have fallen? Panic tightened her chest.

No.

As an immortal, he'd simply be hurt, right? He could survive.

Andel, please.

The closer Evelyn got to the jagged edge, the harder it became to breathe. Looking past the rocky precipice, Evelyn scanned the shore below.

He was nowhere in sight.

As Evelyn turned back to the forest, she recognized the last target on the course. The tree it hung from grappled to hang onto land with its roots. It half-dangled over the abyss. A black arrow had pierced the red center of the bull's eye, and a sheet of paper had been tacked underneath it, fluttering in the wind. Evelyn ran to the target and wiggled the arrowhead out of the wood. Yanking the paper out of the wind before it could be carried away, she noticed handwriting on one side.

The script was elegant like calligraphy, and it definitely was not Andel's handwriting. Evelyn glanced at the bottom of the note where the signature read *Diana*. Forcing her eyes back to the top of the page, she read…

Dearest Evelyn,

I believe it is time we meet. To ensure your cooperation, I have enlisted the help of your friend, Andel. Benjamin is escorting him to London, where I am awaiting their arrival. Your less than civil encounters with Benjamin have led me to believe that a simple request would not suffice. So, if you hope to see your beloved Cupid alive, you will arrive in St. James Park tomorrow night by sunset.

Ειλικρινά,

Diana

Evelyn's lungs felt like they were full of sand, and no matter how much air she breathed in, it wasn't enough. She'd successfully led Andel into a trap, and something Jude had said clicked with her. Evelyn had learned to follow her heart, but she still needed to see the big picture if she hoped to stay ahead of Diana. She needed Jude's help, not just physically but strategically. Together, they could save Andel and hopefully stop Diana. Evelyn felt a supernatural war brewing, and she was willing to do whatever it took to see love win in the end.

To be continued…

Acknowledgements

Unbreakable made me, and my words stronger. Writing this third novel also strengthened many of my relationships in the wordy world I call home. Morgan, Gaby, and Amber challenged me on a daily basis to dive deeper into the words, while my Dynamis girls cheered me on and gave great advice. Kelly kicked my butt into gear and Melissa provided therapy when I felt like I might go bonkers. S.M. Boyce, you helped me set my sights and walk the path this story laid out. I am eternally grateful to and for each of you.

My husband, Scott, is a constant reminder of what real love is, so readers are always guaranteed an inspired romantic element in my books. My children are the best creative minds to brainstorm with, and they always encourage me to keep on writing. Kay and Kassie, we are our own wacky version of the Gilmore Girls and life would be so boring without you. I am blessed.

A special thank you to my cover/graphic designer, Drew Rodgers, and my editor, Maria Pease. You are both so good at capturing my vision and bringing it to life.

Finally, I want to thank the readers. Love is the real inspiration for this new series. I adore a good book, I obsess over characters who steal my heart, and I cherish turning the page into a riveting world. Thank you for taking the time to read Unbreakable. I hope you've fallen in love with Evelyn, Andel, and the others in The Cupid Chronicles.

About the Author

Writing unique adventures with heart.

Kallie Ross has a passion for writing that has become an adventure in itself. She desires to create unique young adult fiction that incorporates legend, conjecture, fantasy, and conviction.

In addition to loving her life as a writer, Kallie adores being a wife, mother, friend, and teacher. She began her creative journey with books, a blog, podcast, and lots of caffeine. Ross never imagined her own adventure would be filled with so many wonderful people or words!

Find Kallie online at www.KallieRoss.com

Also by Kallie Ross

Evelyn: A Cupid Chronicles Novella

Descent: A Lost Tribe (Book 1)
Defend: A Lost Tribe (Book 2)

www.ingramcontent.com/pod-product-compliance
Lightning Source LLC
Chambersburg PA
CBHW061947170626
46813CB00006B/2559

* 9 780099 353203 *